COLOUR
ME IN
LYDIA
RUFFLES

COLOUR ME IN

LYDIA RUFFLES

First published in hardback in Great Britain in 2018 by Hodder & Stoughton
This paperback edition published 2019

1 3 5 7 9 10 8 6 4 2

A CIP catalogue record for this book
is available from the British Library.

ISBN 978 1 444 93768 8

Typeset in Garamond by Hewer Text UK Ltd, Edinburgh
Printed and bound in Great Britain by Clays Ltd, Elcograf S.p.A.

The paper and board used in this book
are made from wood from responsible sources.

Hodder Children's Books
An imprint of Hachette Children's Group
Part of Hodder and Stoughton
Carmelite House
50 Victoria Embankment
London, EC4Y 0DZ

An Hachette UK Company
www.hachette.co.uk

For Florence

No matter where you go, there you are.

Confucius

ONE

Memories of the little forest at the bottom of the swimming pool flood Arlo the second the plane flings its great bulk into the sky.

His brain conjures the heavy moon strung up by a crane, suspended over the roof, the city. He can see it all. The dusting of blossom on the ground, the shoelaces. The thing they'd been trying so hard to make, ruined. Phone calls and crackling radios. The way a door had unhinged inside his head as time stuck, glitched, restarted.

Familiar black weeds start to crawl inside him. He forces his eyes open and watches the plane blip across the screen in the back of the seat in front of him, inching off the edge of land until it's hovering over water.

There are better maps of Mars than there are of the oceans. You've got to go to sea if you want to get really lost; find somewhere deep and watery, somewhere that doesn't even have a name.

Not that he can see the ocean below. The windows are choked with clouds. He's nowhere. Off-map.

Maybe he doesn't exist if nobody, not even he, knows where he is.

Arlo sniffs.

I stink.

The plane banks left, pushing him back into his seat. His life is going one way while he goes another.

Forgot to write on the blackboard.

How will Luke know where he's gone? Arlo taps a message into his phone ready to send to his friend when he lands.

Closes his eyes again, blocking everything out except the pain in his hand.

A day later, half a world away, the plane descends through a bloodshot sky and he is lost.

TWO

Twelve days earlier

On this rooftop no man's land between the city and the clouds, Arlo has almost everything he wants. A friend, an escape, the chance to make something that matters.

He leans back on his elbows, long legs hanging like dead weights over the side of the swimming pool. Luke's thicker body next to him, his feet closer to the cracked tiles. They breathe deep, armpits and temples damp from their labour. Their fingers are raw and their shoulders throbbing from the hefting and heaving and sluicing and scrubbing.

Darkness pours itself across the basin of the empty pool. It trickles into the dry splits like syrup, leaking over their mismatched shadows until the whole thing is full of soft night.

It's a gentle dark, the kind that trusts that light will follow. Safe to wallow in for a while.

'I can hear you thinking,' Luke tells him. Arlo laughs. His friend cuffs the side of his head. 'Want to tell me what's going on in there?'

'You remember when your mum made that rank black treacle thing?'

It's Luke's turn to laugh. 'Well, that's not the response I was expecting. Not that I don't welcome some respite from your usual existential commentary.'

'It was an abomination. You really don't remember?'

'I don't think so.'

Arlo can't recall why Mrs Swanson had been making the weird cake, but he remembers being in the Swanson kitchen up at the big house, watching the syrup ooze into the mixing bowl, like the darkness sliding into the swimming pool. The sticky, crumbling cake, its surprising claggy bitterness.

'What about it anyway?' Luke asks.

'Nothing really. You asked what I was thinking about and the answer was treacle.'

'Just casually thinking about snacks from fifteen years ago. No big deal.'

'Ha.'

'If we ever had a normal, linear conversation up here, I think I'd fall off the roof in shock.'

Arlo smiles. The thought of them eating cake together as children is somehow funny. Luke's shelves in the fridge are stuffed with Tupperware boxes, labelled with things such as 'Huevos', 'Treatz', and 'Chix Titz'. The kitchen is stocked like a nuclear bunker, with bottled water and various nutritional powders and supplements. They definitely won't be malnourished in the event of a zombie apocalypse.

Luke takes two bottles of beer from the six-pack behind them and opens them on the side of the pool.

'Finally got the hang of that then,' says Arlo. They've been perfecting the art of using the pool and various other bits of the roof as a bottle opener since they first came up here.

The tarp that they use to cover the pool flaps by the railing. The wind shakes the blossom on the potted trees they'd ordered and lugged up to the roof to try to make it look nice up here.

'What are we going to do with them when they grow?' asks Luke.

'What do you mean?'

'When they get too big for the pots.'

'Good question,' Arlo says. 'Make some stealth donations to the park across the street?'

'I don't think we thought this forest of ours through.'

Quiet settles again.

This is where they have their best conversations and their best silences, looking out over their adoptive city. The skyline ever-changing with its creaking cranes and low-flying planes. Mobile landmarks. A million doors and windows opening and closing in the sprawl below while they sit, talking, thinking.

Nobody knows they're up here, the secret pool and the two of them. Just a shallow oblong and two warm dots in the grand scheme of things. There are no auditions, no agents, up on the roof. No 'Why did you quit the *The Beat*?' or 'What's next?' Up here, they are kings.

Arlo wonders if Luke is thinking the same: *We've come a long way.*

'Here.' Luke hands him a head torch. Arlo had bought them so they could work on the secret project at night. His friend had humoured him, as always.

He takes the torch and fixes it to his head, leans on the rusty pool steps to his left. No need to explain to Luke that he's not quite ready to turn it on. That the orange glow of light pollution is enough for the moment. Arlo's 'Thanks,' is shorthand for all this.

Luke stretches the thick elastic strap of his own torch around his head but doesn't switch it on either. Arlo is grateful; he's fortunate to have someone to talk with and not talk with like this. Someone who will let him sit quietly in the dark for a while but come in and get him if he stays too long. On good days, Arlo knows Luke is lucky to have him too.

They gaze over the endless city, past the chimneys of the older houses and the designer slate tops of the new builds. The concrete ecosystem that they belong to reaches further than their eyes can in the dark.

The air is threaded with chlorine. Luke will have been at the gym pool all afternoon.

'We've still got an hour before we need to leave,' Luke says. 'We could finish it.'

Arlo snorts.

Luke concedes, 'Well, maybe not *finish* it.'

Now that they're so close to completing their project, Arlo's not sure he wants it to be done. They have no real idea what they're doing and it's probably illegal but what started on a whim has become important. Something to focus on.

'Let's finish tomorrow,' Arlo says, grabbing the beers and his hoodie and standing up. 'It's too windy today and I need a shower before we go out. I'll get the tarp.'

'The trees are getting battered there. Let's move them away from the edge,' Luke says, switching on his head torch.

They shift the heavy pots one by one away from the railing and into the middle of the roof where they continue to shake and shed their blossom in the breeze.

'Well, that made absolutely fuck-all difference,' says Arlo.

'Yup. Literally none.'

'We could put them in the pool.'

Luke laughs. 'Oh, you're serious.'

'Just while we figure out what to do with them.'

'Or we could just send them back,' Luke says.

'I don't think that's how tree-buying works. At least not when you get them off Amazon.'

'OK. Let's do it.'

So they shuffle the trees over to the edge of the pool, then Luke climbs in. 'I'll lift them down. You hold the branches steady so they don't capsize.'

They get all the trees into the pool and line them up side by side in the middle.

'Looks pretty good,' says Arlo. He takes a quick photo of their mini wood and sends it to his mum. She likes to hear from him, to know he's having a good time. *She needs me to be doing well.*

They fix the pool cover in place with Luke's kettle bells, tucking the trees away for the night. Arlo gets to the other side of the roof before Luke says, 'Are you wearing that out?' He taps his own head torch. 'It's a strong look but . . .'

Arlo rests his stuff on the ledge and takes off the head torch, laughing. They shove both the torches into their bag of supplies behind the chimney.

By his side, Arlo feels Luke draw in a deep, slow breath.

He knows what's coming.

Luke tips his head back and pushes out a thunderous howl from his chest.

Arlo had refused to join in the first time, but weeks of howling later they're at the point where it's actually more embarrassing for him not to.

'AwoOOOooo,' they howl.

'Shut. Up. You. Animals,' a voice yells from one of the windows across the street.

'Shit,' says Arlo. 'What if he comes up?'

'Relax, he won't. Your turn.'

'AwoOOOooo,' whimpers Arlo.

They laugh.

'Come on. Let's go down.'

They reach for their beers at the same time, knocking hands and sending one of the bottles over the ledge. It plummets. The smash echoes up to them.

'Shit,' says Arlo again.

'There's nobody down there,' says Luke.

'We could have hurt someone.'

'But we didn't.'

'OK, new rule, no glass bottles on the ledge.'

'OK, boss,' says Luke, and sucks in another deep breath. 'AwoOOOooo, awoOOOooo.'

'AwoOOOooo,' Arlo answers.

They're still laughing as they clamber down the steps off the roof.

An hour later and six floors down, they step over the drift of blossom that's heaped like popcorn on the doorstep and head out into the early night.

Down off the roof, Arlo's mind turns the colour of city rain. The thought of crawling through traffic on a bus seems unbearable.

'Shall we walk?'

'Sure.'

The street lamps wear the spring cold like halos and Arlo shoves his hands into his pockets. He's borrowed a jacket from Luke. His own wardrobe is sparse, as if someone has unpacked a few things in a strange place on a weekend away. His whole room has an air of temporary about it, even two years after he moved in.

'Not filming tonight?' he asks Luke.

When he's not swimming oceans' lengths at the gym, Luke makes videos for his YouTube fitness channel. It's unlike him not to document his every move, something Arlo learned the hard way to avoid. Someone had leaked some of his old photos just after he'd got his part on *The Beat*.

That had hurt, seeing pictures of him and his parents being picked over by trolls – especially the ones of him and his dad from when Arlo was a baby, building sandcastles, him pulling his dad's beard. Snapshots of things he was too young to remember happening were violated by people who didn't even know him. The worst thing was, he wasn't sure who had leaked them.

Lottie, the publicist at *The Beat*, runs his social accounts now. Arlo had deleted all the personal content and now 'he' says things like, 'So pumped that I get to work with this AMAZING cast every day! Dreams really do come true!!!' and 'Great ep tonight! Gonna miss my Beat bros ☹☹☹.'

'Can't film myself going to the pub,' says Luke. 'That would be way off-brand. I did a vljog earlier anyway.'

Vljogging is something Luke claims to have invented. Basically, he straps a video camera to his chest and goes for a run.

They pace on.

In the quiet, the memory of the self-tape audition that Arlo did that morning surfaces. It would be a big deal if he got the part and the chance to be part of something special and important. He also needs to be able to tell people something when they ask what's next for him. All he can do now is wait for Russell, his agent, to call or not call.

'Shall we play Doors?' he suggests.

Arlo and Luke have a lot of games, some old, some newer. They all involve some kind of adventure or magical maps; some kind of being somewhere else. This one had started as a joke last summer. It felt familiar to Arlo, as if he were born knowing the rules. He'd pointed to a tiny door in the side of a bakery and said to Luke, 'Borrowers' Bakery.'

'Nougat Narnia,' Luke said.

'Pavlova Portal.'

They'd evolved the rules over the last year. You could call out any door, any size, and say it led anywhere. The only rule was no duplication; you couldn't call out the same door or the same fantasy place more than once. Heavy forfeits and sanctions were applied in the case of repeats.

'Vomitsville Vestibule,' says Luke.

'Where?' asks Arlo, before clocking a car door being puke-splattered by a drunk guy. 'Never mind, I see. Do you actually know what a vestibule is?'

'No idea.'

The guy retches again.

'Bit early to be that shit-faced, isn't it?'

'To each their own,' says Luke. If he were any more open-minded, his brain would fall out of his head. 'Tiny car though. I'd have to leave my body outside and put my legs through the sun roof to drive the fucker.'

Arlo points down at a grate as they cross the road. 'Fatbergia Gateway.'

'What?'

'Fatbergs. They live in the sewer.'

'What the hell is a fatberg?'

'Massive lumps of fat and other stuff that people flush that doesn't break down. Nappies and condoms and stuff.'

'Savage,' says Luke.

They pass the familiar shops. At first it's all pound stores and fried chicken places but after twenty minutes of walking these give way to grand empires with revolving doors and shiny lobbies. They weave in and out of bankers, journalists, lawyers, faces lit only by the lights from their phones. Real grown-ups with the kinds of jobs that Arlo hopes never to have. He'd been a waiter for a while but it was too much, having to carry actual things and all the other stuff in his head at the same time.

'Shall we try a new route?' asks Arlo.

'Obviously.'

Another game, this one from childhood. It doesn't have a name but if it did it might be called Run Until You're Lost Then Try to Find Your Way.

They leg it the wrong way down the street, zigzagging down random roads, doubling back, turning corners, unofficially racing until they reach the end of a narrow alley.

Both stand catching their breath.

Arlo closes his eyes for a few seconds, inhaling the thrill of being temporarily lost in the tiniest of adventures.

'Where are we?' asks Luke.

There are sixty thousand streets in the city. A handful have fake names on maps. Copyright traps. Maybe this alley is one of them; it's too small for mislabelling to be of real consequence.

Arlo has drawn the city hundreds of times in various forms in the last two years, always fragments, never a whole. He imagines the paper of his notebook spread out in his mind, all the places he'd once been lost, sometimes with Luke, sometimes solo. All the subways and tunnels he's been through, one path linking to the next, the next, the next, until he's home.

He opens his eyes. Luke is already moving.

'We need to get to the river. This way,' he calls from the end of the alley, rounding to the left.

'Straight over's faster,' Arlo says.

'I'm telling you, it's this way.'

Stalemate.

This has happened many times. Each thinks he knows the city best.

'Divide and conquer?' asks Luke.

Another game.

'Walk don't run.'

Their usual rules. Whoever gets to the river first will wait for the other to catch up and be declared the victor. They shake on it and part ways.

Arlo fights the urge to quicken his pace. Luke is competitive but, above all else, a good sport. Neither will cheat.

Arlo passes a man sleeping on a filthy duvet in a doorway and tucks some cash under the side of his blanket, being careful not to wake him. He does this a lot. He tells himself he's being kind and tries not to see the bit of himself that doesn't think he deserves to keep the money.

It takes just a few minutes to wind his way to the river. Luke emerges at the same time as him.

The ideal outcome: each of their private routes proved right and each safe in the knowledge that nobody walks The Smoke quite like he does. *Maybe Luke doesn't call it The Smoke.* It's not an original name for the city, granted, but it's what Arlo's mum calls it so he's sticking with it.

They stride along side by side playing Doors, following the river further into the city, away from home and their home before that. They call out Portaloos, a cat flap, gates holding back a rabid-looking dog. Any door, leading anywhere.

It's a pointless game but Arlo likes the feeling he gets when they play it. When they arrive at the bar flushed with cold and laughing, he's sad that they have to stop. The feeling is slipping away already, as if he can't hold the echo of having fun in his body.

Arlo points to the pub entrance. 'Hell Mouth.'

'Forfeit. You always say that.'

THREE

Later, a girl – sorry, a woman – named Jessica lies in Arlo's lap, feet tangled in a rough blanket.

He lifts his knees to balance them both, cradling her head and shoulders as he leans back against the inside of the rotting shell of the row boat, its mulching wood lending the air a whiff of wet playgrounds.

The warm moment lifts her veins to run like swelling rivers under her skin, lines the colour of algae on a map he cannot read. And in these minutes, while he's alone but not alone, reminding himself not to think of her body as landscape, he pretends they are lost, lost, lost.

His back tenses as he supports her sleeping weight; a loose oarlock pushes between his shoulder blades, but he doesn't mind.

She must have been drunker than he'd thought to fall asleep like this. It does something to him that he can't name, to be holding her in his lap like this, pretending it could last, that he won't find some way to pull it apart.

He shifts their weight and the boat protests, lilting forward, threatening to eject them on to the greying sand. He tightens his hold on her, cheeks clotting with a pink shyness as he surveys their bodies.

She is the seventh woman he's held, excluding his mother; though maybe Jessica thinks she's one of many more. Or maybe she hasn't thought about it at all. Not everyone thinks as much as he does; not everyone wonders where their thoughts go when they've reached the end of them.

He takes in her make-up, thick and peeling like wallpaper at the edges. Lips dry and blackened with jammy wine. The biscuity smell of fake tan on her skin.

She looks younger while she's sleeping. Awake, she had seemed so mature, running rings around him with words he had heard before but whose meanings he couldn't quite pin down. Now he sees she can't be much older than him – maybe twenty-one or twenty-two.

How old does he look when he sleeps?

He'll be twenty soon.

Twenty and retired at this rate.

He'd played the resident bad boy on *The Beat*, a soap about rural police families, for two years before he quit. They've already hired new blood. A younger actor, supplied by the same arts school he went to – some kid hired to play his long-lost cousin.

Why hasn't Russell called?

What if he never works again? He already has to wear T-shirts for bands he hates and shave twice a day with a razor he's sponsored to use – it has seven blades though he only has one face – to keep his fandom 'Arlo's Army' interested.

Maybe Russell could talk *The Beat* into taking him back. His last episode hasn't even aired yet. It's a good one: his and Valerie Pitch's characters disappear during a school trip to the coast. Their dads – policemen with grudges against each other – are forced to unite to try to find them. Nobody knows if they're runaways or if their bodies will wash up somewhere. It was the strangest kind of fiction for Arlo to play – a world with a girlfriend and a dad.

He pushes thoughts of work away.

Don't ruin it.

Their skin glows in the moonlight. Almost blue. *Like aliens.*

In a film, he might throttle her while she sleeps or maybe she'd already be dead from some terrible tragedy.

He hates films, at least the ones he's supposed to like. The violent things they put in his head. Films about war; a reminder that most countries would rather send their sons to die than their daughters.

Cold air pushes away the warm and the map lines sink away. Jessica's dress glimmers. Arlo imagines he will think about her inky smile for the rest of his life.

It seems unfair that Jessica should be exposed while his body is covered by hers so he frees a hand and unbuttons his shirt to even things out. It billows in the wind and the sleeves fill with air but it doesn't have quite the same effect; his chest is furry and his nipples are useless and stupid-looking, like mouse noses.

The breeze carries down voices from the walkway above. Words in English. One of the three hundred languages the city speaks.

'That must be the cathedral. Isn't it beautiful?'

'It seemed different on the map.'

Arlo smiles at this. If there's one thing his and Luke's games have taught him it's that everything looks different on maps. Huge adventures look tiny; places are not as they seem or aren't there at all.

His mind is full of tales of fabled mountain ranges and inland seas. Places summoned into existence on maps by lies and rivalry between empires, weather and wishful thinking, mirages and mistakes.

There's a bright memory of Luke and him playing with an atlas they found as kids. They'd taken it down to the beach and found all the places with silly names and scribbled 'Existence Doubtful' over them, drawing their own countries and worlds, dreaming of all the places they'd go together when they were adults. They took it in turns to take it home, drawing surprises for the other to spot when it was their turn. *What happened to that atlas?* One of them had lost it.

The walkway voices get closer.

Sinking down further into the boat so they aren't spotted, Arlo looks out over the small beach. It's nothing like the ones at home. More of a silt strip, a line, between the river and the city. A resting place for drained bottles. This is not how the beach imagines itself, of course, but it's undeniable: vodka, supermarket-brand cola, something called Spirit Drink. The light mingling in the glass and plastic creates something dazzling for a second, like half-buried jars of magic. Quickly, it's pollution again.

Arlo casts his eyes further down the sand. No summer deckchairs yet, just the husk of another abandoned vessel like this one, which they had climbed into an hour or so earlier. (He's being generous. It was more like thirty minutes; he'd been hard before they hit the deck and Jessica's been asleep for almost fifteen of them.) It had seemed so temptingly out of place, decaying in the middle of the city, a relic of someone's adventure.

Arlo walks his mind through the buildings on the north side of the river. Running through the names he's given them. The Pear. The Castle. The Disco Ball. All made of glass, like him. What if they shattered? He sees streets, cars, people covered with glittering glass. That's how he imagines his insides sometimes; sharp, broken.

Jessica stirs in his lap. She wakes, stretches, her long hair trailing like string across the boat floor. She wriggles her feet to shed the fabric tail.

'Sorry,' she yawns. 'Too much wine. And I can sleep almost anywhere.'

Arlo can sleep almost nowhere these days, not since he left *The Beat*.

Some part of me doesn't trust the rest of me enough to let go any more.

There have been phases like this before. Long nights stretching, elastic and electric. 3 a.m. used to know all his secrets. Are they still up there, whispered into the various ceilings he's stared at?

'We should get back inside,' Jessica continues, wide awake now.

She stands up in between his legs, rolls her dress down her thighs to her knees like a snakeskin. Confident, older again. The moonlight catches the fabric, sending splinters of shimmer into his eyes, blinding him for a second. *Punishment for staring at her while she slept?*

The boat rocks and his hands find her hips to steady her, his fingers lumpy and clumsy. He closes his eyes while she rearranges the top part of her dress, though the gesture is ridiculous given that neither of them has behaved shyly so far. And why should they – didn't everyone keep telling him he was young and having the time of his life?

His eyes open again and she smiles down at him, swaying from the wine and the spring wind. 'What did you say your name was again?'

It had been her idea to leave the bar and sneak down to the so-called beach. She'd started talking to him inside, choosing him over Luke it seemed. After two or three songs, she had drained her drink and pushed her hard little tongue into his mouth, darting it in and out, the sour tang of alcohol on her breath.

'I didn't. It's Arlo.'

'Arlo? What kind of name is that?'

'My dad thought it sounded like a god's name. He wanted me to be famous.'

'Oh.' Her laugh rings out like a warning bell. 'Good luck with that.'

Does she really not know who I am? He feels like a douche for wondering. He's not *that* famous.

'Come on.' She pulls him to his feet and stares while he does up his jeans and rebuttons his shirt. Her gaze is unsettling and he wonders if she was awake the whole time, feeling his eyes on her. He hates being looked at unless he's in character and maybe she does too. He wants to tell her he's not a pervert, that he just thinks she's beautiful, but she seems impatient so he doesn't.

He had spread Luke's jacket out on the base of the boat for

them to lie on. Jessica picks it up, shakes off the muddy sand and shrugs it over her shoulders like she might have seen in a movie. It suits her.

'You're friends with Luke Swanson, right?' she asks.

Arlo's body clenches.

'What's he like?'

Her tone is conversational but the words push everything into place. It stings and he snaps.

'He's a fucking sociopath.'

And fuck you if you think I'm going to introduce you.

He grabs for the blanket that Jessica swiped from the pub. Now transparently a tablecloth, its maritime magic dissolved.

'Leave it,' she says, leaning on the side of the boat to pull on her pointy shoes. 'Someone might want it.'

'We can't just leave it here,' he spits. Static crackles in his head.

'Are you OK?' She smells like sex, pulls at her hair. 'Did I say something wrong?'

Her embarrassment floods the space between them, seeps into him. More stinging.

Arlo swallows down the tight humiliation advancing over him, unable to answer her. *Why am I like this?*

He stoops to fold the cloth and when he stands up she's halfway down the shitty beach, striding away without him, her dress the colour of arsenic.

He wants to try again but is missing the bit that would allow him to risk it.

'Sorry,' he says to the wind. Imagining he hears what she's thinking: *Are you coming to get me now?*

The river looks heavy, a thick black blanket pressing down on the riverbed, keeping the cold and dark in.

The beach shivers. Tablecloth too small to cloak it. The borrowed jacket on Jessica's shoulders, gone. A tug at the back of his throat. Can't keep the world warm, can't even keep himself warm.

FOUR

'Where've you been?' says Luke, as Arlo slinks back to their table inside the bar half an hour later. 'People have been asking after you.'

'What people?'

'Just people. Guy. The others. Were you with that girl I saw you with earlier?'

Arlo nods but doesn't elaborate. He doesn't want to get into a debrief right now. Everyone has one friend who has no idea how to whisper and Luke is his.

Luke is used to Arlo's disappearing acts so he gets back to holding court, laughing and slapping backs with his giant hands.

'Cheer up, mate. I know you're devastated that I'm leaving, but try to get your shit together.' It's Guy, one of Luke's friends from swimming. Guy is leaving for a month-long trip to find himself and had decided to throw himself going-away drinks, the reason they are all there. 'Sucks to miss people.' He clashes his pint against Arlo's. 'Cheers.'

The people on *The Beat* had given Arlo a leaving party. It was OK at first, then all the colour got sucked out of him and he'd gone for a walk so the party had to middle and end without him.

'You're only going for a month, Guy,' Arlo mumbles into his pint. It's warm but he's thirsty so glugs it down. Luke hands him another.

'Five weeks, mate. And it's longer than you've ever been anywhere for,' says Guy in his banter voice, then adds, 'Absolute craic about your army, bro.'

Arlo has no idea what he's talking about so just nods and says, 'Yeah, they're great. Really loyal.' It's the sort of vanilla thing he's used to saying when asked about his fans.

'There's loyal and there's batshit, mate.'

'Yeah.'

Guy turns to Luke, asks, 'What's up with the kid?'

'Nothing, he's fine.' At almost twenty-three, Luke is three long years older than Arlo.

What is up with me?

Things that used to feel like luxuries have started to feel like problems and he hates that. He won't let himself become spoiled. He doesn't think he feels sad this time, not yet anyway, but he's definitely sinking again. Arlo doesn't mind some sadness anyway. It's not as easy to share as happiness, but it fills him up more than numbness and it's better than dread and not knowing why he gets so angry. Why he's so claustrophobic in his own life even though it's a good one.

That was why Jessica's invitation to go outside had been so

24

appealing. That and the fact that she was funny and smart and wearing a shiny dress that rippled when the pub's disco-ball lights rotated over her. She was a lighthouse.

He looks over to where she's rejoined her group.

She and her friends take turns in pouring beer into each other's open mouths, letting themselves be filled like petrol tanks. An athletic-looking guy, maybe a footballer, fawns over her, at once cocky and obedient.

Arlo's stomach groans from the volume of beer he's tipped into it.

She never once looks over to him.

It's worse than if she and her friends had pointed and laughed. He feels for sand under his fingernails to check that he didn't dream it all. An imprint of one of her eyebrows rests in a smudged frown on his cuff. Proof.

Arlo downs his drink, summons his charm. One of his tricks; he can really turn it on when he tries, even while his brain is doing something else completely. With the right number of drinks he can be light and witty, even make fun of himself, all while a part of him feels like he's on fire or drowning.

He flirts with everyone, grabs a pool cue and joins a game that isn't his. Buys huge rounds of shots, bottles of champagne though he hates the stuff. All with a smile as wide as the sea. He laughs until he starts finding things funny. Fake it till you make it.

A couple of girls, clearly underage, ask him for a photo. They press up against him, sweet perfume clogging his throat. He feels a hand on his hips and another invading the back of his neck. It's contact, but it's empty.

They take five, six, seven selfies with him until they get one that they're both happy with. Arlo's face is frozen in a well-practised smile in all of them. Tongue on the back of the teeth to stop the grin from wilting. Rebecca, the kindest make-up artist on *The Beat*, had taught him that. 'Tits and teeth,' she'd laughed. 'At least you only have to do the teeth bit, love.'

'Get in here, Luke.' He calls his friend over and pulls him into the pictures.

'You must be mashed if you're volunteering for photos.'

The girls thank them with hugs when they're done. The suffocating perfume again.

'You smell great,' Arlo tells one or both of them. They leave happy, charmed.

Arlo gets back to the party. He's brighter, louder, more out of control than anyone else. Crashes into a table, sends glasses flying, a roar and applause, he stoops and bows but can't get back up again. Luke apologises on his behalf and helps him on to a chair.

'Maybe you should sit this round out.'

'We should go somewhere,' Arlo tells him.

'You can barely stand up.'

'We should go on a trip. We've been talking about going to places that people never go since we were kids but we never actually *go* anywhere. Let's go somewhere.'

'OK, buddy, we will.'

'I mean it.'

'I know you do,' says Luke.

'Shake on it.'

They shake.

Arlo downs a coke, calms down a bit.

Jessica is having the time of her life on the other side of the bar. He should go over there, say sorry.

'Do you know who she is? Her full name, I mean,' he asks Luke.

'Who *who* is?'

Arlo nods over to Jessica.

'Nope.'

'Jessica something. Reality star,' Guy butts in.

Jessica Something and Maybe Footballer Guy clink glasses and chug.

If they've noticed Arlo they don't show it. Men never ask him for a selfie. And if their girlfriends do, the guys usually pretend they don't know who he is. Arlo gets it; he's always been proud of the show, it entertains millions of people and gives families something to talk about, but by some people's standards he's not a cool actor.

Suddenly he can't do it any more. 'Can we get out of here?'

'Sure, buddy. You OK?'

'Great. I think I lost your jacket though.'

It takes Luke ten minutes to say goodbye to everyone. Finally, he hugs Guy, engulfing him like a giant mattress. 'Love you, man, have a great trip.'

Guy hugs him back, says, 'Love you too, bro,' though they're not brothers.

Arlo always wanted a sibling to take care of, to take sides against his mum with. Maybe he'd be better at making friends if he'd had one from the start, but it never happened. Maybe his dad hadn't been home enough. Had his mum begged him not to leave? It didn't matter. His father had left anyway; many times on purpose and then, finally, by accident. Dead by the time Arlo turned four.

'Night cap?' Arlo asks Luke when they get home.

'Nah.'

The stagger home has sobered them up. Maybe they'll head up to the roof.

Instead they go into the lounge and battle digital demons for a while.

They play a game similar to one the army uses to train recruits, hammering the consoles and staring at the flashing, blood-drenched screen until Luke eventually calls Arlo out in his gentle Lukish way, 'So, you were a bit much tonight. Everything OK?'

'Fine.'

'You sure? You've seemed off lately.'

Arlo keeps staring straight ahead at the giant screen. 'All good, man.'

'Just checking because last time . . .'

Last time, shadows and black weeds twisted through Arlo's brain and body, pinning him in his bed. He was exhausted and hopeless and trapped in a spiral of hateful thoughts. Last time, he'd lashed out and folded inwards. Last time, his hurt had injured his mum in the most unimaginable ways. She'd absorbed it as if it were her own.

The low had lasted almost four months. He's two-and-a-half years clear of the worst of it now but it left a trace.

But last time was the last time. It had come out of nowhere and he won't let that happen again. Life is still desaturated, its colour downgraded, but he's alive. He has medication when he needs it and exercise and drawing and Luke, and Luke's chicken and broccoli. He has acting and making things and their project on the roof.

'Just blowing off steam,' Arlo says. Better to be too much than not enough, surely.

'OK.'

'Cool.'

Luke has stopped playing to ask him the question.

Arlo can't resist. He thumbs the console and shoots a hole in Luke's avatar's head.

If Luke is hurt he doesn't show it. 'Right then, I guess I'm done.'

'One more game?'

'I'm wrecked, mate. Night.'

'OK. See you tomorrow.'

And just as he's done every evening since he left *The Beat*, when the next logical step is to go to bed, Arlo feels the cold arms of panic tighten around him. Imaginary itches start to crawl his skin and he knows the door to sleep has closed with him on the wrong side of it.

He flicks through his phone. A message from his mum, just checking in. He admires her for starting again in a new country but they subsist on texts now. It's the time difference. That's not true; it's only an hour. The truth is Arlo pushed her away. He sends just enough messages to keep her from worrying, few enough that she can't sense when he's hurt.

Arlo looks out of the window. Luke's car sits a few doors down, shining like Jessica's dress in the moonlight. If only he hadn't been so cold to her, that his ego wasn't so fragile. That he could be a tank like Luke.

Arlo has always been thin-skinned. All the things that make him a good actor leave him poorly equipped for real life.

Just go to bed.

In the bathroom, he pops out a tablet from its silver sleeve and swallows it with lukewarm water from the tap. He was proud of himself for going to the doctor when he first felt himself slipping again. She'd been kind and suggested a short course of sleeping tablets to see if some sleep could get him back on track.

Arlo counts the remaining pills. Only three left. If he doesn't feel better when they're gone, the doctor said to come back to discuss trying something else.

You need to get control of this.

Don't let things get bad again.

He forces himself into bed.

His notebook is on the bedside table as always. He unpicks the knot in the twine that holds the pages together and starts to draw. Simple lines – the alley with the dead end, a few wrong turns, the suggestion of a beach. He adds a rowing boat and a fatberg. Then he makes a tiny sketch of the homeless man; now at least someone knows where he is.

Arlo reties the knot and puts the notebook back in its place. Drawing helps to empty his head sometimes. It's part of what the doctor calls his toolkit.

It's gone 2 a.m. but he checks his phone again.

Seven missed calls from Russell and a message that reads, 'CALL ME.'

'They thought your tape was interesting,' his agent blurts as soon as he picks up.

'They liked me?' Someone has put a balloon inside each of Arlo's lungs and is inflating them to bursting point.

'They want you to fly out for a screen test. They've cast the female lead and the other guy already, so you'll be reading with them.'

'Who are they?'

'They won't tell us yet. Big names, apparently, so they don't want it leaking.' Russell pauses. 'Arlo, they really like you for the part. This could be big.'

'Big,' Arlo echoes.

'Feedback was that you completely disappeared into the character.'

His directors at school used to say the same. He was soluble; ready to dissolve and reform into a different version of himself at any moment.

'This thing is going to be massive,' says Russell. 'I'll get your flights booked.'

They hang up. A little door opens somewhere in Arlo's head and doubts tear through it like bats. He tries telling himself that he earned the audition, that his life is more than a series of flukes and coincidences, snakes and ladders. He's worked hard for this.

His brain talks to itself while he lies in the bare bedroom pinned by the scratching lick of night. He waits for the sleeping tablet to suck him down the plughole until, finally, he's pulled down through the mattress into the wrong kind of sleep.

FIVE

'Sorry about shooting you in the face.'

Arlo hollers the apology before Luke has even finished climbing the last steps on to the roof. It's getting dark. The day has passed without him noticing.

'That's OK,' Luke calls back, 'it didn't hurt. I have extraordinary facial strength from talking so much. My mug can withstand any impact. You forgot to wedge the door, by the way.'

Arlo hears the clatter of the old patio chair that they use to keep the fire door closed so nobody hears them or gets curious as to why it's open and wanders out.

'I wasn't sure if I'd hear you knock if you came up.'

It's the first time Arlo's been up here by himself since the night he found the pool. It was the night of his leaving party from *The Beat* about a month ago. They have his insomnia to thank for the discovery. At around 3 a.m. he'd found himself exploring their building and pushing through the 'EMERGENCY USE ONLY' door at the end of the corridor on their floor.

To the left of the fire escape outside he'd found the crumbling steps that lead out on to the raised terrace. It runs across the top of what used to be a hotel and is now three separate buildings internally.

At the far end of the roof on the city side, Arlo had found a huge double sheet of tarpaulin. His stomach juddered as he'd peeled it back. *Please don't be a body underneath.* Logically he knew a body was unlikely – that would have made a human-sized lump under the tarp where instead it was sagging with the weight of itself. The sheet was heavy as he'd dragged it away. Underneath was just a hole. Or rather, a half-constructed swimming pool about the size of three Jacuzzis but rectangular, with the two longer sides running parallel to the edge of the roof. It stank and was full of fetid leaves despite someone's attempt to cover it. Arlo knew immediately that he had to convince Luke that they should clean it out and try to fix it up.

Imagine, their own private rooftop pool. The 'we've made it' version of the paddling pool they'd had when they were younger.

Shoulder to shoulder, they've spent weeks scrubbing out the inside of the filthy basin, turfing out sacks full of rotten leaves and moss, filling in the cracks with heavy duty Polyfilla.

Luke stops wrestling with the patio chair and comes out on to the roof as Arlo hauls himself out of the pool to sit in their usual spot. They always sit on the long edge facing out on to the city with their legs dangling into the empty basin.

Luke flops down juggling two bowls, beers and his camera. A cloud of chlorine lifts from him. 'Here.'

Arlo takes one of the bowls. 'What's this?' he asks, though it patently contains chopped chicken and broccoli.

'Chicky titties.' One of Luke's many names for chicken breasts. 'You smell like a bar mat, by the way.'

'I haven't showered yet.'

'No shit. Have you been up here all day?'

Luke doesn't wait for Arlo's answer before turning on the camera and recording himself talking about 'fail to prepare, prepare to fail' before training the lens on the contents of his bowl. He produces a small plastic bag of ground red powder from his pocket and waggles it in front of the camera. 'Now for the secret ingredient. Recipe in the link below. Let me know in the comments if you try it.'

He points the camera skywards then flips it round to film the inside of the pool, telling his subscribers about their secret project, showing them their mini forest. Luke knows better than to point the camera at Arlo. He understands Arlo doesn't want any of his private life made public ever again. Sometimes it feels like Luke is the only person who doesn't need Arlo to be a performing seal.

Recording done, Luke flaps the bag at Arlo. 'Want some?'

'What is it?'

'Steroid powder. Been sponsored to do a vlog about it.'

'What?'

'Just messing. It's sumac,' says Luke.

'What the hell is sumac?'

'A spice, I think. I don't actually know.' Luke sniffs the bag, brain rotating like a rotisserie chicken. 'Like lemon maybe?'

'You mean lime?'

'Since when is lime red? I mean sumac. Try it.'

He shakes some into Arlo's bowl before he can protest.

Arlo picks up a piece of the now red-coated chicken and inspects it before putting it into his mouth. 'This almost has flavour,' he says.

'Hmmm. Almost.' Luke laughs. 'I'm starving.'

'It's right on the cusp of flavour. It's flavour adjacent. Thanks.'

Luke doesn't let chewing get in the way of talking. 'I had the most batshit dream last night. It was you, me, Guy, Jessica from the bar who you may or may not have had literal sex on the beach with, and we were all . . . what the fuck have you done to your hands?'

Arlo's eyes follow Luke's down to his fingers. His nails are rusty with drying blood and the skin on his right palm is split and still bleeding. He wipes both hands on his jeans. 'They're fine. Your dream?'

Arlo can't remember the last dream he had. Not an actual, all-the-way-down-the-ladder dream. When he actually gets to sleep, there is nothing.

'What've you been doing?' asks Luke.

'Just cleaning the tiles.' He gestures a stinging hand to the end of the small pool where the most damaged tiling is. 'I forgot to put gloves on.'

'Jesus.'

In truth, Arlo had been on the roof working for hours, full of a strange energy that he needed to get out of his body somehow. Exercise is another part of his toolkit.

He couldn't face the gym this morning; it makes him feel

trapped, running miles on the rubber road of the treadmill, going nowhere. The guys with 'roid rage hulking about at the weights station. Flex, flex, flex. The locker room talk. Sweating, grunting, crowing.

Those bodies take real effort, he knows. One autumn it seemed that all the boys but him came back to school with different bodies. His new one didn't arrive until two summers later and by then it was too late for his mind to get in step with it.

'Let me see,' Luke says, grabbing Arlo's cut hand.

Luke seems so annoyed that Arlo asks, 'Are you pissed that I came up here without you?'

'No, but we'll both be pissed if you lose your fingers because I wasn't here to supervise you.'

'Sorry, I should have waited until you got home.'

'I don't care about the pool, Arlo. I mean, I do care, but you're the one who's obsessed with it.'

'I'm not obsessed with it.'

Luke glances at Arlo's hands as if to suggest otherwise. 'Just don't get sumac in the cuts. It'll sting like fuckery.'

They laugh, tension resolved.

'You got a lot done today,' Luke says.

'Yeah.'

He'd scrubbed a significant portion of the damaged tiles. Smoothed off their chipped edges and filled in the gaps in between them the best he could with the tools they have. There was something rhythmic about it. Something satisfying about seeing the ugly, broken tiles made new.

The sun slides behind the tall buildings to the west. Luke hands Arlo some gloves, grabs his own, and jumps down into the pool sending up a small shower of the tree blossom as he lands. Despite their efforts to fix it securely, the tarp cover still doesn't keep everything out.

The trees need to breathe anyway.

They get to work. Arlo's mind drifts back to the paddling pool that was inflated every summer on the caravan park when they were kids. Its squashy walls were patched together with strips of masking tape and sprung a leak every time someone climbed into it.

If Arlo ever got it to himself, he used to lie back and pretend that the water lapping over him belonged to some strange planet. In this new world, everyone had smooth parts and he wasn't scared of the girls because there weren't any genders.

He was five when he and his mum had first moved to the caravan site owned by Luke's parents. Luke was older, cooler, and had invited him to paddle before they'd even unpacked the car. It was summer solstice. Hours and hours of heat and laughter and barbeque. Skin puckered from endless soaking and splashing. Eyes stinging with sun cream and pollen and whatever Mr Swanson put in the pool water to keep it clean. Arlo can still see the cartoons on the side of it – animals chasing each other in an endless circuit.

By the time he got his scholarship seven years later, the creatures were faded, their toothy grins defaced and peeling. He never saw it again; it must have been consigned to the bin when the heat faded not long after he got to the school.

'Here.' Luke hands him a head torch when the sun fades completely. Between the torches and the never-dimming glow of the city, they do some of their best work after sundown.

They don't talk much while they brush on the sealant, but it feels sort of intimate anyway.

'Let's take a break,' Luke says after an hour or so, grabbing two beers.

They climb out of the pool and Arlo follows Luke to the railing at the edge of the roof. The high street is two roads over from them. One of six hundred roads that make up fifty kilometres of high street linking one side of the city to the other. Somewhere over there, construction workers had dug up bowling balls, coins, skulls, jewellery, while they tried to build a railway. Further away still, there are green spaces and shimmering glass buildings.

It's a beautiful, humming view. They're so lucky to be here, to be starting out in careers that they love, able to get enough rent together to live so centrally in the capital. Arlo knows all this.

'Do you ever think how weird it is that we're just allowed to live here and nobody checks on us?' he asks.

'Well, technically the landlady inspects the place once a quarter and I'm sure she'd be round in a shot if we didn't pay the rent.'

'Rent is paid up for the year.'

'I still can't believe you did that,' says Luke. 'I'll pay you back.'

'Only if you want to,' says Arlo. They had paid him good money on *The Beat* and he couldn't think of anything to do with it other than make sure the flat was theirs for the year and drip feed the rest to his mum. 'Anyway, you know what I mean.'

'Like we're responsible for ourselves?'

'Yeah, I guess.'

'Nobody rings your mum to check you're OK if you don't turn up for work now. You just get fired,' Luke says.

That's sort of what Arlo means but not all of it. He's trying to say that sometimes he feels like he's just playing at being a man, that someday someone will figure out he's still just a boy trapped in a slightly bigger body than the one he had a couple of years ago. Nobody will make him apologise to Jessica – *Do you have something you'd like to say to her?* – and the sorry he owes her hangs in the back of his mind like a wonky picture. Either way, he's glad to be here with Luke, of all people.

'I'm glad we're friends again,' he says, pushing the skin on his hand together as if trying to undo cutting it on the tiles.

'Seems a shame to throw away years of friendship because you forgot to wear gloves.'

'I don't mean that.'

'I know you don't,' says Luke. 'I'm glad too.'

That's enough for them to both know what they mean. They talk about most things but not the years that they weren't friends.

Nothing dramatic had happened. The three-year gap in their ages had just widened and started to mean new things at some point, then Arlo had gone away on his scholarship at the age of twelve.

That school hadn't worked out in the end and he'd gone back to his old one for his final year, but Luke was long gone by that point. He wasn't around the black summer when Arlo's brain seemed to break, though they've talked about it since. It wasn't until he got his job on *The Beat* and followed Luke to the city two years ago that they'd reconnected.

'Cheers,' he says to his friend.

Planes blip across the sky, wing lights flashing, white puffy trails behind them. They disappear. He'll be on one soon; flying towards his future, or his failure.

'I've got something to tell you,' Arlo says.

'Yeah?'

Arlo tells Luke about Russell's call and the screen test.

'Holy shit, we need to celebrate. We should have a party.'

'I haven't even tested yet. They could be seeing a hundred of us,' Arlo says, though he knows they won't be. Too expensive.

'You'll get it. I know you will. Arlo's Army are gonna cream themselves.'

'You know most of them are, like, twelve, don't you?'

Luke just howls in response. 'AwoOOOooo.'

They look up at the pollution.

'Are you nervous?' Luke asks.

'A bit.'

'But you want it?'

'Yeah. Yeah, I want it.'

'I wasn't sure if you were over the whole acting thing. No offence, but you didn't seem to enjoy it very much towards the end of *The Beat*.'

'No offence' is one of Luke's favourite sayings. In all honesty, Arlo had sometimes felt like a talking meat prop that was wheeled in to hit its mark and spout a few lines, but he could never be over it. It was all real to him; he was just using his character's name. When he got it right and felt that crackle of connection, it was like finding new colours inside himself.

'I want it,' he repeats. It feels good to say it out loud, as if it cements it in his mind. 'I want to make something that matters.'

'You will,' Luke says.

Arlo can't always feel his friend's love and sometimes he feels too much but tonight it's just right. 'We both will.'

'Hey, I want you to have something.' Luke yanks his wallet from his back pocket and pulls out a small medal on a striped ribbon.

'Your lucky medal?'

'Been carrying it around since I was nine.'

'I can't take that.'

'Have it.' He reaches over and hangs the medal round Arlo's neck, wallops him on the shoulder. 'There you go, champ.'

'Thanks. I'll give it back to you after I've tested.'

Luke tips his head back again and Arlo follows his gaze. The medal ribbon is tight around his neck. The clouds are atomic-bomb thick. Arlo yawns.

'No offence,' says Luke, 'but you look wrecked. Have you slept?'

'I closed my eyes when I sneezed earlier.' A piss-poor joke but it deflects Luke's concerns long enough for him to change the subject. 'It's going to rain. We should cover the pool.'

'I'll do it,' says Luke. 'Go to bed.'

The tarpaulin is in a heap by the railings.

'I'll help,' he offers.

'I want to film a bit more. I'll be down in a bit.'

Arlo is too tired to disagree.

It's spitting now. A leaky, layered sky, soaking up the glow from a million offices, flats, hospital rooms. Arlo counts cranes on the skyline instead of sheep to prepare himself for bed. It looks like the moon is hung on the hook of one of the taller yellow ones. One swing of that boom and the moon would lose its grip on the sea. Tides would turn.

We're all made of water.

Vertigo.

The floor wants him.

He shakes it off, turns back to Luke.

'Thanks,' he says, tapping the medal.

'Hey,' Luke calls, 'tomorrow we have to talk about where we're gonna go on our trip. Maybe that island you used to draw all the time. The one with all the foxes.'

Rabbits.

'We'll have to get a new atlas.'

'Yeah, or we could use this thing I've heard about called the internet.'

'Hilarious,' says Arlo.

'AwoOOOooo.'

'Night.'

Arlo lies in bed with his feet out of the end of the duvet.

It was nice of Luke to lend him the medal. Luke with his endless patience and enthusiasm. Arlo has an idea and grabs his phone. The screen illuminates night-time shapes in his room as he searches the internet.

Two luxury lilos with cup holders. And a pump. They can get rid of the shitty sun lounger and keep the chair for wedging the door closed. Luke could use the cup holder for his protein shakes. Next-day delivery. Perfect. A drone should come by and just drop them straight on the roof.

Is Luke still up there?

He listens for a howl or a snore. Nothing.

Rain starts to tap on the window. April showers, his mum would say.

The sleeping pill is starting to take hold. He's so tired. The small room so empty.

Arlo slips his hand inside his boxer shorts and starts to run a film of him and Jessica in his head. He summons her dress first, fills it with her body. Gives her hair, feels her breath on his neck. She opens her sleeping eyes to look at him as if to remind him she's not some creature made for him to lie down with until he falls asleep. *What's my name? I'm a real person. I'm on reality TV.*

He tightens his grip. Makes her close her eyes, open her inky mouth. Minutes later, he wipes stickiness from his stomach and the idea of her heavy make-up seems sad.

Rain hammers harder on the glass as his thoughts fold into empty sleep. Cold as swimming pools in winter.

SIX

Arlo runs so far and so hard the next morning that his legs feel weak when he stops. His head is clearer. Moving usually helps a bit, he just can't always remember that.

He stands panting on the rain-soaked doorstep as he pulls his key from his sock. Once inside, he finds a cardboard box with his name on it in the hallway. The lilos.

After a shower, Arlo helps himself to a couple of boiled eggs from one of Luke's Tupperware boxes, peeling the shells on to the breakfast bar.

He sits tracing out the route he just ran. The pages of his notebook are almost full of line drawings, half art, half cartography. His own secret atlas. Will he get a new one when he gets to the end – what will he do with this one? It would be cool to have something special to draw before he runs out of space.

Arlo dates the corner of today's sketch and shuts the

notebook. He sets it on the breakfast bar next to a pile of bills and the blackboard that they write nonsense messages to each other on.

'Gone for firewood.' Confident, green letters. Luke's words, from days ago. Arlo had written 'Gone vljogging' underneath in blue earlier, then stuck a thick line through the 'vl' and added 'like a normal human'. Old, half-rubbed-out messages – 'gone to the moon', 'gone diving', 'gone to the farm'. There aren't any rules to this game, other than they're always going somewhere and Luke is always green, Arlo blue.

The bills remind Arlo he'd been meaning to send some money to his mum. He transfers it to her and messages her to let her know. She calls him straight away.

'Thank you, love,' she says. 'Are you sure you don't need it?'

Arlo is not a big spender. He still has plenty of money from the show.

'I want you to have it, Mum.'

'I still can't get used to you having all this cash. Why don't you use some of it to come and see your auntie and me?'

'I will. I just can't at the moment.' The request annoys him, probably because he hates the feeling of letting her down. 'I have to work.'

'I thought you were taking time off?'

'I'm preparing. I have a big audition coming up.'

'You do? That's wonderful.'

He imagines his mother's face, the way she used to look at his as if she could see herself together with his father in it. She is the reason he absorbs other people's sadness and takes it on as his own. She's a magnet for it.

'Are you looking after yourself?'

'Of course.' He smiles while he says it. A trick he was taught for radio interviews to lift the voice. 'Don't worry.'

She tells him about a market she and his aunt have found. They've been practising their haggling.

'I have to go, Mum,' he tells her.

She hasn't quite finished her story about negotiating a discount on some lace curtains but he knows where it's going and is impatient.

'OK. Thank you for the money. I'm so proud of you.'

'OK. Bye, Mum.'

'Call me again soon. And let me know what you want for your birthday.'

'I will.'

He hates talking on the phone. His mum was so sad when he went away to school, maybe sadder than he was because she was left behind, and Arlo can still hear her missing him in her voice.

They hang up.

Why is it so hard to say real things to her? He had only ever spoken to his father as a child; they never had a conversation as men. He doesn't even know what drink his dad would order in a bar. But Arlo's an adult now, he should be able to talk to his mum. He texts her to say he loves her and wonders what she's doing now they've hung up.

He decides to take the lilos up to the roof so they're ready when Luke gets home. Arlo rolls one out on to the breakfast bar and inflates it. The mouthpiece is uncooperative and it takes all his patience to get it closed again once he's finished blowing it up.

'Shit.' *Should have taken them up to the roof first, then inflated them.*

He shoves a lilo under each armpit, one big and buoyant, the other folded and manageable.

The fire door is stuck when Arlo pushes it.

'Fuck's sake.' He sets the lilos down and pushes all his weight against the bar on the door. It doesn't budge.

'Luke,' he calls, feeling like an idiot. 'Are you out there?'

Silence.

He gives the door one last heft and hears a clatter on the other side. The chair. *Luke must be out there.* He presses down on the bar again and the door swings open.

'Luke, it's me,' he calls.

Still no response.

He leaves the lilos propping the door open and takes the steps to the roof two at a time. Any second now Luke will leap out and lurch towards him like a zombie. Arlo holds his body stiff so he won't jump when it happens.

'Luke. You're not funny.'

The rooftop is as slippery and blossom-coated as the streets below. Arlo skids, feels himself blush.

Nobody's up here.

But the door was wedged shut.

He looks towards the ledge. His eyes land on a beer bottle on its side in front of the low railing.

He feels himself sway.

Dread blisters over his shoulders and down his back.

Somehow he gets himself across the roof to the railing and steels himself to look over the edge, knowing he will see Luke's crumpled body on the street below or crushed into the roof of a parked car. Blood will trickle from his broken nose. Dislocated limbs will jut and twist. Dead, fishy eyes.

Will Arlo be able to see all that from up here or will the detail come afterwards when he tears down six flights of stairs to the road – will he be the first on the scene?

Everything will change, that much he knows.

Arlo plants his feet back from the ledge so he doesn't topple over and leans forward.

His eyes sweep and search.

No body.

Nobody.

'Get a grip,' he tells himself.

He picks up the bottle and holds it up to the light. Things float on the surface – bits of plant, maybe a bug or two. He swills it. Beer dregs diluted with last night's rain. Sets it down again. Luke can clean up his own mess.

He throws one last look over the railing and goes back down to get the lilos. He'll blow them up and stick them in the pool with the trees for Luke to find later.

'Oh, shit.' The pump is downstairs in the kitchen.

Arlo blows up the second lilo without it, challenging himself to do it without a break no matter how dizzy he feels. He seems to make no progress at first then, all of a sudden, it unfurls and pings into shape. Done. He wobbles to his feet, enjoying the head rush.

The view up here is really something.

Maybe they'll pay someone to fix the pool properly so they can actually use it this summer. He can imagine being buoyed up by water, bobbing away, a tiny dot on the horizon. Maybe he'd invite Jessica Something to swim up here. It feels as if it would be easier to not fuck it up if they were lifted out of the city. They could get to know each other. It's his birthday next month. Twenty. They could have a party up here. String some lights in the trees, get a barbeque or something.

He can see now that the pool isn't quite covered. The tarp is over it and the kettle bells are in place but the far edge has slipped and draped itself into the basin. That end of the pool will be wet and full of sludge again – trust Luke not to finish the job properly after all the effort they put into emptying and cleaning it. Too busy filming himself probably.

It starts to spit and only now does it occur to Arlo that perhaps he's so fixated on sorting out the damn lilos because they're a distraction from what he should be doing – making a doctor's appointment and preparing for his trip. But having wasted this much time, he may as well see it through, so he pulls the lilos over to the side of the pool and lifts the kettle bells off the rain-slick tarp. It's heavy without Luke's help so he turns round to drag it behind him as if he were a cart horse.

He bundles the cover into a heap and turns round.

And there, face down among the trees and blossom at the bottom of the pool, is Luke.

When the police arrive, Arlo is in the pool trying to get Luke's shoes off his stiff feet. A faint voice issues instructions from his phone, but he ignores it. He'd called 999 and the voice had told him an ambulance was on its way and started talking about checking airways and breathing into Luke's mouth, but Arlo had put his phone on the pool basin.

He hasn't checked his friend's pulse or lifted his head to look at his face. He doesn't know if there's blood leaking from Luke's nose, if his eyes are glassy or his mouth is open and silent as if he doesn't know the answer. He'd just looked so broken lying there in the mulch that Arlo had to try to make him comfortable.

Nobody sleeps with their shoes on.

He works at the wet laces but his fingers don't seem to belong to him.

A man and woman in police uniform appear at the side of the pool above him, mouths moving. He'd heard them cross the roof calling out to him. The fizz and sputter of their radios.

He's finally got one of Luke's huge trainers undone but can't get the foot to bend right to pull it off. Tiny balls of pollen and dismembered blossom are ground into the grooves and lines of the sole. He grips Luke's ankle and pulls at the shoe. 'Help me,' he whispers, partly to Luke, partly to the police.

Two paramedics in green jumpsuits arrive. All but one of the uniforms drop down into the pool next to him and Luke. One of the green jumpsuits unzips her bag while the other goes straight to Luke's head, pressing fingers against his neck.

Pointless.

They'll crack his ribs trying to resuscitate him. Bone can come loose from the rest of you when someone does that, breaking off like slabs of ice detaching from their poles. It didn't work on Dad either. There was fluid on his lungs.

Arlo notes the hot white tear of his heart breaking. His veins feel bright and full as he tells them, 'He's dead.'

Something happens to time once the paramedics confirm what Arlo had already told them.

He's helped out of the pool and led to the other side of the roof where time sticks, stops. A door unhinges in his head and he slips inside, deeper and deeper. A portal. He's been through this door before, the summer of the black weeds. Away from the shapes and their voices, and clocks that only truly go forward. Time slides with him, trips backwards. He looks up to the sky. Tired. Closes his eyes and conjures pollution, a low moon, Luke sitting backwards on the patio chair next to him. They'll cover the pool and the trees together, then they'll both go to bed. Whoever gets up first will write something green or blue on the blackboard.

'CID will be here shortly,' someone tells him.

Time restarts.

'CID?'

'Criminal Investigations Department. They're on their way.'

Luke's not a criminal though.

The beer bottle is lifted into a plastic bag and sealed.

My fingerprints.

The paramedics say things to Arlo in a consoling tone. One writes something on a pad and hands the piece of paper to the police.

Time stops again until two more police officers arrive, this time without uniform.

They sit him on the top step with his back to the pool. He pushes the palms of his hands into the chipped stone, gripping, shredding his nails on its sharpness. Knuckles white. If he lets go, he will slide off the earth.

There are questions.

'What's your relationship to the deceased? Are you a relative?'

For a second he can't remember. 'Flatmate,' he chokes. 'He's my friend too.'

'How long have you lived here?'

'Two years. It'll be two years next month.'

It'll be my birthday next month too.

They ask him questions about what he found. When Luke and he had last seen each other. How did he seem? Whether he'd moved the body. *Call him Luke, not the body.* They take notes. They ask about Luke's state of mind. His next of kin. His GP.

The lilos shine in the sun and drizzle. Brilliant, useless.

Please don't let there be a rainbow.

A voice calls from the pool, 'Come and look at this.'

Arlo feels his brain send a message to his legs to try to lift him off the steps but someone has cut the cord that connects them. His fingers won't uncurl either. Another shape gets up and goes towards the voice. A hand on Arlo's shoulder keeps him where he is. They don't mean for *him* to go and look.

A tall shape suggests tea. Does that mean they want him to make it? Arlo doesn't understand.

Arlo is taken downstairs to the flat. It buzzes with respectful, purposeful activity. Luke's phone and laptop are seized. *Will they tell his mum if they find porn on it?*

They photograph the messages on the blackboard.

'The green is Luke,' Arlo explains.

'*Gone for firewood,*' a shape reads Luke's words out. 'Any significance?'

'I don't know,' says Arlo. 'I don't think so. No.' It feels as if he's lying.

The eggshells still sit on the breakfast bar next to the bills.

When Arlo moved to the city, Luke had to show him how to pay one. His fingers itch to touch the envelopes to plug himself into the memory.

'This yours?' the shape points to Arlo's notebook next to the envelopes.

'Yes.'

'Diary? Journal?' A neutral enquiry.

What's the difference?

'Sketches.' The shape doesn't ask to see inside but doesn't stop Arlo as he unpicks his special knot and flips through the pages to show there's nothing written inside, just pictures. The last ten or so pages still blank.

The shape nods as if to confirm, yes, these are clearly devoid of any meaning.

A call is made to Luke's parents.

Arlo imagines Mrs Swanson on the other end of the phone as she slides through her own little door. Hand to mouth, skin draining like dishwater. A sick feeling as she sinks into a world without colour. On her knees: too late to pray.

Where will they take Luke?

Arlo went through a phase of wanting to give his own body to medical science when he died, but then someone told him that they send it back to your family when they're done with it. Imagine that, his empty body arriving at the small farm house overseas, his mother or his aunt finding it on the doorstep. What do they send it in? In this scenario, he always dies before his mother.

The police look in Arlo's room too.

'Moving out?' asks a shape, motioning to the handful of boxes by the window.

'No.' How can he explain that even after two years in this flat, he just likes to feel contained and portable?

Someone tells Arlo not to worry; his name won't appear in anything that's released to the press. *Oh. They know who I am.* He'd forgotten himself for a while. Maybe they watch *The Beat.* It is about police after all.

People come in and out, some in uniforms, some not. Arlo can't keep track of who's who, though they all explain their roles in hushed tones, their heads tilted forty-five degrees in sympathy. *Which one is the coroner? Who do they think is a criminal?*

Arlo sits at the breakfast bar, eyes mapping the slope of Luke's letters on the blackboard, then following a line of green chalk dust down over its bottom edge and on to the floor.

The lower part of the fridge is grubby. Greasy tidemarks grow up from the base, peaking and troughing in a ghostly mountain range. He's never noticed the grime before. There are crumbs all along the edge of the cupboards. Everything looks greasy, filthy. Arlo's skin stretches as if trying to escape to somewhere clean.

Luminous numbers on the oven clock change while he blinks: 11.57 a.m. He prepares himself for the three tiny beeps that will mark midday.

One floor above, Luke is wrapped and strapped to a stretcher and carried down off the roof in slow motion.

SEVEN

Ten days later, a hollow numbness that he can't name chases Arlo to the airport before dawn.

The check-in desks heave with migrating backpackers. They clump together in tribes, flashing their access-all-areas passports. All self-assured, millennial mettle. Arlo feels a hundred years apart from them.

Everyone told him he'd feel better after the funeral, but he doesn't. He'd got through it by acting as if he were on set – *This isn't real. We're playing pretend* – and now he doesn't feel anything.

On the other side of the airport in the arrivals hall, swarms of travellers return laden with beads and eastern philosophies.

All these people looking to find themselves and all I want is to be lost.

The queue crawls forward. Arlo's head is pounding. A heavy weight behind his forehead blurs his vision.

He's barely looked at the pages for the audition, tries to run the lines in his head. Russell doesn't know about Luke yet. He might have seen it on the news but won't have known they shared a flat.

A few desks over, a conversation gets heated. 'You wouldn't be allowed to enter the country when you land. You'd be sent back. I'm sorry but we cannot allow you to fly with us today.'

There is misunderstanding, mistrust. People grow impatient.

One speaks, alone in their panic, and the loud voice replies, 'I'm sorry, I don't understand you. A translator will be here shortly. Please step aside.'

Another voice says, 'Desk number eleven, please, sir. Keep the queue moving. Number eleven.'

'Sorry,' Arlo says and shuffles forward, so tired that he feels like a hologram of himself. The beginnings and ends of objects, and which colour belongs to which, are unfixed. Even pulling and pushing air in and out of his lungs is harder than usual.

He hands over his passport and is asked if he has a seat preference. No interpreter required.

Arlo would like to sit next to the person who looks least likely to die in an accident but just says, 'Aisle.'

'Go straight to security. Gate thirty-seven. Have a nice flight.'

Laughter reaches Arlo and he hears his name whispered. 'That's Arlo Thomas.' A kid, about eleven or twelve, and his mother have recognised him.

He freezes.

Please don't come over. Don't talk to me. Not today.

They don't.

Why not?

The kid holds his phone out in front of him and pretends to read a message. Arlo shifts to face the other way, seething. The unmistakeable click of a photo being taken. *Should be illegal to take people's pictures without asking.*

Still, Arlo doesn't move.

I can't do this.

His ears hum with high notes like emergency whistles.

Luke's dead.

The thought rolls through him, ripping, tearing at his insides, smashing all the air out of his lungs and pinning him against an invisible wall.

Luke's dead Luke's dead Luke's dead Luke's dead Luke's dead Luke's dead Luke's dead Luke's dead Luke's dead Luke's dead Luke's dead Luke's dead Luke's dead Luke's dead.

Arlo is at the end of himself. No thoughts left other than that he can't be here any more and he can't go where he's supposed to be going either. He just can't. He has to escape.

'Can I help you with anything else, sir?'

A protracted conversation follows. Arlo's sentences won't come out right but eventually he gets what he needs, hands over a credit card, and one piece of paper is swapped for another.

Russell is going to kill him but he had to do it. He can't risk another black summer, even if he has to stay lost for ever. Even if it means he never makes anything again.

Once on board his flight, a woman whose badge indicates that she speaks five languages, announces that an exceptional crew will tend to their safety and comfort during the twelve-hour journey.

Twelve hours.

An hour longer than the flight would have been if he'd been able to make himself go where he should be going. Instead, they will hurtle eight thousand kilometres in the other direction to a place without a shared language. Somewhere he can get lost until it stops hurting, somewhere he and Luke had dreamed of.

This isn't the first time he's run away. He did it all the time as a kid, shouting 'Leave me alone!' when he meant 'I'm scared, come and get me, show me you love me.'

The plane heaves itself into the sky. The city below reaches for him, strangled and forced upwards by the tight green belt around it.

They bank right, through a break in the cloud. Sun slices through the small windows and Arlo spins through a kaleidoscope of Luke and talking shapes in uniforms. Paramedics, police. The way they'd fixed a ring of official tape around the forest in the swimming pool. The way they'd called Luke 'the body' and taken away the kettle bell that Luke had tripped on and seized his camera's memory card.

Arlo sees Luke's parents and Guy at the funeral. Hears the heartbreak in his own mum's voice when he'd called to tell her, the quieter pain when he told her not to come to the service. It would be easier without her, he'd said. What he didn't say was he knows she needs him to be well, to be coping, and he couldn't guarantee that. He has to protect her.

The aircraft banks back to the left. His hand aches. He should take some painkillers but all his medication is still in the bathroom at home.

The motion makes him woozy. He's barely slept all week,

just keeps thinking that it doesn't make sense that someone so strong could be dead.

If he closes his eyes, he can pretend he's in the back of his mum's car with Luke on a grand adventure.

He can hear her telling the story about the place where his grandpa was from and how it wasn't on maps any more. He had migrated across the country before Arlo was born when the valley he came from was drowned to create a reservoir. Most of the houses and the cemetery were submerged. The year that Arlo was born, a drought had dried out the valley and the village had reappeared but they never went back.

He and Luke sat in the back of the car, their hearts full of the idea of a disappearing village, the huge pages of the road atlas spread over their knees like wings as they counted down junctions. Mum didn't really need them to read the map, it was just something they did together to make the journey more of an event. He and Luke shared it until one day it disappeared and each blamed the other for its loss.

Twelve hours later, it's morning again and the plane lowers itself through a red sky. As soon as they land, Arlo presses send on a message to Luke.

Trying a new route.

He flexes his sore hand.

Last night after the funeral he'd gone back up to the roof for the first time since he found Luke. The crane that seemed to hold the moon up the final night they'd spent up there had moved. Arlo thought he might say a prayer or a poem for his friend but a wave of something violent took over, something dark and wild.

The shame of hurling the sun lounger across the roof, watching it bounce and slide to a halt when it hit the wall on the far side. When it didn't break, he'd grabbed the patio chair by a leg and heaved it against the ground, smashing it again and again and again until it was mangled and twisted. If only he had stayed to cover the pool with Luke. *If only, if only, if only.* The chair's metal seat fell off and he flung it down into the pool forest, shattering one of the pots. He doesn't really remember destroying the rest of them, just the blossom flying like ashes as he wrenched the trees from the soil and swung their terracotta houses against the side of the pool.

He'd sat in the dirt and roots, holding Luke's medal, waiting and waiting for him to come back and tell him it was all a game.

Arlo sends a second message.

Sorry I hurt our forest.

It doesn't seem right that the letters aren't chalky and blue but he supposes it doesn't really matter. He won't get a green one back.

EIGHT

Hours later again, Arlo wakes in a hotel bed.

There are seven circles on the ceiling. One looks like a smoke alarm. Two are lights. Another could be a sprinkler. He can't tell what the others are but is certain planets are missing.

Luke's dead.

What am I doing here?

He's really dead.

His stomach gnaws on itself. The last thing he ate was salty plane 'beef'.

It's 9 p.m. here, lunchtime at home. He needs to go out and find something to eat.

Arlo turns left, at random, out of the hotel. Spring warmth, soft rain.

Just down the street before a huge junction, a sign blinks with two words: 'Insomnia Cookies'. *A pharmacy? Can't be.* It's a bakery.

There are people everywhere but the chaos comes from the buildings not the humans. Their neon facades are electrifying. Giant walls glow and pulse. Stories written in characters that Arlo can't read run up and down the street. He's illiterate again, a baby.

At a junction, buildings with huge screens burst with competing music. On one side, a teenage metal band screams incomprehensible lyrics.

Every second person he passes is wearing a white hygiene mask or carrying a transparent umbrella. Their clothes are plain, not as he'd imagined. He'd seen girls in music videos with their platform shoes, knee socks and pastel hair. None of that here.

A train glides over a bridge up ahead as cars and motorbikes rush under it. Going, going, gone. More come.

The buildings are high, not just the odd one here and there, but all of them. Six, seven, eight storeys up at least, and lit from top to bottom. Kinetic air buzzes in his lungs.

Luke would love this.

Luke's dead.

The black and white stripes of the crossing are shiny with rain, reflecting the whole neon jungle back on itself. Arlo's eyes blur until there are only strips of colour on the ground: white, bright blue, pink, orange. A wet neon underworld he could drop into.

In some ways, it reminds him of home. Not the home he's just flown from. The one before that. The one by the sea. That faded little place that still manages to cast a glow.

Under a bridge where it's darker and less busy, Arlo turns round to soak up the light.

Bright, bright, bright. He could eat it.

He still needs dinner. Or breakfast. Food. He cuts down a

wet side alley littered with small restaurants with lanterns outside and curtains across their doorways. He can't play Doors without Luke.

There's a busy, well-lit, twenty-four-hour place on the corner. Arlo slips inside. Fellow diners remove their masks, folding them carefully into pockets. Chopsticks clink like bionic fingers.

He tries to ask for ramen without pork belly, pointing at the menu, miming. The waiter smiles and nods. Arlo does his best to communicate and says the word that he thinks means thank you three times before taking a seat on one of the stools by the window.

The ramen arrives, with pork belly. It's no different from how he communicates at home really; trying to ask for what he needs but somehow getting it wrong.

An old man with soft folds on his face glances at Arlo's bowl then back to his own smaller dish of broth. There's hunger in his eyes. Arlo slides the bowl over to the man who gestures a no to him. Arlo insists and orders another for himself. It tastes like heaven and acts like medicine. Sweat slides down his temples as he listens to the man slurping next to him. The windows of the café are wet with condensed broth. Tiredness starts to creep. The man eats quickly, bows and leaves.

Afterwards, Arlo walks and walks. It hurts less when he's moving. He zigzags across the city until he's entirely lost. He grows exhausted from his toes up. Tiredness crawls over his feet, climbs his ankles, legs, up through his torso into his eyes and mind.

He's really lost now. Needs Google Maps. Feels in his pocket for his phone. Shit. Left on the bedside table.

What was the name of the hotel – even the name of the road? He'd asked the taxi driver at the airport to take him to a hotel in the centre. *Fuck.* Arlo sinks to the curb. People glance but don't linger. Nobody offers help. Too polite for that.

He sits for a few minutes, staring down the road into the dazzling lights.

Nobody comes to rescue him because nobody knows he's here.

'Get it together,' he tells himself.

He pushes himself to his feet, a plan forming. He'll just check in somewhere else and find the other hotel in the morning, when he can think straight and it's light.

He walks back towards the busier area. The thought crosses his mind that it could be a red light district. Among the blinking signs he sees 'Capsule Hotel'. Strange name but who cares.

A man stops him at the door.

'Please put your shoes in a locker.'

'I don't have a reservation.'

'We have space. Please put your shoes in a locker.'

'OK.'

Shoes exchanged for a small key, Arlo pays for a room at reception. It's much cheaper than he thought it would be unless he's got the exchange rate wrong. The man hands him a photocopied map of the hotel, pointing out where the showers are, the TV area, where he can get breakfast.

'This is yours.' The man points on the map. 'One five seven. Men's stairs are over there.'

Men's stairs?

An underground hotel.

'Thank you.'

He follows the staircase down and is met with a wall of

smoke. It's all men, all ages, wearing matching brown pyjama suits. Arlo has to walk through a lounge to get anywhere. Ash and sweat in the air. A wall of old graphic novels written in characters. Rows of tatty reclining chairs pointing at a TV.

What is this place? It feels like a city submarine.

Arlo walks as if he knows where he's going. Through a door, past a shower room, yet another door. Locked. He pushes it again. It won't open.

'Luke, it's me.'

There's an access pad with a picture of a key on it. Arlo presses his key against it and the door buzzes. He pushes it, heart jangling.

'Luke. You're not funny.'

Inside there are rows of double-stacked, human-sized microwaves. Some with a closed rattan shutter, some open. The lower-level ones are divided by small ladders up to the top row. Each hole has a number.

Luke's dead.

A few metres away, a man in brown mounts one of the ladders and swings himself into one of the top cells. A hand reaches back out to pull down the shutter. The man doesn't reappear.

Arlo takes a few steps down the corridor and peers into one of the cells. Inside is a mattress and some bedding. It's marked seventeen.

He pulls the crumpled map from his pocket and locates himself on it: 'Zone A: Capsules 1–60'. These are sleeping capsules, not cells. The strangest dormitory he's ever seen.

It must be gone midnight by now. Too late to go somewhere else.

As he goes deeper, snores rumble and bounce off the narrow corridor. There are others wandering through the burrow looking for their capsules but they don't make eye contact. It feels like a subterranean morgue.

Arlo moves into Zone B and finds the hundreds. Passes 110, 120, keeps going. 157 is on the bottom row. Above it, 158 has drawn his shutter down. Anyone could be in there. His mum. No, not his mum. No women allowed down here.

Luke.

Dad.

Ashes.

Bones.

Arlo crawls into his capsule. There's barely room to turn around, and just a few centimetres between the top of his head and the ceiling while he's sitting up. The walls are hard, white plastic with nothing but a light switch and a small shelf on them.

He pulls down the shutter and ties its string in his special knot around the hook.

The biggest journey of his life so far and he's left his notebook at the other hotel. He tries to trace the route into the knee of his jeans but gets lost.

There's a set of brown pyjamas folded with a sheet in the middle of the mattress. Too tired to change, Arlo kicks them to the end of the cell and eases himself under the sheet. He takes a deep breath, turns off the light, closes his eyes. Pretends to be on the moon or Pluto.

Isn't this what he wanted – to be lost in some faraway place until it stops hurting? To be far enough away from his mum that she won't feel his pain.

Arlo hears nothing of the neon city above but its coloured lights still play inside him.

His hand reaches back to check the knot. It reminds him of his mum. She used to tie their home to a tree so it didn't slip down the shore into the sea in rough weather.

NINE

In the daylight the next morning, the name of his hotel comes back to Arlo as if it had never left. He finds a cashpoint and slides unfamiliar money into his wallet. A cab delivers him back to the hotel in time for breakfast.

The receptionist presses maps of the city and transport networks into his hands and bows. Colourful spaghetti lines, secret icons. Arlo asks her how to say please and thank you and vows to himself to learn a few more phrases. He balls the maps into a bin on his way out.

It's an easy city to dissolve himself into but, to ensure his anonymity, Arlo goes into the first pharmacy he sees and buys a packet of plain hygiene masks. It takes a minute to get used to the elastic behind his ears and feeling his breath trapped in the paper pocket round his mouth and chin, but he soon forgets he's wearing it.

The ache in his stomach is starting to creep so he decides to walk the city. In the back of his mind is the idea that if he walks long enough he'll just fade away. Somewhere else in his body is the hope that someone will start a fight with him, give him a chance to get some of the tension and hopelessness beaten out of him.

The neon is flatter by day and there are vending machines everywhere. Arlo passes electronics stores, stationery shops, toy emporiums. The biggest games arcade he's ever seen. There's a 7-Eleven on every corner. Karaoke bars, open but unpopulated. Themed cafés: robots, maids, cats. Even an owl café. *Aren't owls nocturnal? How do they teach them to sleep at night?*

He rounds the edge of a park, a riot of spring colour. Over some steps, down the other side. The tremor of subway trains underfoot. This is a city of many levels. Underpasses, overpasses, footbridges, towers, trees, planes.

Supermarkets with nothing he recognises in their windows. A make-up shop with a robot customer assistant. Art galleries. Museums. Bookshops with architectural displays of paperbacks that look like a game of Jenga.

Another new district. A labyrinth of pastel backstreets selling leather, lace, layers. Clusters of people about his age in bright clothes, pastel hair, shading themselves in huddles from the Sunday sun. Others all in black, leaning, smoking. It's like the set of a music video where all the performers are taking a break. He itches to take a photo, but knows how invasive that quiet click of a camera phone can be.

If Luke were here he'd have his camera out in a heartbeat.

His heart doesn't beat any more.

Keep moving.

Arlo soon hits a stream of people with picnic baskets and blankets, heading towards what looks like a park up ahead.

At the lips of the green space a wooden structure straddles the path. Two horizontal beams, held up by a vertical pillar on either side. Arlo has heard of these: gates. An entrance to a space containing a shrine. In front of it, a huge tree heavy with pale pink blossom shades the corner.

As he approaches, the air seems gentle. Other visitors stick to the edges as they pass through, as if they'd disturb something or someone if they walked through the middle of the gate. Some bow as they enter. Arlo follows their lead to be respectful and dips his head as he walks under the arch into a forest.

A few paces in and the city behind him is forgotten. Columns of light fall between the trees.

He walks for a few minutes then rounds a corner. There's a spicy sweetness in the air. Everywhere he looks, groups are gathered on tarpaulins and blankets under trees heaving with blossom. Some lie on their backs as petals float down to them, sticking to their lips and eyelids. Others share picnics and hot things on sticks brought from the sizzling stalls that line the paths. Others dance in lines or circles, joined in synchronised, unfamiliar movements. Music, laughter.

Two girls dressed in shades of blossom stroll by, each cradling a large rabbit; a small boy pushes a puppy in a toy pram. Kites and balloons fly while kids play Twister and a game with giant blocks. All around him: badminton, guitars, chimes, street dancers, human statues, painters, even two harpists at the edge of some still water.

Hundreds of people celebrating something; Arlo has never felt so alone.

Every other person is taking photos of themselves or the flowering trees. Their bowing branches weep pink into big ponds, small lakes. Great pompoms of flowers burst on the breeze. Everything is soft, or maybe cruel. Untranslatable.

In another universe, this could be Luke's wake.

'Sorry to bother you, mate. Do you speak English?' says a man in front of him, his accent distinctive. One of the few that Arlo struggled to master in Accent Arts at school; a mix of long and short vowels. Tricky.

'Yes.' The clearness of Arlo's own voice surprises him. He hasn't spoken more than a handful of words since the funeral. The conversation at the airport seems like another life now. Just a few words since – in the taxi, at the diner, the place with the capsules.

'Would you mind?' The guy holds up his phone.

He wants a photo.

The Beat airs in his country.

'Sure,' Arlo says, recovering himself, remembering to be gracious. He pulls his mouth into a humble smile, unhooks his mask and gets ready to crack out the 'arm non-threateningly slung around shoulder of stranger' pose that he's adopted so many times before.

He doesn't want to. The thought of it makes him feel dizzy.

You're an actor. Fake it.

'Great,' says the man, handing him the phone. 'Usual button.'

Oh.

71

Arlo is to be the photographer, not the subject. The temptation to put the mask back on to hide the embarrassment staining his cheeks is strong.

The man gathers his family and says, 'Could you be sure to get the trees in the background?'

'Sure.'

After a few snaps, they thank him.

'When did you get here?' asks the woman.

Was it yesterday?

'Yesterday morning.'

'Perfect timing,' she says.

For what?

'Mummy, look at me,' cries one or both of the kids.

'Coming,' she calls.

Arlo hands her the phone and feels for his own in his pocket. He should turn it on and check in with his mum and respond to Russell's inevitably livid messages.

Later.

Bodies, sounds, scents whirl around him in motion but he's stuck, can't take another step. He looks down to the ground to steady himself. Drifts of petals with browning edges chase each other like miniature moths at his feet.

He should go home. The audition is tomorrow. He could still get there if he went back to the airport now. Nobody would even need to know he'd been here.

Even as he thinks it, he's noticing the girl.

She's alone. Familiar. Maybe because she's dressed in black like the uniform they wore at school because the governors thought that it made the pupils look like real artists.

A proper camera hangs round her neck. Her hair falls in dark slices over her black scarf.

She stops once or twice to examine things through the viewfinder of her camera. Arlo watches the lens zoom in and out as she refocuses. A ring on her engagement finger catches the sun as she trains the lens on various potential shots but her thumb never presses down on the capture button. Nothing she sees seems worth preserving to her.

Arlo had taken a photography class at boarding school. He knows what it feels like for something not to translate into a picture the way you want it to. In sleepless phases, he'd wander the school grounds at night looking for things to photograph.

He'd found a dead baby fox once, fur still perfect. He felt as if someone should mark its passing so he'd taken off his T-shirt from under his jumper, lain it over the animal like a black shroud and covered the mound with handfuls of dirt. He was sure nobody had seen him but somehow a rumour got started that he kept dead things in his studio to photograph so he'd retired his camera and stuck to acting and drawing.

The girl stops under one of the trees, drops to her knees and lies down on her back. Arlo watches as she looks up into the branches through the camera.

He realises it's actually two trees. One planted in the shadow of the other. The larger one is white with a pink crown. Two shades of blossom in the same tree. A hybrid. *Is that normal?* In its shadow, the smaller one's branches twist through small bronze leaves like arteries through lungs.

The girl takes picture after picture until finally she sits up and leans against the trunk.

Arlo realises he's been watching her like a creep for a good couple of minutes. He wishes he could see her photos but takes one last look and leaves her to it.

He's not sure what to do with himself now so starts another lap of the park. It had seemed so urgent that he get as far away from the roof as possible and something inside him had made him choose here. Grief logic. But now he's not sure it was the right thing to do.

He misses his mum, misses Luke. Misses the city, misses the sea. He's missing a layer of skin. Raw.

He'll take one last look around the park then head back to the hotel.

Following the path back the way he came, he passes the double tree again. The girl has gone. Part of Arlo had been hoping she might still be there. He steps closer to it, looks up to the sky through its leaves – bronze, white, pink. It's pretty but nothing special. Maybe he just doesn't have her eye for a photograph. He finds himself sitting down in the spot where she'd sat. It's a long walk back to the hotel.

'I'm so sorry, but do you think you could take a nap under another tree.'

'What?' He must have fallen asleep. *It's her.* 'You speak English.'

'Well observed,' she replies. Her accent is from the place he is supposed to be; the place without real weather on the other side of the world. 'So do you.'

'Of course.' It comes out like that's some kind of achievement, though of course it's a total accident. He gets to his feet. 'Here, have your tree back.'

She smiles. Small teeth like a row of closed doors behind her lips.

'I like your camera,' Arlo says. 'My friend has one like that.'

Had one.

A young girl dressed in what looks like traditional dress skips by them as fast as her wooden shoes will let her.

'It's her birthday.'

'How do you know?' he asks.

'Those are birthday shoes. She's seven. I had the same ones.'

The conversation is happening in the wrong order.

'I'm Arlo. What's your name?'

'Mizuki,' she says.

He wishes he had given a fake name. Then again, Arlo is an actor and an actor can make himself into anything – un-sad, un-lonely, un-homesick.

Mizuki watches the girl until she reaches her parents. She takes a few quick photos of the family's backs as they walk away, long shadows stretching out behind them. A shiver crosses her face and streaks down her neck.

'Are you OK?' he asks.

'Fine. Just déjà vu. I should go.'

'I thought you wanted your tree back.'

'That's OK, I'll be here again soon enough.'

The thought of being alone makes Arlo brave. 'We could get a drink. I mean, would you like to get a drink with me?'

'Best of three.'

'What?'

'On three,' she says. She puts a hand behind her back as he watches, confused. 'One, two, three.' She pulls the hand back out and holds it out flat in front of her. Arlo catches up too late to join the game. 'Well, paper beats nothing, so I win that one. On three. One, two, three.'

This time Arlo makes a fist and she plays scissors.

'Rock blunts scissors,' she says. 'This one's the decider. One, two, three.'

They both play scissors.

'Again. One, two, three.'

He holds out two fingers in scissors again and she holds out a flat hand as paper.

He's won.

'Come on then,' she says. 'Don't gloat. And don't worry, it's normal to feel sad about the blossom. They die when they're at their most beautiful. I'm coming back in the fall when the other trees are red.'

TEN

A couple of hours, some tea and a significant portion of the city by foot later, Arlo has worked up the nerve to ask Mizuki why she agreed to get a drink with him.

'Isn't this what people do when they're travelling? Meet another human in a hostel or staring at tree porn then hang out with them for a while?'

'Seriously?'

'I don't know. Maybe you looked sort of familiar.'

He can't tell her he thought the same because it'll sound like a lie now.

'And you looked a bit lost,' she adds. 'How long are you here for?'

'Not sure yet. You?'

'I'm here until fall; hopefully I'm meeting someone then going home,' she says. 'Did you come for the blossom?'

'It was an accident.'

There was an accident.

'I'm not into this spring madness.'

Now that Mizuki says it, Arlo knows he saw something about it in a magazine on the plane. It's a special time of year here, and then again in autumn when the leaves turn red, like she said. He's lucky to have caught the blossom. Perfect timing, the lady in the park had told him, as if he'd planned any of this.

Mizuki carries on, 'I lived here from when I was two until I was seven. This is my first time back in the country.'

'You seem at home,' Arlo says.

'I've been here a couple of months.'

'How come you moved away?'

'My dad's parents got sick. I don't think my mum wanted to leave but what could she do.'

They're in some older streets now. They pass a row of teahouses with tidy rows of shoes outside. *Don't they get stolen?* Arlo imagines the people inside, napping on mats. They wonder about getting more tea but decide to buy some fruit instead.

Mizuki chooses an apple, a process she takes very seriously. They get some pears, two oranges, and Arlo adds a bag of cherries. He pays to say thank you for her tour-guiding. It's expensive.

'You can get square watermelons here. They cost thousands of dollars. And giant strawberries,' Mizuki tells him.

'Why would you want a square melon?'

'Why wouldn't you?'

They find a quiet bench to share some of the oranges before continuing their walk.

A bee beats its wings at his side.

Mizuki translates a sign. 'They make honey up on the roof here.'

At school there always seemed to be insects everywhere, things with too many legs behind the radiators, buzzing at windows.

'I've never been to this part of town before,' she says.

'Don't look at me, I'm new here.' Though he's already starting to get a sense of the shape of this part of the city, connecting together in his mind all the neighbourhoods he's seen so far.

Mizuki stops to look in a shop window full of antique maps and globes. Star charts for mariners.

'Let's go in,' he says.

She follows him.

A huge antique atlas is spread over a lectern. For a second, he's in the back seat of a car in the dark. Mum at the wheel, Luke by his side. Big pages hang over the sides of his lap like wings or the curves on an anchor. A magic book for flying away, instructions for finding your path. Maybe his mum knows what happened to the lost atlas. He'll ask her.

'Useless,' Mizuki says, spinning the top of an old globe.

'Harsh.'

'The world doesn't look like that any more. Bits have broken off and parts have melted.'

Ribs crack in Arlo's ears as, somewhere, great slabs of ice and earth slide away from their homes.

He lays his hand on the globe to still it. It's room temperature. He presses, feels a pulse of pain, but isn't sure if it's him or the world that hurts.

Back out on the street, he asks Mizuki if she's a student.

'I'm an environmentalist.'

'Cool.'

'Do you know what that means?'

'Of course.' Though now that she's said it he's not sure he does. 'Did you always want to be one?' he asks.

She shakes her head. 'What did you want to be when you were a kid?'

'An actor.'

She laughs.

'Why is that funny?'

'I don't know. Just the idea of you wanting all that attention seems kind of wrong.'

It's not about wanting attention.

It's about making something that matters, connecting.

Escaping monochrome.

'What did you want to be?' he asks.

'First I wanted to be a pony. Then a doctor and a mum.'

'But you became an environmentalist.'

Mizuki lifts her camera to zoom in on a zigzag crack in the pavement. Takes a photo, checks it, deletes it. Arlo stares at the split stone; it looks like the remnants of a tiny earthquake.

'For now. What did you become or are you still becoming?'

'I'm a student,' he says, then changes the subject. 'Do you know where we are?'

'Nope.'

'Me neither.'

They cut through a botanical garden. The signs are all written in multiple languages.

'*No jogging or running in the park*,' reads Mizuki. 'There's an order I can get on board with.'

Arlo hasn't run since before the roof. That's not true; he's run eight thousand kilometres away from home.

'Should we ask someone for directions?' he says.

'I usually just keep walking if I'm lost. Eventually you'll hit a bus stop or a subway station, or something more interesting.'

She's right. They find a subway station five minutes later.

'Where are you staying?'

He tells her the name of the hotel.

'This station will work.'

He follows her underground feeling as if he were in *Alice's Adventures in Wonderland*.

Two minutes until the next train. Underground minutes always seem longer than above-ground minutes. His heart ticks along with invisible clocks. After precisely two minutes, a train pulls into the platform, slamming out a tunnel-shaped train of air first. All around the network, ghost trains are shunted along by metal tubes with seats in them.

The motion bounces their shoulders together as they sit down. Contact. Arlo shifts in case it's making Mizuki uncomfortable. She smells of fruit.

The aluminium surfaces and poles are so clean they're almost lilac in the white light; it's like being inside a UV tube. The carriage is quiet except for the automated announcements and the sounds that play in the stations as they pass – *Is that electronic birdsong?*

Both slump back in their seats, tired from their long walk. Mizuki folds her hands in her lap, twisting the engagement ring round and round. Arlo notices her silver bracelet and the charms dangling off it – two cherries, an old-fashioned camera, a leaf. He can't see what's hanging on the underside. His fingers toy with the hygiene mask in his pocket, coiling and releasing the strap.

They sweep along under the city in easy quiet. Nobody tries to take his picture. The rails don't screech.

Mizuki flicks through the photos on her camera. She favourites the ones she took lying on the ground looking up through the two twisted trees and deletes the rest.

'Yours is the next stop.'

Arlo has under half a minute to ask what he wants to ask. 'Would you . . . would you maybe want to meet up again tomorrow?' Before she can decline, he adds, 'On three?'

She puts a hand behind her back and counts, 'One, two, three.'

His paper beats her rock. Until now he'd always thought it was kind of stupid that a piece of paper could defeat a rock but he wasn't going to disagree with the rock, paper, scissors gods now.

'Do you want to put your number in my phone?' he asks.

'I've lost mine. I'll meet you at your hotel at nine a.m.'

He gives her the name again. 'You want me to write it down for you?'

'I can remember two words,' she says, 'especially when one of them is "Hotel".'

He likes the way she teases him; it's not mean and makes a change from all the people at home who try to suck up to him.

The train pulls into the station. Arlo pushes himself to his feet and yawns.

'That means you need oxygen,' Mizuki tells him. 'Or you're scared.'

'Just tired.'

'Jetlag or can't sleep?'

'Both.'

'They have a proverb here: "If you can't sleep it's because you're awake in someone else's dream."'

Arlo is pleased with his response, 'Well, if you see me in one of yours, tell me to go back to bed.'

He gives her the rest of the cherries and gets off the train.

ELEVEN

Arlo flops on to the bed wishing he'd asked Mizuki if she wanted to hang out tonight too. It's not even 5 p.m. *What now?* He can't spend the rest of the day haunting his hotel room.

He feels empty again. Maybe he'd feel better if he sorted some things out at home.

First he'll deal with Russell, then he'll call his mum.

He has a bunch of emails from Russell when he switches on his phone. The most recent one has 'WHERE ARE YOU?' as the subject. The message reads:

You missed your flight! Are you OK? Audition at 10 a.m. tomorrow.

Russell has always had his back and it feels awful to let him down. There are consequences for wrong moves like this. The studio will be fuming and it'll be embarrassing for Russell.

Arlo knows all this but it doesn't move him enough to fix it. He just can't at the moment. He's only keeping his shit together because he's away from everything that reminds him of Luke. He wants the role, to be part of making something special, but he wants to protect his mum more.

He emails Russell back to tell him he won't make the audition and that he's taking some time off. A sincere apology. Tells him not to worry.

Next Arlo emails Guy and a few others to say he's gone to visit his mum. Uses a tone that makes it sound like an inconvenience, a chore. He'll call them for drinks when he gets back.

He wants to message Luke again, so the universe knows he hasn't forgotten about him, but he feels guilty for having fun with Mizuki. He hadn't told Luke about the thing where he can feel like he's drowning and carry on doing other things at the same time, so he might not understand.

He's dead.

Finally, his mum. This is best dealt with face to face, of sorts, so Arlo gets his story straight in his mind and video calls her. It's breakfast time there.

She is all questions. 'I've been trying to call you for two days. How was the funeral? Where are you? Are you OK? Why haven't you called me back?'

He wants to tell her everything; the words are ready to rush out of him, to beg her to come and get him and make everything better. But he made a promise not to hurt her again. 'Sorry, Mum. I'm fine. I had to move out of the flat. It was weird being there without Luke and it was too late to call last night.'

'You've moved? I thought you'd paid a year upfront.'

'It's just for a bit; I'm staying with a friend. I'll give you the tour of my room.'

Arlo holds the phone up to show her the bed and the TV.

This calms her down. 'I like to be able to imagine you if I need to. What if you went missing and I hadn't known where you were – what would the police say?'

'They'd be more worried about finding me than whether I'd given you a tour of my bedroom, I imagine.'

But he knows what she means. Evidently he likes to be able to imagine people who aren't with him too.

'How was the funeral?' she asks again. 'I wish I hadn't let you talk me into not going.'

There'd been a complicated game involving prank calls and banned words on the radio as Arlo got dressed for the service. All the sadness was caught at the back of his throat, making his jaw ache. He'd swallowed everything down and tightened his tie close against his neck, trapping it all inside himself, fighting the press and push of tears.

It's the hymns that get you at funerals – something about the music tells you how to feel – but he knew the worst bit would be watching the coffin as it was lowered into the ground. He remembered that from his grandpa's funeral. He hadn't wanted them to put Grandpa into the hole but couldn't think of a single thing they could fill it with instead, so down he'd gone.

'It was a cremation,' Arlo tells his mum. There was something unfinished about watching the enormous coffin slide back and the curtains close around it at the end of the service as if it were just the end of a day, not of all Luke's days. All Arlo could think

about was Luke's stiff feet in soft socks pressing against the end
of the box.

Was he wearing shoes?

Nobody sleeps with their shoes on.

'I sent Bobby and Mary a card. Did they say they'd got it?'

'I think so.'

He can't remember.

At the wake, Arlo shook Mr Swanson's hand. They hadn't
seen each other for a couple of years. A tower of a man, like
Luke. Bones made of scaffolding keeping him upright. Mrs
Swanson had hugged Arlo so tight his ribs cringed. He'd had
Luke's medal in his pocket, ready to give to them. Hadn't his mum
handed him Neon the dog's collar in exactly the same way when
Neon had been put down? He should have given it to them.

Instead he'd given them Luke's key to the flat in case they
wanted to come over and bury their faces in Luke's things, maybe
climb into the wardrobe with his clothes, or lay them out on the
bed and imagine Luke were in them. Except he'd said, 'In case
you want to collect anything. I'm going away for work tomorrow.'

It was then that he'd looked them in the eye properly, so
they'd know he was sad too but that he had to keep moving. He
saw the redness around Mrs Swanson's eyes and nose. The burst
blood vessels, tiny explosions of grief under her skin.

They were all members of a special club now. You don't sign
up; membership is automatic. The benefits are minimal: an
excruciatingly heightened sense of empathy and holes that won't
be filled no matter how much dirt you pour into them. Arlo
wanted to tell the Swansons he wished it had been him who'd
died in the pool.

'There can be nothing worse than losing your child,' his mum is saying.

He had to shut himself down so Mr and Mrs Swanson couldn't see him wondering if they could still be parents without a child. Maybe this will bring them closer together. Did they have sex when they got home? Death makes people want to do that. Isn't that how intimacy works? He'd heard stuff about his mum and other men after his dad had died but he'd never met any of them.

She must have been so lonely.

'It must have been so sad,' she says.

It's still so sad.

Arlo reassures his mum that he's doing OK and listens to some stories about her and his aunt. There are always crucial bits of her tales missing. Parts of the facts and folklore of the family that she thinks he knows, which the stories don't make sense without. Things he was too young to be told that she imagines he somehow knows by in-utero transference. Emotional osmosis. He asks a wrong question. They swing towards each other, lost in space, but always miss, too far apart even to feel the displaced air rush.

He paces as she talks, listening to the slurps of her tea, being careful not to get anything in shot that could give away his location.

'It's a bit bare, love,' she says. 'Will you put some pictures up?'

'Mizuki is a minimalist.' He wants to say her name even if he has to lie a bit more.

'Mizuki? Have I met her?'

'I haven't known her long.'

'Are you together? You can tell me if you are. I was your age when I met your dad, you know.'

'She's engaged.'

'Oh, shame. She sounds like a nice girl.'

He laughs despite himself. 'I've literally told you nothing about her.'

'You don't mind it being small anyway.' She's talking about the room again now.

She knows him.

In big rooms, Arlo clings to corners. Nurture taught him to live small. He can see the past clearly; distance has brought it into focus. Their static mobile home roped to a sturdy tree. They called it the caravan or the van but it wasn't much smaller than his and Luke's flat.

He can see it all: crayon scribbles on the caravan walls, a dead goldfish in a dirty bowl, a Bacardi bottle on the draining board, Sellotaped photos, ants marching by the door, the teabag mound by the kettle.

Later, cigarette smoke curling, summer fires burning.

Later still, clumsy first touches, getting a handjob behind the gas shed from one of the summer girls, worrying that he wasn't doing it right (though his active role in the proceedings was minimal, to be fair) and that he made a weird face when he came.

Arlo steels himself against homesickness and switches on the TV. Mutes it, keeps one eye on its flickering while his mum talks.

The clock rolls round to 5 p.m.

'What will you have for breakfast?' she asks.

Another swing past each other in space.

'Mizuki is making something. I better go and help.'

Something tells him that Mizuki doesn't cook breakfast for strange guys she meets in parks.

Then he adds another lie, 'I'm flying to the screen test tomorrow. Russell has loads of meetings lined up for me so don't worry if you don't hear from me for a few days.'

'You'll have to slow down at some point,' she says. 'Luke was your friend. It's normal to be upset.'

Arlo's not upset. Grief won't settle if he keeps moving. 'I know.'

'Are you sure you're OK?'

She's using the voice that she used all the time that black summer. Concern, love, a tinge of fear.

'I'm fine. Well, not fine exactly.' Can't be too fine. That's suspicious too. 'But I'll be OK. It's good to have something to focus on.'

'Well, I'm here if you need me, love. I'll fly over any time, just say the word.'

What word?

The way she calls him 'love' feels like a lie too. He is anger and regret and other things he doesn't know the names of and can't tell her.

'Let me know how the audition goes.'

They hang up.

Something has crept over him. Mothers are supposed to know, aren't they? Even if you're hiding something from them. *Especially* if you're hiding something.

Still, nothing is more important than being the son she deserves. He won't let her down.

His phone juicing up with power, Arlo sits on the bed. Looks to the door and wonders if he should go back out to find some dinner.

He can't be still, but it's too early to eat and his stomach is starting to knot again anyway.

He sits back against the headboard on the bed, swings his legs up, puts them back down again. Stares at the seven circles on the ceiling; too many, yet incomplete. He stands by the window. Moves to the chair, holding its back with both hands. Hovers in the doorway to the bathroom. Sits back down on the bed, imagining his restlessness captured frame by frame by Mizuki's camera.

He jolts up again.

Luke's medal. Where is it?

He tips everything out of his backpack, searches through the zipped sections even though he knows he didn't put it in any of them. He checks the pockets of all his jeans and trousers. Even the smart outfit he'd packed for the audition. Did he have it when he stayed at the capsule place? What if he dropped it in the park? *It could be anywhere.*

'*Have it.*' Luke walloping him on the shoulder. '*There you go, champ.*'

He's furious with himself for losing the last thing Luke gave him.

Blackness is taking over. He needs to go out and look for it.

Arlo grabs his shoes, tries to yank them on without undoing the laces. It doesn't work; he has to unpick the bows.

In an instant, he's right there at the bottom of the pool among the trees, trying to pull off Luke's shoes again. The police radio hums and a voice tells him to check Luke's airways as he stares at the dusting of blossom trampled into the grooves of his friend's trainers. His breath is sticky with pollen, horror.

The hotel carpet crawls with petals like migrating crabs.

Why did I leave him up there?

He hates this. Hates himself. Hurls a trainer across the room. It hits the kettle, knocking it over. It hangs pathetically over the side of the fridge, suspended by its short cable.

He wants to smash up the whole place. Rip the TV off the wall and send it slamming through the window. If there were sun loungers and patio chairs and rooftops pots to annihilate again he would.

He flings the other trainer against the wall. It bounces back and hits him in the chest, knocking the wind out of him. He sits, gulping, banging a fist down on the carpet, then pummelling his knuckles against the edge of the mattress until the skin is raw and split again. His breathing is quick and shallow. He can't get control of it.

It hurts, it hurts, it hurts, and he keeps smashing the mattress until his arm is as heavy as lead and the rest of him is as empty as home.

TWELVE

Arlo's whole body shakes. The bed and the building vibrate with him, under him, around him.

It's the end of the world.

The only light in the room comes from the neon glow of the small clock. 6.37 a.m. Morning. He'd always thought the apocalypse would come in the dead of night and on any day but a Monday, if at all.

Violent rumblings roll across the floor and up the walls to the rooms above him; 199 other beds lurching like boats in a storm. A deep wave rises inside him.

Coat hangers fall from the hooks on the back of the door. Bottles clatter into the sink in the tiny bathroom, rolling like spinning tops, landing in a heap over the pristine plughole. His hoodie slips from the back of the chair; he hears it land lightly in a heap at its four feet.

The jolting intensifies, shaking all the rooms in the hotel and in his head.

There is thunder inside the aching hotel skeleton.

It's coming from below.

Something is forcing its way up through the earth under the hotel, through its stacked floors and ceilings. Roots loosening and lassoing. Gnarled, mossy arms reaching for him through twenty-three layers of beams and carpet. A huge tree exploding upwards only to suck him underground and suffocate him with its powdery fingers. Lungs full of petals, he'll drown in springtime.

He can feel the flexibility in the building as it creaks and sways. It was built for this. There are memories of it happening before in the walls.

An earthquake. It's an earthquake.

He should be under the desk or in a sturdy doorway but grips the duvet instead.

It'll stop in a minute. How long do earthquakes last? He'd always thought of them as violent but brief acts. Devastating but short, like a car crash. *Is this the centre of it – what if there's more coming this way?*

Arlo sits back against the vibrating headboard to ride it out in the dark. Air is caught at the top of his lungs. A deep breath forces it down and back out again. Repeat.

'OK. It's OK. It's going to be OK.'

A few final bumps and the building settles.

He waits for the longest minute to see if it starts up again.

He should stay away from the window but for some reason he's worried about touching the light switch so he needs to open the curtains to be able to see. He feels certain a gaping crack will

94

have ripped through the world outside, that trains will have collided on tracks and people killed by falling debris.

He feels his way over to the window. A slight trembling of aftershock shivers through the carpet and his socks into the soles of his feet. His hands reach out to yank the curtains apart.

Outside there is nothing.

Did I imagine it?

Maybe it was a seizure.

I don't get seizures.

No, the mess in the room is proof that it happened. Why isn't anyone calling to see if he's OK?

Everyone thinks he's away at his mum's, except for his mum who thinks he's safe with his new friend Mizuki. *Mizuki.* He doesn't have her number to check if she's OK.

He finally thinks to turn on the TV. Keeps flipping till he gets to an English news channel – it's confirmed by the breaking news that scrolls across the bottom of the screen. Earthquake. There's a tsunami warning at the coast.

He wants to talk to his mum. Or Luke; Luke would have a joke to make it all seem funny and not scary. Instead, Arlo returns the coat hangers to their hooks, lines up the bottles by the sink, shakes out his hoodie and hangs it back on the chair. Puts the kettle back on the stand he'd knocked it from in his outburst yesterday.

Next he makes the bed, smoothing the covers as if healing the cracked earth with his hands. Boiled white fabric. Hotel linen has that in common with hospital sheets. They should get some patterned ones instead. Something geometric maybe. Nothing floral, no stripes. He shakes his head to disperse the image of

Luke's striped duvet from his mind. Then there is nothing left to rearrange or resettle apart from his mind.

Did it happen because he hasn't drawn his maps since he got here? That's the jet lag talking. Magical thinking. *Why haven't I drawn them?*

In the sudden stillness, Arlo remembers he has left another life elsewhere. Checks his phone to confirm it. There's another email from Russell reminding him of the stakes. The studio really wants him to read for the part; they can push the screen test a few days. *It's not too late after all.* 'Your fans miss you,' Russell says, 'don't sabotage yourself – chances like this are one in a million.'

Two in a million. The Beat *was the first chance.*

Arlo is still breathing fast but can't tell if it's from the earthquake or the thought of wrecking his career.

There's a link to an article.

WHERE'S ARLO?

ARLO'S ARMY TAKES VOW OF SILENCE UNTIL
THE BEAT ACTOR IS FOUND.

What the hell? He skims it – some bullshit about various fake sightings of him since Luke's death. A blurry selfie with 'TRAGIC YOUTUBER LUKE SWANSON' and the two perfumed girls from the bar. A cartoon map with cut-outs of Arlo's head with question marks for eyes stuck on a Where's Wally body and superimposed into various locations across his home city.

There's even speculation that he's holed up with Valerie Pitch in the countryside somewhere. The press was always keen to create a relationship that didn't exist there. The article says something about #SilenceForArlo trending.

Wait. They're talking about him, not his character.

But he's only been gone two days. Unless they've been looking for him since Luke died, in which case, 14 days.

All he knows is that Lottie at *The Beat* will be wild with the good fortune of it all; a potential tie-in with his and Valerie's disappearance on the show.

The article ends with a quote from Jessica Something whose real name, it transpires, is Jessica Start. The 'reality stalwart and aspiring actress' had met him in a bar, it explains. She wishes him the best and hopes they might even act together one day.

There's a quote from someone he doesn't remember from school describing him as 'cool and distant'. He didn't want to be cool; he wanted to be warm, have friends.

Arlo keeps scrolling. The magazine invites readers to send in photos if they spot him.

They've reused the leaked photo of him and his dad building sandcastles for apparently no reason other than to make him seem more tragic. Those memories are his and not theirs to take to sell magazines. Arlo flings the phone down and grips the side of the bed.

What if his mum sees it? She has a Google alert set up for him even though he's asked her to repeatedly please cancel it.

Arlo sends her a message.

Ignore press about me being missing if you see it. PR hype for the show! Xx

She'll probably look it up now. Still, it's only one magazine and why would she believe them over her son? She wouldn't.

The clock beeps: 7 a.m. No chance of going back to sleep after the shock of the earthquake and his anger at the photo.

An aftershock rattles the bathroom mirror while he's showering. He's inside a snow globe being shaken by a giant. There's the briefest of gaps in the water pressure and a gurgle from the plug as if something were trying to escape. These small sounds are somehow more terrifying than the movement of the walls.

In this moment Arlo decides he'll leave the city today.

What am I doing – where can I go?

Luke's voice is in his head. *'Hey, tomorrow we have to talk about where we're gonna go on our trip. Maybe that island you used to draw all the time. The one with all the foxes.'*

That's it. He'll meet Mizuki to tell her he's leaving then go straight over the road to the station and head south to the island.

Arlo hops out of the shower and throws on some clothes without drying properly. He doesn't want to die naked if there's another aftershock. Especially if Mizuki might come to find him.

Arlo takes a last look around the small room and at the seven circles on the ceiling before swinging his bag over his shoulder to take down to breakfast with him. He's ready to go as soon as he's apologised to Mizuki for abandoning their plans.

He jumps when the ice machine in the corridor lets out an existential howl that reminds him of Luke. A man bows to him in the lift.

The lift doors open and deliver them into a crowd of frantic tourists waiting for earthquake advice at reception. Arlo wonders why he didn't just come down and ask for help earlier. Asking for help is not really his thing.

He has an hour until Mizuki gets here. If she gets here. He's starting to wonder if he imagined the whole of yesterday or hallucinated her in some sort of jet lag fever.

But then the crowds thin out and there she is, backpack and duffel bag at her jiggling feet. Camera stowed away somewhere. *Is she crying?*

'Mizuki,' he calls, crossing the lobby as she gets up to come to him. She's not crying but she might have been earlier. 'Are you OK?'

'I just came to say that I can't meet you today. I have to go.'

She sounds different to how he remembered. Maybe this is her morning voice.

'Go where?' he asks.

'Is that your stuff?' she asks.

'I'm leaving.'

'Where are you going?'

'South,' he says; he's even more sure as he says it out loud. 'Seriously, are you OK?'

'I *hate* earthquakes.'

'Nobody *likes* earthquakes, do they?' he says.

'I mean I really hate them. Anyway, I wanted to say goodbye.'

This time he asks her where she's going.

'I'm kind of on an unofficial tour,' she says. 'There are places I want to see before Thanksgiving, then I'm going home for good.'

Is he brave enough to ask her? He is. She said it herself: people meet and travel together for a bit. He has nothing left to lose. 'Do you want to come with me for a while? I'm going south.'

He looks her right in the eye for the first time. Her pupils are wide. She's still scared. 'Let's go,' she says. No rock, paper, scissors this time.

The train looks like the future, gliding into the station with its long white nose, slick as a dolphin. A man with matching white gloves hurries passengers on to the train.

Arlo wonders what would happen if someone got pushed under it. Would it still leave on time? These thoughts don't surprise him any more. He just goes through phases where he has to peer through the crack into the darkness of the worst possible thought just to make sure it's not true, that he doesn't want it. *These thoughts aren't mine. Whose are they then?* He ushers Mizuki on to the train, a protective arm hovering behind her but not touching.

He's lucky that she knows the transport networks well and that just a quick google had helped her figure out the best route to take to the island. He would have felt bad trying to convince Mizuki to come but she seems desperate to get out of the city and the prospect of going there with another person, even one he's only known a day, feels less strange to him than travelling alone.

The train seats are wide and warm, at odds with the hi-tech outside. Arlo watches a shiny pink train pull in to the platform next to them. It doesn't look real.

There's no delay. This country seems built to withstand the earth's plates shifting under it better than anywhere. Not like home, where the wrong kind of leaves or snow or sun on the tracks grinds everything to a halt.

They don't talk but both their breathing begins to settle as they leave the neon jungle and the earthquake behind them. Only now that he feels safe again does Arlo wonder if Luke was scared when he tripped into the pool. How quickly did he die – did he know it was happening? Everyone reassured Arlo that his dad won't have felt anything when he went but they hadn't said the same about Luke.

Arlo wants to message him to tell him he's finally going to one of the places they always talked about. He starts to tell himself a story – that he's taking this trip for Luke; that his friend would want this adventure for him – but he doesn't believe it.

Mizuki finds a newspaper under the seat in the otherwise spotless train. She flips through, looking at the photo credits.

The message he sends to Luke says:

I'm sorry.

'Could I borrow your cell?' Mizuki asks.

He hands her his phone. 'Sure.'

'What's the passcode?'

He reaches over to type it in.

'That's the lamest passcode ever,' she says. 'A chimp could remember that.'

'You're not supposed to look.'

'You might as well just have one, two, three, four.'

'It's not that bad.'

'It's pretty bad. You should change it. I hope your bank PIN is a bit more imaginative.'

It isn't.

He watches over her shoulder while she logs on to a news photography site and flicks through the pictures. Maybe she's looking to see if there are any pictures of the earthquake. The images don't look that interesting on the tiny screen, at least not to Arlo, so he looks out of the window to watch the world go by instead.

Mizuki returns his phone.

'Find what you were looking for?'

'I never do,' she says.

She gets out an orange, breaks the skin open with her fingers and peels back a strip. Her fingers fumble. She shakes her hand out, making her bracelet tinkle, then starts again, steadier this time.

Out of the window, Arlo sees a big, white-tipped mountain and understands why people worship it.

'You don't want a picture?'

'Nah,' she says.

It passes out of view.

Mizuki has pulled the tray table down to eat her fruit. She holds up the peel in one piece that's unmistakeably the shape of a trunk and two large ears.

'An elephant,' he says.

She arranges the peel flat against the tray table. 'Citrus safari.'

He smiles as Mizuki wipes juice from her fingers and the bright ring on her left hand. He imagines her type of guy – powerful, international, self-assured.

'Doesn't your fiancé mind you being away this long?'

Her mouth opens in surprise. 'I don't answer to anyone.'

She twists the stone side round to face her palm and he knows he's said the wrong thing.

He tries again, 'I just mean that you must miss each other. Doesn't he worry where you are?'

'I try to let everyone who might be missing me know exactly where I am.'

Is that a wish that they'd come and get her, or a warning shot to let Arlo know he'd be found if he hurt her? He'll never get used to the idea that his body could be a threat to someone. Either way, the conversation has been terminated. He won't bring it up again.

'What happened to your hand?' Mizuki asks.

Touché.

It hurts where he'd smashed the roof furniture and pummelled the mattress but it's nothing compared to the ache that made him do either of those things. 'Nothing.'

Mizuki tears the orange flesh apart. Zest stings the air and she hands Arlo half. 'Here.'

He palms it as if she's handed him half the sun.

She dismantles the elephant peel. 'Go on then, eat it,' she says.

So he does, thinking about how in junior school kids would mouth, 'Elephant's juice,' to look as if they were saying, 'I love you.

Mizuki wants to show Arlo a museum before they make the final leg of their journey.

It was built to document a bomb. Not like one of the ones that sometimes happen at home. Much worse.

They visit colourful trails of paper cranes that must have

taken hours and hours of stiff fingers and cramping hands to fold.

Inside, they see a charred children's tricycle. Arlo had seen a picture of it in a textbook before but this was also so much worse.

A peace flame glows outside. It's been burning for over fifty years and will burn for many more, it seems.

'Let's go to the island now,' he tells her.

THIRTEEN

Arlo and Mizuki take another train and cross denim water by boat. They watch the water in gentle silence. He wakes up cotton-mouthed when the boat stops, his head lolling on her shoulder.

'Sorry,' he says.

'That's OK; you must have been tired.'

They disembark and she says, 'I'm going to work while I'm here.'

'OK.' He just wants to know if this place really exists, this island he and Luke had been obsessed with as children. The government used to leave it off maps. It was top secret.

Mizuki stops to get something out of her rucksack. He'd assumed environmentalist was a euphemism for protester or something like that but now he's thinking maybe she's brought test tubes or litmus paper so she can collect soil samples and test the water.

She pulls out her camera.

'Oh, that kind of work.'

'Always,' she says. 'Ready?'

'Ready.'

They leave the small ferry terminal. Arlo shakes off the idea that he's somehow cheating on Luke's memory by being here with someone else and follows Mizuki on to the path.

'Hello, Rabbit Island,' she calls into the wind. 'I must have heard about this place as a kid but I don't actually remember it.'

The island is bigger than Arlo thought it would be and the atlas had not prepared him for the smell.

'I guess if you keep a thousand rabbits on an island, you're going to end up with a lot of rabbit shit,' he says.

Bunnies – a great bank of them – are lined up to greet their visitors. Most of them have pale ginger fur with white bits, like patchy blonde foxes. As Arlo and Mizuki follow the path, the animals lope forward to meet them. They're bold and greedy.

'They want food,' Mizuki says.

A young boy lies in the grass nearby covered in twitching, nibbling rabbits. They're fearless and it feels good to know that probably means nobody has hurt them before.

'There's loads more over there,' Arlo says. 'This is nuts.'

They pet a couple of the bunnies then keep moving. Mizuki stops now and then to take photos, crouching and zooming in on rabbits' hind legs, lifting paws to capture the undersides of their feet, even lying down and shooting upwards to the darkening sky. She seems incapable of taking a normal photo from a regular angle.

Arlo gets out his phone to take a picture of her while she's working. A photo of a photographer. Sometimes when he was out at home and paparazzi followed him, friends would tell him to photograph them back, like that was the first time anyone had ever thought of that – the fastest way to turn the whole thing into a circus. Arlo just thought Mizuki might like a nice picture of herself doing something that was important to her.

None of Mizuki's images satisfy her.

'It's not how I imagined it,' she says.

'How did you imagine it?'

'Fewer people. More magical. I know it's stupid, I just didn't think there would be so many tourists.'

'That's not stupid. Although I am a tourist.'

Her face is flushed. Frustration maybe. 'I need to get a photo.'

'OK, let's keep looking then,' Arlo says.

'I heard someone on the boat say that there's a factory here somewhere.'

'There's a map over there.'

They walk over to a big board on posts hammered into the grass.

'Got any paper?' she asks.

He only has his notebook full of sketches. He wants to say no but pulls it from his back and eases out one of the pages so the whole thing doesn't disintegrate. 'Here.'

'I could have just written in the pad. Pen?'

She takes the pencil he offers and sketches a quick route to the factory.

'May I?' he asks.

She gives him her drawing. The scale is a bit off.

'So we need to circle back towards the dock first.'

They retrace their steps then turn away from the sea and follow their handmade guide.

'Through here, I think,' she says and they head into a short concrete tunnel marked with yellow and white symbols. They could be official warnings or graffiti. More rabbits dart from side to side in the tunnel.

'Look out.'

On the other side stands what's left of the factory. A hollowed-out space with grim black outer walls and long-shattered windows. Three floors' worth of window frames but no actual floors within it and a shorter block at one end, plus a smaller outbuilding with saplings growing through the windows. Both sides of the main building are cradled by thick woods.

'This must be it,' Mizuki says, uncapping the lens of her camera.

A double-runged barrier blocks their path to the building. They glance at each other and vault over it.

One of the building's doors hangs from its hinges, fringed by wild fronds that shine like fibre optic lights in the strange island sun. *Portal to the Past.* The game is not the same without Luke.

History pulls Arlo and Mizuki through the glowing greenery into the factory shell.

Inside feels like somewhere being very slowly digested by Mother Nature. Roots crawl over parts of the floor, thick and impenetrable in places. A shelf of weeds grows along the top of the doors and every window, demolishing whatever paint used to cover them. The metalwork is rusted to the colour of autumn leaves.

The sun has bleached door-less doorways on to the wall on one side, projections of the window frames. Doors for ghosts to slip through. The wall on the other side is dank and crawling with vines, the bare bits of the wall marked with sweaty patches. Leaves are piled in front of the windows and a huge plant has sprung up at one end. Bright, bright green.

Arlo looks up. Dark moss carpets the ceiling above rusting beams. The ground is blue-grey stone like a stormy sky. The world is upside down. There are stories in all the structure's surfaces but the silence is profound. The walls are crumbling but still more solid than anything inside of him.

'This *is* it,' Mizuki breathes.

'What was this place?'

'It used to be a poison gas factory.'

The click and zoom of her camera unsettle the air. She takes at least a hundred frames. She goes outside again to get shots through the glassless windows, comes back in and squats in front of the vines, then asks Arlo to hold her legs while she mounts the window ledge to take pictures of its upper edges.

There's a plaster with bananas on it where one of her shoes has rubbed her ankle. He stares at her dry shins and listens to her sighs until she jumps down.

They both survey the big space. Arlo finds himself in a corner as is his default. Mizuki strides from end to end, snapping as she goes.

Ideas wash over him. He feels like someone else. How well someone would have to know him to look for him here; he wouldn't even look for himself here.

But why is Mizuki here? He doesn't quite trust her yet.

She crosses from the other end of the room towards him, minding her way through the camera's viewfinder. When she reaches him, she lowers the camera. He watches as she flicks through the images she's captured.

'These are really cool,' he says.

She sniffs. Tears begin to roll down her face.

'Are you OK?' he asks. 'Shall we go?'

He's not sure he wants to leave though. This wreck and ruin seems right to him; he would shoot down roots through his feet and tether himself here among all this strange green life if he could.

'I've seen all these pictures before,' Mizuki sobs.

'What do you mean?'

She can't speak for crying.

He tries again, 'I don't understand. What's wrong?'

'There's nothing original here. This whole thing is pointless.'

She sinks against the wall and he leans next to her, wondering whether or not to put an arm around her or if he should ask her first.

'What whole thing?'

'I need to tell you something,' she says.

'OK.'

'I'm not an environmentalist.'

'OK,' he says. 'Wait, you're not in some kind of cult, are you?'

'No, I'm just not an environmentalist. Although I do care

about the environment because I'm not a cretin. I'm sorry I lied. I hate liars.'

'Well, it's not as if you've been keeping this a secret for years. We literally just met yesterday.' He wants her to feel better. 'And, no offence, but I don't really care whether you're an environmentalist or not. Sometimes I even put stuff in the wrong bin. I mean, not on purpose, but it happens.'

No offence. Luke says that all the time.

Said that all the time.

She laughs the sort of laugh people do when they've stopped crying and the tension has burst. 'That's the most you've said in one go since we met.'

'So why are you here if it's not to fiddle with the soil?'

'The soil?'

'Never mind. That's what I thought environmentalists did.'

'I'm trying to take a photograph.'

'You've taken about a thousand since we met,' he says. 'Mission accomplished.'

'I'm trying to take one nobody has taken before.'

'Why?'

'It's for sort of a photography competition. It's really, really important.'

She reminds him of all those obsessive kids at school, completely consumed with making whatever was in their heads into something tangible. He gets it; he still wants to make something that matters, though the chance of that happening seems to be getting further and further away.

'I need to make a name for myself. I need to be noticed.'

'I get it,' he says.

'I've been going to all these places, trying to find the perfect view or an amazing portrait, something no one has ever seen before, but it's not working.'

Their puzzle pieces shunt into place; they're looking for the same thing but for different reasons – to be totally lost for a while.

Hair hangs in her face; he longs to brush it out of her eyes.

A small, furry face appears at the door. It freezes as they notice it, then twitches its head like a mechanical donkey in a nativity scene. A blink and it's gone again.

'Are you OK?' Arlo asks.

'I'm OK. I think the quake just set me on edge and I'm getting frustrated but I'm fine. Are you OK?'

'I'm OK.'

'Do you want to tell me why you're really here?' she asks.

He wants her to know but he doesn't want to have to be the one to tell her. Maybe she would understand; sometimes it's more painful to stay than to leave everything. Most likely she would have questions that he doesn't yet know the answers to: 'Where are you going next? Don't you want to be an actor any more? Are you ever going home?'

'I just didn't want to do a typical gap year,' he lies. 'I guess I want to see things most people won't see too.'

'We're looking for the same thing.'

'Yeah.'

More rabbits are gathering on the other side of the windows but they don't approach the door.

'Let's go?'

'OK.'

They step through the wild-green neon framing the door back out into the open.

'How did all the rabbits get here anyway?' he asks.

'I read about this while you were snoring on the ferry. You want the nice-ish story or the grim story?'

'Both.'

'One theory is a school got bored of their pets and released them here. Kind of irresponsible pet ownership but pretty cute. The other is they were used for testing the gas and they took over when the humans left because of contamination.'

'Oh. That's savage.'

'Yeah.'

She takes one last photo of the husk of the factory then they walk back to the terminal both finding their way through their thoughts. Arlo folds Mizuki's wonky sketch into his pocket to put in his notebook later. There can be no doubt the island has earned its place on maps.

They wait by the shore next to the small dock for the catamaran. The sun hangs low and heavy over the horizon as if sinking under its own weight.

The wind is picking up.

'You OK?' he asks Mizuki. She nods and hugs him from the side, clamping one arm in front of him and the other behind.

'Thanks,' she says. He rests his chin on the top of her head and lifts his hands to cradle her front arm. Holds on tight. The shape they're making probably looks stupid but it feels good. Warm. Over too quickly.

A pair of row boats knock against the jetty, jostling to be ridden. The knowledge that he and Mizuki need the same thing makes Arlo brave and he's seconds from asking her if she wants to borrow one with him when the catamaran comes into view.

On the other side of the troubled water, the mountains are just dark shapes now. Sleeping giants already awake in another planet's dream.

The sky goes on for ever and for the first time in his life Arlo doesn't know which way is home.

FOURTEEN

The island gave Arlo and Mizuki something that they both needed. As the boat ploughs through the dark water back to the mainland they decide to visit more places together.

They check in to a hostel close to the dock and stay up most of the night researching and planning.

They find whole websites dedicated to exploring abandoned relics and derelict sites; places to distract and lose yourself, places to find something nobody else has seen, places to outrun all the people and things that hurt you or that you might do to hurt them.

Mizuki tells Arlo that the name for the explorers translates to 'ruinists'. It fits.

They trawl through the posts and comments, debating the pros and cons of the sites they find listed. Old gold mines, a bowling alley, abandoned schools. A derelict strip club and a crumbling tower with an altar of skulls inside. Stranger and stranger places.

There are threads on how to avoid security, which places have dogs, which have fake cameras and so on. Few give specific locations and almost all of the photos have the full names of the places blurred out.

When they dig deeper, they realise there are clues. Topographical hints, pieces of history and detail about the layout that they can piece together and triangulate with the help of Google Earth. The irony that they have to use maps to get lost does not pass Arlo by.

Eventually, they find a couple of forums where less discreet contributors have posted advice on exactly how to get to places. Arlo isn't totally sure of the rules of play – other than 'take nothing but pictures, leave nothing but footprints' – but this step-by-step help feels like cheating. He's not sure if these people are sharing or showing off.

'But how else would we find these sites?' Mizuki asks. 'And how would we not get caught?'

'Both excellent points,' he concedes. 'I'm thirsty. Are you?'

'Yeah. There's a vending machine in the other lounge.'

Arlo goes to the machine and comes back with a selection of drinks.

'You're quite the bartender,' Mizuki tells him. 'Although, aren't you underage?'

'I'll be twenty next week and these are all non-alcoholic.'

'We have to do something special for your birthday.'

She's so kind that it hurts. Letting a bit of it in means allowing everything else to rush in and out of him. 'I'm not much of a birthday-er.'

'They're important though,' she says. 'I'm already counting down the days to mine.'

They work their way through all of the drinks as they pore over threads, routes and train timetables. First up is coffee in a can, which magically heats itself up and tastes pretty good after their long day of earthquakes and rabbits and ruins. Next, a fizzy energy drink with too much added vitamin C.

'Tastes weird. I think I like it though,' she says. It's like citrus, but powdery.'

Sumac.

The bird's nest juice is a step too far. Mizuki takes a sip from the bright blue can and spits it straight back out again. 'Que le fuck is this stuff? Tastes like spit and twigs.'

Arlo tries it.

She's right, it does. 'Toothpaste spit with a hint of forest floor.'

Luke and the trees take over Arlo's head. He refocus on their task.

An hour later, Mizuki declares them done. They have a list of places to visit and routes planned as far as they can without local knowledge. They've made their final destination the most ambitious one – storming a castle in the dead of night.

'I have to sleep,' Mizuki says.

'Me too,' Arlo agrees, though he knows he's too wired for that.

'Could I borrow your cell again quickly? I just want to email home.'

'Of course,' he says. 'You're welcome to use mine but I'm sure we could pick you up a cheap one.'

'I'm liking life without one to be honest.'

Arlo watches as Mizuki taps out a message.

'You don't want to let people know where you are?' she asks.

'Yeah, I should.'

He texts his mum to say he didn't get the part, but is staying for more meetings. *I'll be busy so don't worry if you don't hear from me,'* he tells her.

It's the only contact he can handle at the moment: anything else and he wouldn't be able to pretend he was OK.

'Let's go to the dorm,' he says.

'You have to try my toothpaste first. It's melon-flavoured.'

It's weird being in a room full of snoring and snuffling strangers with Mizuki lying in the narrow bunk next to his. Arlo hadn't packed any pyjamas, in fact he doesn't own any, so sleeps in his boxers and T-shirt, tucking the thin duvet over his legs.

They whisper.

'Night.'

'Night.'

'Sweet dreams.'

'You too.'

Mizuki falls asleep immediately.

Arlo stares up at the bunk above him, waiting for his eyes to adjust to the dark room and wondering who's asleep up there. It's nicer than the capsule hotel. A surprise – he'd assumed all hostels smelled like bong water. But then everything is cleaner, more efficient, here.

He runs his hands over the cool metal slats above his head, then down the smooth wall to his side. His tongue tastes of synthetic fruit from the toothpaste.

As a child he'd laid in his cot fingering the planets on the mobile strung above him, batting them, smacking them out of orbit, watching them tangle.

Later, at school in the dorm, the planets were replaced with a papier mâché pterodactyl dinosaur made from a washing-up-liquid bottle and a coat hanger. As it aged and crumbled to pieces, Arlo would wake up with flakes of its khaki paint on his bed. He'd wanted to use the rainbow to paint it but something told him it had to be camouflaged. He knows now he was wrong to use green; pterodactyls have wings so he should have done it blue, like the sky.

One day he'll make another one, or something even better. Something perfect, something that matters.

Mizuki turns over in her sleep, faces away from him. If only he could fall asleep like that and trust he'd be safe. He imagines three prongs growing from the back of his head and slotting into a socket in the pillow where he'll power up overnight.

Stupid.

Arlo pulls the pillow out from under his neck and slams it down next to him. It lands in the suggestion of a body beside him. He doesn't move it. If he closes his eyes, he can almost convince himself it's someone curled up next to him. Jessica, Mizuki, maybe someone else.

He'll have to get some sleeping tablets if he doesn't manage some rest soon.

Do not let this get bad again.

In the end, he dozes a bit but doesn't dream, never fully lets go. It would be too much to see Luke or even his dad and wake up to find them not real.

FIFTEEN

It's more complicated for Mizuki to take pictures when it's dark but the payoff is greater, she tells Arlo. He wants her to win the photography competition. They decide to do their exploring at night when the chance of capturing something original is higher. She explains about manual focus and long exposure. He remembers bits from Photo Arts at school but likes hearing her explain.

After a fruitless trip to a crumbling house on the outskirts of a small town, they ditch some of their heavier stuff at a hostel and buy a foldable tripod and a couple of sleeping bags to make their night work easier.

Mizuki won't let him carry the tripod as they sneak out of their hostel for the night to take a look at an old school house.

Their arrival disturbs the school's inhabitants. Scuttle, slither, hide. Creatures hold their breath. Roots stop their creeping. Fight, freeze, flee.

'Look at this place,' he whispers.

They take in the clean blackboard, books tessellated on the shelves like ornaments. There's hardly any dust.

Mizuki sets up the tripod and a small portable lamp in front of the rows of desks and asks him to hold up a light reflector while she tries a few shots. She's not interested in making these places look apocalyptic. 'Stock images of dystopian wasteland,' she calls those types of photos. 'No thanks.'

Instead she infuses the sleeping room with light and life, capturing a cool sliver of moon on the floor boards, the swish of the curtain riding a blast of air through the broken window. Flowers in the old walls. Giant frogs leaping through pulverised brick on to text books.

'I feel like something's here,' he says.

'Big Mother is always watching us.'

'Do you believe in ghosts?'

Arlo's skin prickles and he starts to freak himself out but tries not to show it. Evidently he doesn't do a very good job because Mizuki says, 'Don't stress – everyone knows all the ghosts here are women with long hair and they only hang out in toilets.'

It's true; he's seen it in those films he's supposed to like.

Arlo wanders round the room to distract himself; moving is the best way he's found to make himself feel better.

It's so tidy and well kept.

Did the children know when they packed their books away and said goodbye to their teacher that final time that it was their last day here? When he'd left boarding school, Arlo didn't know he wasn't returning. He didn't know the black weeds were coming for him. If he had, he'd have tried harder to leave a bright path to follow back.

'It's like someone has been in to clean it,' he says.

'Maybe it was your ghost.'

'Maybe someone local can't bear to watch it rot,' he says. Or maybe this was another of the ruinists' rules – you were supposed to help preserve these places any way you could without interfering too much.

As they creep out an hour later, they come across some local kids doing dares outside. He and Luke used to sneak out and do the same thing sometimes.

'Tell them we're not the police.'

'I think that's fairly obvious,' Mizuki says but reassures the kids anyway and they scuttle off.

The thrill of their first night-time exploration follows them all the way back to the hostel.

Two nights later, they sneak into a rotting strip club. They'd caught a bus as far as it would take them then walked the rest of the way following one of Mizuki's sketches. When he's moving like this, it's easier for Arlo to outrun his thoughts.

Somehow Mizuki convinces him to pole dance on one of the dusty platforms inside.

'Come on, I thought you used to want to be an actor,' she says. 'Act like a dancer.'

Arlo has his back to her camera so the lens only catches his silhouette against the 1970s wallpaper. He looks out over the rows of wipe-down seats while Mizuki calls out instructions.

'Strut, bend, blow kisses, freeze.' He can almost see the men who must have sat here, staring up, adjusting their trousers. Ghostly characters graze through his head like a slow-mo parade as he tries to push away the idea of their loneliness.

The camera clicks a hundred times before Arlo jumps down.

Mizuki shows him some of the pictures, shot in black and white this time and sadder than her usual style.

'You have to swear to me that you will never show these to anyone,' he says.

'I would never do that.'

He's worried the suggestion has offended her so when she offers to delete them his voice says no, while the rest of him begs yes.

A thing that nobody told Arlo about travelling is that in the still moments shadows can still creep in. His and Mizuki's exhilarating nights are punctuated by watching endurance programmes on hostel TVs and washing clothes in hot laundry rooms, sitting on floors with their legs out side by side in front of them, maybe slightly closer than they need to be or maybe Arlo imagines it. They spend hours traipsing to and from train stations and on various forms of transport, losing time looking for places that aren't there any more.

Sometimes they watch films on his phone. He suggests *Titanic* one evening while they're waiting for dark to fall. Mizuki lists five reasons why it's a masterpiece of misogyny and irresponsibility.

'Well, maybe it's not that bad,' she concedes. 'But Jack basically hits on Rose after she's just contemplated jumping off the boat into the sea, then twenty minutes later he's all but dangling her off the front of the boat encouraging her to fly.'

They keep themselves occupied with endless rounds of rock, paper, scissors, incorporating ever-more complicated variations.

'Hole punch beats paper.'

'Obviously.'

'Wait, does moss beat rock?'

'There is no moss in this game but rock beats floss. Slices right through it.'

'Right, floss is no match for rock.'

'Or scissors.'

Arlo still hasn't taught Mizuki how to play Doors though. Some things are sacred.

At night, he messages Luke some of the things he can't say out loud. He wants the universe to know he hasn't forgotten about his friend and what happened.

I'm sorry I lost your jacket.

I'm sorry I lost your medal.

I'm sorry I left you on the roof.

I'm sorry, I'm sorry, I'm sorry.

He deletes the messages as soon as he's sent them since he's basically sharing the phone with Mizuki now. Not that she would read them, of course.

She uses the phone for three things: emailing home,

obsessively scrolling through photography sites and sketching out walking routes for the final legs of their journeys.

It's a relief that's she's taken on that role. Arlo hasn't drawn his maps since he got here, maybe he doesn't want to make his adventures without Luke concrete.

All the same, when Mizuki starts dating the corners and signing them like an artist, he wishes he had the nerve to ask her if he could keep them.

She sleeps through the night when they aren't out exploring. For Arlo, night-times are an infinite string of 'what ifs' and slow seconds staring up at the same old things on new ceilings.

It's in these quieter moments waiting for sleep that he thinks about why the ruined places are empty and who has run away from them. Are they still lost – and did anyone try to find them?

SIXTEEN

Inside three weeks, chasing ruins has become like an addiction for them both.

Arlo has recast himself as a student traveller/photographer's assistant and has almost started to believe his new role. They live out of their backpacks, subsisting on noodles and sliced apples. The earth's sweets, Mizuki calls them.

They make lists of the things they miss from home because it's easier than talking about the people they miss. It hurts less to talk about biscuits and beer than it does guilt and dead friends.

Occasionally they get their hands on some of their holy grail items. Arlo had barely seen anyone as triumphant as when Mizuki found actual peanut butter instead of the 'peanut cream' that's usually on offer here. 'A violation,' she'd called the latter before eating half the jar of the real stuff with a spoon.

'Try it,' she said. 'So good.'

When she was done, Arlo had rinsed the jar and wrapped it inside his backpack.

Despite all their planning, the path they're taking is not the one they imagined. They know they want to end up at the castle but keep reading about new places that sound exciting along the way so they change direction, circle back, go off on tangents. Just two warm dots zigzagging up and down the country.

Tonight it's a dilapidated clinic that Mizuki read about on one of the forums. They've travelled hours off their planned route to get here, meaning they'll get to the castle a day later than planned.

Arlo can't help but be happy about the diversion. The castle will be their final stop and they haven't talked about what will happen after that.

The clinic door opens easily.

Fear prickles over him. 'What if there's a body?'

'Why would there be a body?' Mizuki whispers. 'And even if there was one at some point, someone would have found it already.'

Stinking mattresses and strange pieces of metal litter the clinic's stained halls. Most of the damage is through age and abandon rather than through vandalism. Each room is marked with a yellow sign above the door. Mizuki translates the words she knows: reception, consultation room, X-ray, even a dentist.

Inside each room are everyday things made terrifying by neglect: filthy gauze, trays of rusted surgical instruments, capsized wheelchairs, folders with scans of body parts belonging to people who might now be dead, jars of more body parts in formaldehyde with peeling labels.

'Funny how all this stuff used to save lives and now it just looks like instruments of torture,' he says.

They jump every time one of them brushes against something or accidentally knocks something on to the floor.

This is a better buzz than Arlo ever felt acting or acing auditions. Being scared is the most alive you can feel, especially this visceral, physical kind of fear. Cold sweat. Eyes popping. Nerves jangling. It feels new.

They find themselves singing stupid songs and making jokes to keep the tension at a bearable level.

Mizuki picks up a pot with an ear floating in it and pretends to read. 'This one is sashimi. Want some?'

His stomach churns and he can't keep his face from grimacing.

'Sorry, have you got a weak stomach?'

'If it's weak not to want to eat a fifty-year-old pickled ear then, yep, I definitely do.'

'Isn't it amazing they haven't all been stolen?'

She hands the jar to Arlo. He clutches its oblong edges, reassured by the tightness of its silver lid. Would it be weird to tell her that he and Luke had a jar like this when they were kids? They'd filled it and buried it. Not with an ear in it but it was almost exactly the same. Jars are jars, he supposes, not much scope for deviation. Even the peanut butter jar is more or less the same.

'Do you hear something?' she asks.

They freeze. Listen. Laugh when his stomach gurgles.

'There's nobody here.'

They find an old pharmacy, the floor carpeted with decaying documents, maybe prescription papers and medical notes. Diseases and secrets strewn about the place. A shelf of textbooks full of outdated drawings. The plaster on the walls peels, the wooden shelves sag, deep in dust. Rows and rows of more jars, all different sizes, some still filled with pills, lotions, ointments.

'Don't say "ointment",' Mizuki says. 'Such a gross word. Almost as horrifying as "moist".'

'Dear god. Please never say that again.'

'Exactly.'

'Please consider both words banned if this friendship is to continue,' he says.

They swing open the door to another rotting room. Someone has arranged anatomical mannequins and skeletons in compromising positions on an old gurney. Mizuki is laughing so hard she can barely get out her joke about boners.

The metal beds look like old sun loungers and there's a beaten-up baseball boot on one of the mannequins' stiff feet. *Nobody sleeps with their shoes on.* Just when Arlo's mind had drifted from Luke, the universe serves up a symbol to remind him.

Luke's dead.

When it hits, it's as if a seatbelt comes undone and he sails through shattered glass into a brick wall.

'I have to get out of here.'

'What?'

He says it louder, 'I can't be here. I'll wait for you outside.'

'I'll come with you, just let me collapse the tripod.'

Arlo can't breathe as he's running down the corridor to the clinic exit. Dust and old chemical smells choke him. The place is full of death.

'Wait,' Mizuki calls.

He doesn't slow down. Needs air.

It's OK. Almost there.

He stumbles on, almost at the door, Mizuki behind him trying to catch him up.

Arlo's hand has already opened the door when he hears her trip and land with a yelp.

'My camera!'

Arlo turns around and drops to the floor with her.

'Get my camera.'

He passes her the camera, still breathing hard. It's dusty but fine.

'Your leg,' he says.

'Why were you running?'

'Mizuki, look at your leg.'

The fabric of her jeans has a new rip just below the knee but not enough for them to see how badly she's injured.

'Shit,' she says.

'Can I roll this up?'

'Are you OK? What's going on?'

'Your leg could be cut. We need to get a better look at it.'

'Let's get out of here first.'

'Mizuki.'

'OK, OK.'

He inches the tight fabric up her leg, taking care not to hurt her. She looks drained, maybe from the shock of the fall. Arlo tries to make her laugh. 'These are ridiculous, by the way. How do you breathe wearing them?'

'Should we tear them?'

'It's OK. Maybe if you just pull here.'

Mizuki yanks at the knee of her jeans while he shuffles the

denim until they can see what they're dealing with.

There's a small gash at the top of her shin.

Arlo touches the area around it gently, feeling her eyes on his hand as he does. 'Does this hurt?'

'Not really. I think it's OK.'

'I'm so sorry I made you fall.'

'You didn't. That piece of wood did. I tripped on it. But what happened?'

'I just had to get out.'

'Panic attack?' she asks. 'I get them sometimes.'

'Maybe,' he says. 'Do you know what you landed on?'

There's mangled metal and splintered wood all around them.

They both think it: *Infection.*

Mizuki takes an orange from her bag, tears the skin open and squeezes the juice into the cut.

Arlo winces for her. That's got to sizzle.

'Does that work as an antiseptic?' he asks.

'I don't know but I feel kind of badass.'

'Have you had a tetanus jab?'

'A jab?'

'An inoculation. Vaccination?'

'A shot? Yeah, I had, like, a million of them before I left home. My dad is kind of paranoid.'

Is that the first piece of information she's volunteered about a parent? He's been too preoccupied with protecting his mum to consider her family.

'It's getting really light outside,' she says. 'We should get out of here.'

'Can you walk?'

'I think so.'

She lets him help her up and tests her leg. 'I don't think it's as bad as it looks.'

He feels guilty anyway. 'I'm so sorry. This is all my fault.'

'It was just as much my idea to come here as it was yours.'

But if he hadn't freaked out, she wouldn't have been running and . . . a light sweeps over them.

It flashes. They freeze.

A dog barks.

'Shit,' Arlo whispers. 'Security.'

The light sweeps over them again, hitting them in the eyes this time.

They reach for each other's hands.

'Run.'

SEVENTEEN

'Hey,' comes a voice.

'That was English,' Mizuki says.

'Hello,' Arlo calls back.

'Come out with your hands up.' The flash and sweep of the light again.

Arlo and Mizuki raise their arms, still holding hands. He steps in front of her.

Barking and laughter. 'You should see your faces.'

'What the fuck?' says Arlo.

A guy in a red hoodie steps out of the shadows.

'You guys almost shat yourselves. Sorry, I couldn't resist.'

Their arms drop. Arlo isn't sure who is the last to let go of the other's hand.

A young woman appears as the guy sticks out his hand to shake hello. 'I'm James. This is Arisu.'

Arisu nods down to the small dog at their feet. 'And this is Teriyaki. You guys need a ride?'

Ten minutes later, Arlo and Mizuki sit in the back of Arisu's car.

'Thanks for the lift.'

'Sure, man,' says James. 'What are you guys doing here anyway?'

'Just passing through,' says Mizuki. 'What about you?'

'We study at the university. I'm on a year abroad to learn the language.'

Arlo isn't sure whether or not to tell them that they don't have to speak English for his sake. He's learned enough phrases to be polite and let people know he's trying but wishes he could speak more of the language.

The town is already wide awake when they get back.

'Can we buy you breakfast to say thanks for the ride?' asks Mizuki.

'Have you been to the park here yet?' asks Arisu. 'We could get a picnic.'

They haven't been to any of the places the guide books say you should.

Arlo looks at Mizuki like, *Are you up for this?* She is.

They pick up some food and walk to the park in pairs. Mizuki and Arisu lead. Arlo and James lag behind. Teriyaki scampers back and forth between them until Arisu stops to clip on a lead.

James seems to be going slower than he needs to be and Arlo is trying to keep an ear on Mizuki and Arisu's conversation in case they're talking about him or her fiancé.

'So, what are you really doing here, man?' asks James.

The way he keeps saying 'man' is already grating on Arlo.

'Just exploring.'

James stops again, forcing Arlo to do the same. They look at each other. He's seen the look on James's face before. It's the realisation that Arlo's been in his living room but they've never spoken.

He knows who I am.

'You're that guy with the silent fans.'

'No,' Arlo says. *Have they started talking again yet?* He'd forgotten all about them.

'My mum watches your programme. *The Bill?*'

'*The Beat.*'

'I knew I recognised you.'

A cold flash shoots through Arlo. His lie to Mizuki.

'Please don't say anything.'

'No offence but I don't think anyone will have heard of you here anyway.'

No offence.

Luke.

Luke's dead.

'I mean to Mizuki. She doesn't know.'

'How come?'

'I didn't know we were going to turn out to be friends.'

'OK,' says James. 'It's none of my business but she's going to find out eventually. Better to hear it from you.'

'Yeah.'

'So are you here for a movie or something?'

'No,' says Arlo. 'Nothing like that.'

Mizuki and Arisu drop back to them. Arlo catches James's eye. *Did he nod? Does that mean he won't say anything?*

Arlo changes the subject. 'What are you two talking about?'

'The politics of green spaces,' says Mizuki, waving to the park entrance.

'I'm studying art and urban planning,' Arisu adds.

Mizuki explains, 'Environment versus property rights, public health versus municipal services, you know.'

But Arlo doesn't know. Their words bob around in his head as he tries to think of something to contribute. Instead he half-shouts, 'A deer.'

The park is brimming with them. They trot alongside the foursome, pushing their black noses into pockets, nuzzling backpacks and butting at their legs. Arisu scoops up Teriyaki before he can pick a fight.

'They're looking for paper to eat,' she explains.

Even after Rabbit Island, it's amazing to see so many bold animals roaming and sheltering under trees.

They find somewhere to eat away from the deer and swap stories. It feels strange to talk to someone who isn't Mizuki. Arlo keeps looking over to her to check she's OK. She smiles and laughs as they eat. The bit in between Arlo's stomach and his heart feels kind of empty and full at the same time, as if he misses her even though she's right there.

'What happened to your leg?' asks Arisu.

'It's nothing. I tripped on some metal or something. Wasn't looking where I was going,' says Mizuki, trying to push the edges of the rip in her jeans together.

'You should take better care of her,' says James.

'I can look after myself,' Mizuki says. She twists her engagement ring so the stone is on the underside. *She's so young to be engaged. What's his name? Something solid and concrete and normal?*

'Oh, sorry, I thought you were a couple.'

'Even if we were, I would still be able to take care of myself,' Mizuki says. 'We're friends.'

'Just friends?' asks Arisu.

'No such thing as *just* friends,' says Mizuki. 'Friends are more important than anything else.'

'And girls make better friends than guys,' says James.

'How so?' asks Arlo.

'We're better at talking and sharing how we actually feel, for one,' says Mizuki.

Something flickers inside Arlo. *How can she say that?* 'That's such a stereotype.'

'Do you talk to your closest guy friend?' she says. 'You haven't even told me his name.'

'His name is Luke and, yes, we talk about most things.'

Maybe it's true, maybe their friendship was in the minority, but it really pissed him off that she thought guys couldn't be good friends to each other.

'Sounds like a very special bromance,' says James.

'Call it what you want.'

Arlo's words land like awkward spikes between them and Arisu changes the subject. 'So where's the best place you've seen so far?'

Mizuki shows them some of the pictures on her camera.

'These are incredible. They actually look alive.'

She must have taken thousands of photos now. Unexplained

stains by the sides of the beds at the clinic. Broken pins and cracked balls in a decrepit bowling alley. Rows of desks where they'd opened all the lids to create a wave of wood in the decaying school.

Somehow Mizuki has captured the smell, rotting, congealing. The cold concrete, the dead wood, the wild neon of the plants. They speak of the feel of rough rust on old metal, the damp of internal stone walls, the people who aren't there any more.

Mizuki's cheeks pink up under the attention and Arlo has to quash the pride he feels swelling. He can't take any credit.

'These are amazing,' says James.

Arlo tries to catch Mizuki's eye, to make sure she remembers to stop scrolling before she gets to the ones of him posing at the strip club. If Arlo says something, James is just the kind of person who won't let it go until he's seen them. Just when he's resigned himself to the embarrassment, Mizuki puts the lens back on the camera, saying, 'It's just more of the same after these.'

She looks at Arlo like, 'Don't worry, I've got you,' and he's never been so grateful to anyone for keeping a promise.

'You're so lucky to be travelling,' says James. 'We can only go at weekends because of university.'

'Any tips on where we should go next?'

'We went to this amazing old hospital,' says Arisu. 'Have you heard of The Play?'

Arlo and Mizuki shake their heads.

'They're this art collective who've been working since the sixties,' Arisu explains. 'They've done all these things like floating down a river on a raft made out of . . . I don't know the word in English.'

'Say it in any language you like,' says Mizuki.

She does; it sounds to Arlo like 'polystyrene'.

'It's the same,' Mizuki says. 'Well, similar.'

Arisu continues, 'Yes, polystyrene. Shaped like an arrow. They did all these events that most people didn't understand like building a house and floating it down a river then setting fire to it, or moving sheep across mountains. And they made a giant egg and put it in the sea.'

'What happened to the egg?' asks Mizuki. 'I hope it wasn't plastic.'

'It got lost,' says James.

Arisu says, 'They made a thing called Hospital. I don't think that hospital is still there but James and I went to one like it. It was the best place I've been.'

'You want the details?' asks James. 'Developers are buying up land and knocking places down faster than we can get to them, but I think it's still there.'

'We have to see it,' says Mizuki.

Arlo's notebook is at the hostel so Mizuki writes the location on the back of a receipt. She shows it to Arlo and then pockets it. Her handwriting is big and tidy.

James tells them about a trip they're planning to an abandoned luxury hotel on an island. Arlo has one ear on the conversation as he thinks about The Play.

Maybe that's the kind of artist he'll be.

He catches the end of an exchange. 'We're going at the weekend. You guys should come.'

'Great,' says Mizuki. 'I lost my phone but put your number in Arlo's and we'll call you.'

'It'll be a new moon,' says Arisu. 'The twenty-eighth.'

On autopilot, Arlo tells them, 'That's my birthday.'

EIGHTEEN

Arlo and Mizuki stand in the shadows ten metres or so from a high fence. No light.

'We made it,' he says.

'Almost. We'll have made it when we're at the top of the castle.'

They've been planning this since the start and now it's here Arlo wants everything to go right.

'Let's give it five,' he says, 'to let our eyes adjust.'

'OK.'

They are both happy to give themselves a few minutes to prepare. They'd watched the taxi lights fade before walking the last bit to the site in silence.

'Arisu and James will be on their way to that hotel island now,' he says. It's sort of a test to see if Mizuki secretly minds that they'd decided to travel on by themselves instead.

'Yeah,' she says, 'but sometimes you're only supposed to meet people once.'

'Very philosophical.'

'And James was kind of . . .'

'A douche?'

'I was going to say extroverted but we can use your word,' she says. 'Can you believe this place has just been sitting here falling apart for ten years?'

'Do you think there'll be anyone else here?' he asks.

'I don't know. Maybe. All I know is it was just sold and this is pretty much the last chance to see it before the whole thing is bulldozed.'

'Here, get your torch ready, but don't switch it on.'

They adjust the torch straps on each other's heads. Arlo is careful not to get Mizuki's soft hair caught in the clasp. Tendrils. A word he didn't even know he knew. Her head smells clean, like lemons.

'See the cameras?' He points to the top of the fence.

'I doubt they're even on. And even if they are, nobody's going to be watching them. And we're not going to damage anything.'

'True.'

'Let's collect some trash while we're in there. Besides,' Mizuki continues, 'nobody would recognise you with that attempt at a beard. You look like Teenage Jesus.'

'I was actually going for Seventies Dad.'

'Are you literally stroking your beard right now?' Her laughter carries in the dark.

'Shhh,' he whispers. Her teasing doesn't sting the way it would from someone else.

The beard needs some work, it's true, but the wiry feel of it reminds him of touching his dad's beard when he was a toddler – distance has brought this memory into focus too. When his parents split up when he was three, his dad shaved off his beard and for the longest time Arlo thought you could only have one if you were married. He wonders if Mizuki's fiancé has one. Some kind of designer stubble maybe.

'Ready?' she asks.

'Let's do it.'

They jog over to the fence, heads down. There's a patch where the barbed wire has been clipped and bent away by a previous visitor. Mizuki hooks her hands through the fence wire and asks Arlo for a leg up.

He boosts her over and she drops to the ground the other side.

His height is an advantage. He takes a run at it, clings to the fence halfway up like Spider-Man.

'Come on.'

Arlo drags himself over the top and lets go. Pain shoots through his legs and spine as he lands on the other side.

'You've got to bend your knees.'

Too late.

He shakes the pain out.

It's beyond quiet. He can hear things he can't normally. The tick of body clocks; the stretching of his dry lips as they grin at each other.

'Two hours till sunrise,' he says. The adrenaline starts to pick up now that they're in the grounds focused on their mission: they've got a castle to find. It seems like another lifetime that he was sitting on that bleached beach with Jessica searching the skyline for something to excite him. Those shiny buildings – The Disco Ball, The Castle, The Pear. All made of glass, ready to shatter at any moment.

Mizuki looks around. 'I think this place was supposed to be like Disneyland but there was some issue with the licensing.'

'Should have called it Nightmareland.'

They rely on the moon and stars to light their way as they follow the path into the theme park. It's completely derelict. The tannoys lining the path have been claimed by winding greenery, strangling off any chance of them pumping out jingles or announcements. Vandals have clearly spent time here. There are unfamiliar, human-sized plastic mascots everywhere; the ones that still have heads have graffiti for eyebrows. Mizuki gets right in their cracked faces with her camera. The flash illuminates their surroundings.

'This is creepy as shit,' Arlo says.

'I know. Look at that poor guy.' A mascot has been stripped of its limbs and rolled on its side to the edge of the path.

Arlo feels a rush of sympathy, a desire to at least stand the mascot up the right way. *Don't be stupid – it's just plastic.* And it would be embarrassing if he couldn't lift it.

Ahead they see the shapes of some low buildings.

'Let's go in,' he whispers.

They try the left building first. The furniture has been gutted but it's not completely trashed. There's a counter and a space with metal cabinets behind it. Arlo creeps into a backroom and finds it full of old snack machines advertising doughnuts, slushies, nachos. Weeds grow tall in the wet corners.

'This must have been a diner or something,' he says, still

keeping his voice low. It's hard to imagine this dead space filled with people eating, laughing and planning which ride to go on first. Families, friends, birthdays. Mizuki drags her finger along the counter, drawing in the dust.

'What's that?' he asks, looking at her dust art.

'It's supposed to be a castle.'

'I'd stick to photography if I were you.'

They write their names in the dust. He takes a picture with his phone.

'There's nothing here,' she says. 'Let's keep moving.'

They traipse through an abandoned shop. The gifts have long since been looted but plastic animal garlands still hang over the till and are trodden into the floor. Gills and wings ripped by careless feet. Arlo lifts one, smooths it out and sets it on the counter by the tills. When he looks up Mizuki is smiling at him.

In the corner, artificial Christmas trees are piled up, still dressed with decorations from a decade-old celebration. He didn't even know people celebrated Christmas here.

Next, they find an old arcade. A hundred smashed games fill the sad space, an unplugged army. The guns have been ripped from their cables on the shooting games and the steering wheels dismantled from the racing ones.

Sorry about shooting you in the face.

That's OK.

The only game Arlo recognises is Pac-Man. Mizuki is excited by a couple of others.

'I was obsessed with this when I was a kid.' She runs her hands over old coloured stickers then clutches a console. 'It's so sad seeing them like this.'

Seeing all the machines beaten up also seems so at odds with how everyone seems to conduct themselves in this country.

Mizuki asks him to hold his torch light on a few of the games so she can get some shots before they leave.

'Come on,' Arlo says, switching the torch back off. 'We're not going to find the castle in here.'

They march on in a large loop. Past what could have been an old haunted house with things bursting out of the walls – creatures that were once animatronic but now just look lame.

Mizuki spots something up ahead and runs over to an enclosure. She calls back, 'I used to love these too.'

'What is it?' he calls, catching up to her.

'Spinning teacups.'

Arlo wasn't allowed to go to travelling funfairs when he was a child but there was a small theme park overlooking the sea in his hometown. There were a handful of basic rides and a game called the High Striker where you could test your strength by smashing a hammer on a platform. *Step right up! Test the men from the boys!* He never tried it.

He had sat in a teacup in between his mum, his aunt and Luke one summer. His aunt had flirted with the young guy working the ride, hollering to be given an extra spin as if it were a waltzer. The boy had obliged and Mum had tipped him twenty pence. Arlo had been embarrassed but the boy seemed pleased and had held out his hands to help Mum and his aunt out of the cup.

Arlo joins Mizuki to lean on the fence. The giant teacups are cracked and worn. A couple have been smashed, splitting their floral patterns apart. The side of one is missing completely. A giants' tea party turned brawl.

'How tragic,' she whispers.

'Don't you want to get a picture?'

'Too depressing and I've seen loads of photos of these already.'

They set off again.

Mizuki walks a few paces ahead of him, hitching her backpack up every now and then, bending over to sort out a loosening lace or straying sock, then powers on into the night.

He notices still, white shapes to the right. Ghosts? No. Endless heaps of white plastic chairs stacked against railings and tangled round the backs of buildings. Occasionally they hear voices and smashing from elsewhere in the site. Arlo thinks he hears a bear more than once, though if pressed would find it hard to say with confidence exactly what a bear sounds like. He'd like to see one though. From a safe distance.

'Look,' Mizuki says. 'What's that?'

'Some kind of fun-house or day-time disco?' he says.

The building is lined with cracked disco balls, like a string of oversized fairy lights. As they get closer, pieces of mirror crunch under their feet.

'Some of them have been smashed.'

'I've got an idea,' Mizuki says. She's excited and shrugs her backpack on to the floor. 'Shine your torch on them and spin them.'

'That's not going to work,' he says. 'We need to keep the light on them all.'

So she flips on her own head torch and he runs through the disco balls batting them into orbit then diving out of shot while she captures their refracting light as it illuminates the destruction and decay.

'Again,' she says.

He scowls. It's a risk having their torches on for long but it could be worth it for the right photo.

'Please.'

Arlo tears through the disco balls again using both arms to spin them this time.

'Perfect,' Mizuki says. 'Well, not perfect, but pretty good.'

'I want joint credit for that one if you submit it,' he jokes.

'OK, but my name is going first so it's Mizuki Arlo unless we go full Brangelina.'

'You mean like Arluki?'

'I mean like Mizarlo.'

'Sounds like a wizard.'

She's distracted by the frames she's taken. 'One more try.'

'Ugh.'

'Please.'

'Fine.'

He runs through the shimmering globes blinking away thoughts of Jessica Start in her metallic dress being lit up by the disco ball in the bar. Strange that they should find them here too. Maybe the one in the bar was lost.

Arlo tells himself it's just his brain trying to make connections where there aren't any. Human nature. Imagination can only work with what's already in there; it uses things you might not remember seeing but it's all in there already in one form or another.

Next they find the monorail. The train cars are still parked in the platform so they climb into one.

'Gross,' Mizuki says.

The fetid smell of rotting leather fills the uncared-for

carriage. In front of them, undergrowth pushes through the rails. Now it's overgrowth, he thinks. The pale green rails are diseased with orange.

Mizuki clambers to the front of the train and leans out of the broken front window to photograph the roots ripping through the tracks. This is the stuff of future nightmares.

Back on the path, Arlo hears a noise again. Should he say something? Sometimes the night just makes noises, he knows that. Nothing should get in the way of them getting to the castle.

The park is so much bigger than they'd imagined. No wonder the owners had trouble attracting enough visitors to keep it afloat. Paths are longer and play tricks when you don't know where you're going. They have to beat the sunrise so they speed up.

They smell the pirate ride before they see it: four sinking boats with striped canopies rusting to oblivion in thick swampy water. The stench is so bad Mizuki retches as she approaches with her camera. Arlo wraps her scarf over her mouth and nose while she points the lens over the edge of the deck into the murk and reeds. He breathes in lemons.

'Thank you,' she says. 'You're an excellent assistant.'

She's half joking but it means something to Arlo, as if he's a part of her finding the perfect photo.

As the night wears on, Arlo finds it harder and harder to imagine his life before they did this. Hanging around on set at work learning his lines and avoiding Valerie Pitch seem impossible now.

Past the rancid lake, the corkscrew shapes of a rollercoaster mark low lines in the sky.

'Have we got time to climb it?' he asks.

'It's almost quarter to four.'

Sunrise is under forty-five minutes away. They need to find the castle and then get all the way back to the entrance.

They push on. Almost running now, both breathing hard.

Finally, the spectre of the castle looms in front of them, its turrets dark silhouettes against the clouds, though the moon is at its whitest now and the sky is ready to be lit again soon. 'There it is,' Arlo says as Mizuki's hand lands hot on his arm.

'Let's go.'

They run through capsized mascots and smaller ruined rides.

It's tatty, but in the moonlight the castle glows in faded pastel splendour. Explorers before them have removed the door, making it easy for them to enter. They head inside the dome, knowing without discussion that they're heading for the roof. They climb the broken steps, passing an exposed engine room and endless dead power cables.

'Don't trip.'

'Be careful.'

The floor is uneven and the plaster cracked but they make it to the top and step out on to the roof together.

'Wow.'

'Wow.'

'There's the waterpark,' Mizuki says, waving back towards the east of the entrance. They can see the top where three parallel blue slides begin, but not where they end. In Arlo's mind, the slides deliver every rider into a rain-filled pit curdled with algae, leaves and blossom. The coppery green of a rotten penny. No resistance, like bombing through a trap door.

Please don't ask to go in there.

They look out across the strange shapes and colours glowing in the almost-dawn.

'Aren't you going to take any photos?' he asks her.

'In a minute. I'm just taking it in.'

This is the first time she hasn't got her camera straight out. She must be as overwhelmed as he is.

They tread across the roof, staying away from the crumbling edges, checking out the view from all vantage points.

'I'm starving,' Mizuki says.

Arlo laughs. 'Me too actually. We have snacks.'

'We do?'

He pulls grapes and boiled eggs from his backpack. He can't get over being able to buy flavoured eggs from corner shops here.

'You made a picnic.'

'Midnight snack,' he says.

'It's four a.m.'

'Whatever.'

She cracks an egg against the castle wall and picks off the shell.

He peels one, gives a silent toast to Luke.

They finish eating. Mizuki tidies all their rubbish into her bag and takes the cap off her camera.

'The sun will be up soon,' she says, capturing shot after shot of the blue light and the desolation below.

They need to leave in case the developers arrive at dawn.

'One more look,' he says.

Mizuki is by his side again. He throws back his head and howls the deepest, longest howl he has in him

'AwwwwwwwwoooOOOooooooooooooo.'

Luke doesn't howl back. There's no echo from the other side of the world but Arlo does it again. This time fingers brush against his as Mizuki howls in tandem. 'AwwwwwoooOOOooooooooo.'

'That felt good,' she whispers, curling her hand into his.

'And if that didn't raise security, nothing will.'

They laugh then fall back into silence.

Everything is magical as they eavesdrop on birdsong. In the cold blue light of the early morning, they look out over their distressed kingdom and it feels like home.

They look back to each other again; who wouldn't want her when she smiles like that?

NINETEEN

Arlo sets his and Mizuki's shoes side by side at the door when they get back to their room. The new hostel didn't have any mixed dorms so they'd got a twin. It feels strange to be alone in a room with her – a real, solid space that isn't crawling with frogs or a hostel dorm full of snorers.

'We should get some sleep,' Mizuki says.

Arlo is mesmerised by a print on the hostel wall. He's seen it before, maybe in an art class at school. A boat full of men fleeing a giant blue wave, its foamy fingers reaching for them.

'Gives me nightmares,' she says, following his gaze to the wall.

'They're escaping though,' he says.

'You're reading it wrong. The boat is heading towards the wave.'

'Well, shiiiit.'

'Yep.'

Mizuki yawns, scrunching her face as she rubs black smears off her eyes with cotton wool and cream. 'Even my eyelashes are tired.'

'You want to use the shower first?'

They're sharing a bathroom too, just the two of them.

'If you don't mind. I'll be quick.'

Arlo hears the loo flush and the shower spurt on through the thin wall. Mizuki sings to herself. He laughs at her terrible singing voice and tries not to imagine her soaping her body, twisting water out of her wet hair.

She reappears. 'All yours.'

There's a castle drawn in steam on the mirror. Condensation drips from it. Mizuki has unpacked all of her bathroom things though they won't stay long. *Where will we go next?* They don't have a plan yet.

Her toothbrush wears a white plastic hat in a glass by the sink. He picks it up, turns it over in his hand, puts it back. Almost empty bottles of shampoo and other stuff are lined up on the bath. A damp shower cap hangs over the tap. He puts it on, looks at himself in the mirror. He looks like a dinner lady.

He lifts the loo seat to pee and notices specks of blood on the underside. *Does she have her period? Does it hurt?* He puts the seat back down when he's done.

After his shower, Arlo sits on his bed and stares at the metre of floor in between his and Mizuki's. Even after their amazing night at the castle, there is a distance between them that he wants to close before they decide where to go next.

'I have to tell you something,' he says.

Mizuki's hair is wrapped in a towel, her face younger without make-up. 'I'm listening.'

Before he can chicken out, Arlo tells her about running away and not going to his audition, and that nobody knows where he is. It doesn't make a lot of sense when he says it out loud. 'I don't know why I didn't just say I'm an actor when you asked.'

'Well, you didn't know we were going to end up being friends, I guess.' She's saying things that make him think maybe she gets it but she keeps her eyes on her legs. Her fall the other day has pressed a bruise into her knee and he feels guilty all over again.

'I'm sorry. It wasn't meant to be like this big secret. And I'm not even sure if I am an actor any more.'

'Why did you leave like that?' she asks.

He really does want her to know about Luke and about not being able to be himself any more, but he can't bring himself to make it all real by saying the words and answering her questions, so he settles on, 'I really, really just had to have a break from everything. I felt as if I were drowning.'

'I've felt like that.' She looks up. 'I have something to tell you too.'

'You're not an environmentalist?'

The joke falls flat.

'It'll be easier if I show you.'

Mizuki gets up.

She slips the engagement ring off her finger and drops it into the bin.

'What are you doing?'

'It's a fake,' she says. 'I wear it when I'm travelling to save myself hassle.'

'What do you mean?'

'A lot of situations are just easier with that on.'

This seems like the saddest thing in the world. The fact that some stupid fake ring can send so many signals and that annoying and scary things happen to Mizuki often enough to make wearing it worthwhile.

'Were you going to tell me?' he asks.

'Were you?'

Each watches the other determining how angry they can justifiably be.

Stalemate.

'We should get some sleep,' he says.

'Yeah.'

'I'll set an alarm for dinner so we don't sleep through and wake up at midnight or something.'

'OK.'

She pulls the duvet over herself and mumbles one of those platitudes people say to each other to end a conversation at night – goodnight, sweet dreams, sleep well.

He shuts the blinds to block out the day and turns off the light.

'I can feel you staring at the back of my head.'

He blushes in the dark. 'Sorry.'

He rolls over to face the other way. 'Better?'

Arlo replays their conversation while Mizuki sleeps. She hadn't asked any questions other than whether or not he was planning to tell her eventually. Did she already know? Maybe she'd looked him up. *Don't be paranoid.*

Now these secrets have been released, there is room for something else. He sees them tickling blonde rabbits together on an island that he used to draw as a child. Sneaking around in the cold dark, shining torches and singing away their fear. Surveying a faded kingdom from their turret in the low morning clouds. The way he sits closer to her than he needs to sometimes, the curl of her head into his neck and resting his head on hers as they sleep on trains, getting lost, lost, lost.

He experiments with the thought of her, using his left hand on himself so it feels like it could be hers. Still, he knows the only way that there'll be a real first move is if she makes it.

TWENTY

'So I was reading about this place where there are radioactive boars.'

Mizuki looks up from where she's crouching on the floor, packing.

In this instant, Arlo wants nothing more than to spend his birthday tomorrow looking for boars with her so he takes her stare as encouragement and continues, 'There was an energy accident. It was the biggest disaster like that for years – I think I remember it being on the news. We would have been about thirteen; actually you'd have been fourteen. It was . . .'

She interrupts him, 'Why are you talking like that?'

'Like what?'

'Like you're happy that this horrible thing happened.'

'I'm not happy about it.'

Mizuki holds his gaze. His hands start to feel clammy, as if his palms were breeding mould.

'Well, you seem pretty pumped about it.'

'Are you annoyed with me about the acting thing? You kept something from me too.'

'What? No. This has nothing to do with that. I just don't understand how you could be excited about going somewhere where something so tragic happened.'

'We've literally spent a month creeping through tragic buildings and photographing their bones. I just thought it would be cool to see boars – I've never seen one before.'

'They're not going to glow in the dark like some cartoon. If they did get exposed to the radiation then it's probably not going to work out well for them.'

'You don't know that,' he says. 'I'm not saying we should go in the dangerous bit.'

'I'm not going there, Arlo,' she adds, voice flat.

Has she said his name like that before?

'You just don't want to go because it's my idea – you wish you'd thought of it.'

'I did think of it,' she says. 'You can't come to this country and not think about what people went through there. What they're still going through.'

Mizuki rolls up her pyjamas and pushes them deep into her backpack.

Arlo holds out his hand. 'We could rock, paper, scissors it?'

'I think you're having some sort of blind spot about how ignorant you sound right now.'

'OK, forget I mentioned it.' He can't help it coming out sulky even though it's dawning on him that she's right.

Mizuki isn't finished. 'For one thing, people died. Two, being a tourist at a disaster site is about as tacky as you can get. It's like buying postcards at Ground Zero. And three, boars are big and dangerous – especially, I imagine, so-called "radioactive" ones.' She stops packing to do air quotes around radioactive, her fingers thrashing through the air to shame him. 'Four, I can't believe we're even having this conversation. In fact, let's stop having it, like, right now.'

Her face is red at the top of her cheeks and her eyes look wet. Arlo understands this; he finds it hard to separate anger and frustration too.

'I'm sorry.'

She keeps packing.

He doesn't know whether to let her cool off or to try again. 'Mizuki,' he braves. He kneels down next to her and passes her the rest of her folded things from the bed. 'Mizuki, I'm sorry.'

'Are you though?'

He reaches for her hand. 'I get it now.' A thin indent marks the finger she'd removed the ring from.

She looks at him looking at her, stares right into him. He doesn't look away until she sees that he means it. 'OK.'

'And I promise I will never mention boars again for as long as I live.'

He can see she is annoyed with herself for smiling at this.

'Seriously, it's on the no-go list.'

'That was a really insensitive idea, you know,' she says.

He knows.

* * *

Mizuki seems to bounce back from their fight once she can see how sorry Arlo is. He's shown her an ugly part of himself and she hasn't run, but he's still deflated after breakfast.

He recalls the accident more clearly now he thinks about it. Remembers watching it on the huge TV in the caravan. The news had shown officials dressed like astronauts in contamination suits to keep out what was blooming from the energy spill. Another programme with people measuring the ground years later, a strange bird noise from the machine telling them whether or not the soil had cancer. It was a real place and a real thing that happened to real people, just like him and his mum and Mizuki. He won't forget that again.

Arlo fishes Mizuki's ring out of the small bin and sets it on top of her backpack. A bit passive-aggressive maybe but she might regret her throwing away something that's travelled so far with her, though it's a pretty fucked-up talisman.

He flinches thinking about what it means; she hadn't felt safe enough with him to take it off. He's being unfair to both of them; how can she trust him when he's shown her so little of himself?

Mizuki taps away on his phone while he rests. She's not getting her notebook out to sketch maps or reading bits from forums like she usually does. They'd talked about going to the hospital next but it wasn't a definite plan.

'Do you want to carry on travelling together?' he blurts.

'Why are you asking that?'

'I don't know. We don't have a plan for where we're going next and I just wanted to give you an out.'

'You don't ditch someone just because you've had a disagreement.'

It seems to Arlo that's exactly what people do. Hadn't his mum told him about his dad leaving and coming back like a misshapen boomerang when he ran out of money or places to stay or sometimes when he just missed them? The latter hurt the most because it meant the missing was bearable for him the rest of the time.

'So is twenty a big deal back home?' Mizuki asks, trying to make conversation.

'Not as big as eighteen.'

'Twenty-one is the big one for us.'

'I've just always wanted to be twenty.' Twenty had once seemed so old it felt impossible that he would get there.

'I always wanted to be seven. Seven is a big deal for girls here, you know.'

'Can you remember being seven?'

Seven seems hazy and unspecific in Arlo's mental timeline. He can remember lots of things from his childhood but he doesn't know what order they happened in. Some of the things he might just have been told about or seen in photos. A life marbled with ideas and memories that might not even be his.

'Of course. We combined Thanksgiving and my birthday. We got dressed up and went to the shrine and the park, and I got candy.'

'Sounds fun.'

'It was my last birthday here. We had a picnic under a tree. Anyway, back to where we should go for yours.'

'We could go to the hospital that Arisu and James told us about.'

'Do you really want to spend your birthday in a ruined hospital?'

'I guess not,' he says. 'Promise we'll go though.'

'I'd love to see it.'

'OK, where would you want to go if it were your birthday?'

'We can't go to where I'm going for mine. I'm a fall baby and you're an almost-summer baby.'

'I'm twenty tomorrow – I'm not any kind of baby.'

She looks around the small room as if searching for inspiration and picks up his phone again.

'Don't you want to be with your family?'

The way she says family makes it sound as if this big, loud crew of people will be celebrating and his chair will be empty – as if someone else will be called upon to blow out candles in his absence.

'Not right now.'

He'll need to find somewhere he can pass off as home to video call his mum, though – a restaurant maybe. He's hasn't had a birthday with her since he was twelve but they always speak and she'll want to watch him squirm while she sings 'Happy Birthday' at him.

They were apart for all of his teenage birthdays, he realises. She always tried to make up for it at the caravan site's annual end-of-season party before he went back to school. They called it his half-birthday. Mr Swanson always decorated the rec room like it was prom. A different theme each year – underwater, cowboys, tropical and so on, until he'd exhausted all his ideas and started recycling the themes from the beginning.

Five teenage birthdays away at school and the last two in his and Luke's flat. They'd gone for drinks with Guy and the others for his nineteenth. Somehow that seems longer ago than his seventh birthday.

'Let's take a break,' Mizuki says.

He knew it; she wants to go their separate ways.

'I don't mean from each other. God, your face. I mean, let's take a break from ruins for a day or two.'

'OK.'

She tucks the phone into the pocket of his backpack.

'I've got an idea. I could take you to my second favourite place.'

Mizuki wants to hear all about *The Beat* on the train.

'So was it super-dramatic?' she asks. 'Did you have to wear breeches?'

'I don't even know exactly what breeches are. It's a programme about rural police families. I played the son of one of the detectives.'

'Did they kill you off?'

'I quit. My character is missing with his girlfriend.'

She swoons – in role – love-struck and does what Arlo assumes is her impression of a soap star: 'If I have the key to your heart, why does it feel as if I'm picking the lock all the time?'

'Stop it.'

'So do you have fans? Like an army of young women supporting you?'

He can't bring himself to say the phrase 'Arlo's Army'. 'Probably not any more.'

'Oh my god, you do, don't you. That's awesome.'

The train shoots along for a couple of hours. He googles The Play and finds a photo of their Hospital piece. It's black and white. There are six of them, the artists, each blank-faced in the window of an old building. In another photo they stand in a doorway, six reflections on the wet floor in front of them.

'Do you have any water?' Mizuki asks.

'Sure.' He gets his canister from his bag and offers it to her.

'Thanks. Could you grab my bag down or let me out so I can get it?'

He passes her the duffel.

'Forgot to take my medication,' she says.

'Don't you feel well?' he asks.

'I feel fine, but I might not if I forget to take these.' She shakes a bottle of pills. 'For my anxiety.'

'I didn't know you took medication.'

'Probably because I didn't tell you.'

'Don't they make you feel bad?' he says.

'The first lot didn't work for me. These ones are a lot better.'

Mizuki gulps down a tablet with some water and helps herself to his phone, scrolling through photography sites.

'It's just the same as us wanting to visit all these ruins, you know.'

'What is?' he asks.

'You having fans.'

'Oh, we're back on that.'

'People romanticise places they can't go – doesn't matter if it's a geographical place or in the mind. We just want to taste it. That's why we can't look away when people have a public breakdown, it's as close as most of us will get to the dark side,' she says. 'It's why you wanted to go and see those damn boars.'

Arlo gets it. Hacking into something that doesn't belong to you, like eavesdropping on an argument or hearing your housemate having sex.

He feels himself getting red at the thought of bumping into one of Luke's girlfriends in the corridor in the middle of the night on their way to the bathroom or finding them in the kitchen together in the morning, as if he'd stumbled upon something special that he wasn't part of. He doesn't think he'd been in love with Luke. It was more that he wanted to be like him than be with him, but Arlo was definitely jealous at having to share him.

'Is it also why people I don't know apparently give a shit that I'm "missing"?' he asks.

'You do realise that technically you *are* missing? As in nobody actually knows where you are.'

'You know,' he says.

'Actually I have no idea where we are right now.'

'Really?'

'Kidding. Get your stuff together, we're getting off at the next stop.'

They walk for ten minutes; it feels like more in the heat. The May sun blazes through the breeze and sweat starts to soak the back and underarms of Arlo's T-shirt and jumper under the weight of his rucksack.

He plays a game with himself, guessing what their destination will be. If he had to bet on it, he'd say a photography museum or, longer shot, some kind of fruit plantation. 'Do you actually know where we're going?'

'I was here just before we met *and* I'm following the signs.'

He'd stopped looking at them after his first night in the city.

'There's probably a bus we could take if you want?' she says.

Salty sweat lifts from them both. He sniffs his arm; it smells like the sea. 'That's OK.'

'Ten more minutes.'

TWENTY-ONE

The beachfront is lined with campervans and a few people wriggling out of wetsuits when they arrive. The sand is the colour of wheat. The air is warm and salty.

Everything inside Arlo opens when his eyes meet the water. Green, blue, glinting.

'Ta da,' says Mizuki. 'This is my favourite beach.'

He's never seen a bay enclosed by mountains before. The cliffs are not super high, but gnarled and forested enough to make climbing them impossible. Not that Arlo is much of a climber.

'There are bays like this all along the coast here,' she says as they cross the sand, 'lots of indents in the land. We're a few beaches over from a big surf spot.'

Arlo wants to feel the water, to let it hold him up and pull him along.

'Come on,' he says.

They ditch their stuff on the sand and kick off their shoes and socks.

'Careful, the currents are strong here.'

Arlo jogs the last few paces to the ocean's edge. The water is not quite warm. He watches it wash over his toes and drain away. Again and again. Mineral thick, persuasive as anaesthetic.

He wades out to where the water is darker, pushing through pockets of hotter currents. Small fish jump around him. He stands, hopping the low waves, pulling the water through his fingers at his sides.

'You're getting so wet,' Mizuki calls from the shore.

He doesn't care. And he also doesn't want to strip down to his boxers in broad daylight.

'Aren't you coming in?'

'Maybe later.'

He lets the water tug him in up to his hips, feels a sort of pain in his neck as the cold hits his groin. Something happening to one part of him felt in another. Whirlpools of current spin around his feet like planets.

Something wraps itself around his foot. He leaps up, kicking it away. 'Fuck, fuck.' Tangled and gelatinous, the creature envelops his leg. *A jellyfish.* He's freaking out now, trying to get it off his foot and calf without using his hands, without calling for help. No lifeguard. Cold panic. He drags the heel of his other foot down his leg, trying to peel the creature away. Better to be stung on the leg than the fingers.

Arlo can see its shape through the water, transparent white and rippling, inflating each time the tide sucks itself away from the land. He finally shakes himself free from its grasp. It sways up to just below the surface of the sea, body filled with water. He propels himself back to a safe distance and watches it bob.

It has writing on it.

A plastic bag.

Arlo reaches out to grab it and pours out the water, clutching it as he half swims, half wades back to the beach. His jeans start to slide down his hips from the weight of the water.

'This just tried to kill me,' he says in his most dramatic soap opera voice when he gets to Mizuki.

'Sent by your evil twin sister Arlene to murder you,' she swoons. 'Fortunately I just came from the lab and I have the antidote in my side saddle.'

'You came from the lab on a horse?'

'Obviously. That's why I'm wearing breeches and a lab coat.'

Mizuki takes the bag from him and shoves it into the front pocket of her backpack. 'Seriously though, you know there will be more plastic than fish in the sea soon if people don't stop being so gross.'

Arlo wraps his towel around himself, shrugs off the soaking jeans and pulls on another pair. His T-shirt and jumper are damp too. Sea drips from their hems.

They sit back on the warm sand and discuss finding somewhere to stay. Sunset is only an hour off but he still needs his cap to shield his eyes from the glare. Would it be awkward if he paid for them to stay in a nice hotel, he wonders? Then feels like a dick for assuming she couldn't afford to pay for herself.

'We haven't used the tent yet,' he says.

She loves the idea, he can tell. 'Let's do it. We should get some treats too, for your birthday eve.'

'I don't think that's a thing.'

'It's a thing if we say it's a thing. I like to have at least a week-long festival for my birthday.'

'You probably have more friends than I do.'

'You only need one friend, Arlo. More is nice but you only really need one.'

One of his directors used to say something similar at school: *'You only need one yes, Artists, you only need one yes.'*

Wrong, he thinks, *you need to turn up and say yes back too.*

'Beautiful,' Mizuki says, smiling into the breeze.

Pitching the tent in the sand is a shitshow but they find a use for the plastic bag and some others, filling them with sand to weigh down the stakes.

Arlo had walked up to the beachfront shops to get them some supplies. He'd called his mum so she and his aunt could sing 'Happy Birthday' early and then found the perfect gift for Mizuki. It's sappy but he wants to give it to her tomorrow since she likes birthdays so much.

And now they have beers and the sunset.

'Do you know what time you were born?' she asks.

'Two forty-nine a.m.'

'We could set an alarm and wake up to celebrate.'

'Man, you really love birthdays, don't you?'

'They're important,' she says.

'Let's just celebrate in the morning.'

'Boring.'

'I'm an old man now, Mizuki.'

'You're a man-child, that's what you are.'

This could be the first time anyone has called him a man-anything. 'Like Mowgli?'

'You're thinking of man-cub.'

'Oh.'

He grabs two beers.

'Drink this first,' Mizuki says, producing two miniature bottles and handing one to Arlo.

He tries and fails to decipher the characters on the label. 'What is it?'

'A magic potion.'

'Is it going to make me really big if I drink it?'

She raises an eyebrow.

'I didn't mean it like that.'

'It'll help with the birthday hangover.'

They clink cheers, chug, and he opens a beer for each of them. They cheers again.

'You're actually several hours underage to drink here,' she says, 'but I'll turn a blind eye. Actually I guess that kind of makes twenty a big deal here. You going to make birthday resolutions?'

'I don't think so.'

'I just realised we'll have known each other a month tomorrow.'

Can you love someone you've only known a month? 'Our friendiversary.'

'That needs to go on the list of words we do not speak,' she says. 'Immediately, if not sooner.'

They dig their toes into the sand. Mizuki sits back, resting on her elbows, while Arlo leans forward to bury the tops of his feet.

They look so ugly next to hers, even with one of her banana plasters wrapped around her big toe.

They plant a row of beer bottles in the sand next to them. Arlo hasn't drunk since the flight. He lets the alcohol release his neck and drop his shoulders.

Mizuki sinks deeper into the sand before lying back as the sky darkens. She fidgets, sitting up then lying back again as if waiting for someone to arrive. A strip of cloud runs out to sea until what began as a loose puffy belt wraps itself around the sun, stemming the light, until it drops and melts into the water. Soon there is more sun in the sea than there is in the sky. Arlo lies down next to Mizuki, feeling the baked sand cooling beneath him.

Above them a billion pinpricks turn the sky silver.

'It's impossible to drink lying down,' he says, beer trickling down the side of his face. He licks his lips, tastes sea salt. His hands are rough with it. 'I'm a mess,' he says, the hair by his ear now wet with beer.

'Practice makes perfect,' she laughs.

A few other parties of people are dotted along the sand further up the beach, closer to the cliffs. He wishes they had the shore to themselves.

They talk and then don't talk. After some soft silence, Mizuki reaches the end of a long thought. 'I've been thinking about you and your fans.'

Arlo opens another beer and pours it into his open throat. 'Nailed it.' Wipes his mouth with his hand.

She continues, 'I don't understand why you're so dismissive of them.'

'I'm not.'

'Either it's because you think you're not worth their attention or you think their opinions don't matter because they're mostly teenage girls. Both of which are really sad but for different reasons.'

'I don't really want to talk about this,' he says.

'OK.'

She scoops up a fistful of sand and drizzles it into the mouth of one of the empty bottles in between them.

'You should think about it sometime though,' she adds.

'OK,' he says, sitting up. 'Oh my god, look!'

The edge of the sea is glowing bright blue. A thick neon scribble runs all the way to where it hugs the mountains and disappears around the bends at either ends of the bay. They scrabble to their feet. Mizuki grins.

'You knew,' he calls, as they run to the water. She'd been waiting for this. 'Is it jellyfish?'

'Squid,' she says. 'They're not even supposed to be on this side of the country – their migrations patterns are all messed up. I read about it this morning while you were sulking.'

'It's incredible.'

'I wasn't sure if they'd still be here or if it was a false report.'

It's like the pictures he's seen of the Northern Lights but the purest, brightest blue, and underwater, and flashing not swirling.

'Mating season,' she explains, 'but they really shouldn't be here.' He can hear the tremble of excitement in her voice. 'I'm going to get my camera.'

Up close, Arlo can see the creatures are huddled together in glimmering clumps and constellations.

Further up towards the eastern mountain, a small boat with passengers is pulling out to sea. Some kind of tour.

Arlo stands a few steps up the beach from Mizuki so the moon doesn't throw his shadow across the picture she's setting up.

She waits for the right combination of wave, moonlight and underwater sparkling. He stands in awe watching the blue magic amplifying as the moon grows brighter. Her eyes flick around the bay searching for something she can capture in the photographs to show the squid aren't where they belong. She crouches down, pointing the lens up and along the beach towards the mountains.

A cloud bank rides in on the wind masking the moon so the forest is too dark to be seen. They wait in silence for the clouds to drift away. Finally, the trees reveal themselves, gunmetal grey in the moonlight.

Click, click, click.

Mizuki takes photo after photo.

'These must be the perfect pictures for the competition,' he says. A flutter of panic in his stomach – maybe she'll go home before Thanksgiving if she's got what she needs.

'What competition?'

'*The* competition. Your photos.'

Mizuki doesn't look at him.

'Did you already enter something?' he asks. No, she can't have done. They've been together the whole time.

She lets the camera loll, straining around her neck, and looks at him.

'There is no competition.'

Something flops over Arlo's left foot. A scatter of squid have beached themselves. They flip like fringed fingers, panicking. He lifts them one by one and tosses them back into the water, trying not to pinch them too tight.

'The moon confuses them,' Mizuki says, helping him return them to the sea.

Squid dazzle and die at their feet like blossom.

'What do you mean there's no competition?'

It's hard to read her face in the dark.

'I made it up.'

His stomach jerks in tandem with the squid. She's been lying to him. Instinct fires and he turns to walk away from her. The sand sucks at his feet as he tries to get to the road.

'Arlo, wait. Please, wait.'

He waits. Her hand on his shoulder, like the hand of that shape on the roof telling him to sit down while they took pictures of Luke at the bottom of the pool.

'I can explain. Please, let's sit down.'

They drop back on to the sand, filling the indents they made before, the row of beer bottles marking battle lines between them.

'So this has just been one big game to you, I guess,' he says. 'All this finding the perfect photo thing is bullshit.'

'Everything is exactly the same. I am trying to get a photo, there just isn't a competition.'

Arlo tries to get it, he really does.

'Haven't you ever done something that you can't explain – something that just wouldn't seem rational to anyone else?' She's pleading now. He hates that desperate tone in her voice and even though he's mad at her he wants to undo it for her.

Mizuki takes his hand. Can he say it – that he needs her to hold his hand as much as she needs him to hold hers? He makes circles on the base of her thumb with his, hopes that's enough. And then she says something that makes him understand, something that unlocks why they've fallen into whatever it is that they've fallen into together.

'I need to get the photo for my mum. She's missing and this is the only way I have left to find her.'

Her words make a door where there used to be a wall or rock or muscle and they step through into something else.

TWENTY-TWO

Truth comes tumbling out of them both, takes its time to settle, seeds more.

They listen, learning their own parts as they pull them out of themselves, lit by the blue glow of the water's edge.

'Mum was a photographer for a news agency,' Mizuki explains. 'She left while I was at school one day. She walked out and never came back.'

That seems like the most brutal understatement to Arlo, as if her mum were off buying milk.

Just one week in the flat without Luke had been too much to bear. How many times must Mizuki have heard a key in the lock and thought life was about to go back to normal.

Her face is wet. This is bitter crying, as if she hates her mum as much as she misses her. He loves her face and how shiny the tears make it, hates himself for thinking that while she's in pain.

'I threw my phone away just before we met. I was spending all my time searching for her, looking through news sites for her name in the photo credits. She doesn't even work for the agency any more – I must have called them ten times.'

'What about your dad – couldn't he find her?' Arlo asks.

'He says she's not coming back.'

There must have been conversations between her parents that Mizuki was too young to understand, which would be too damaging to relay now.

They look out to sea. The sightseeing boat is way out in the chop, pointing back to the shore so those on board can see the sapphire line of squid stretching along the coast. An old rope like a thick eel carries the anchor down, down, down between its teeth, keeping them steady. People peer overboard at the dark shapes passing below them.

'What about the police?'

'She's not missing to them. She left.'

A tremble passes from Mizuki to Arlo. He reaches inside the tent for a sleeping bag and she bundles it around her shoulders. He pulls on another jumper.

'For a while I honestly thought my dad had murdered her, like that would be easier to handle than her walking out.'

'Do you still think that?' he asks.

'No. I know she left. I opened her bank statement before she had them diverted. She travelled a bit, I followed her path, then the statements stopped coming.' Mizuki wipes her eyes with the sleeping bag. 'I think she's here, somewhere, working under a different name. Sometimes I see photos in the papers that look so much like her work I think it must be her but every lead I follow is a dead end.'

There are layers and layers to the story, Arlo realises; it stretches back years.

He asks Mizuki if she knows why her mum left.

'I think she was sick. She covered an earthquake for the agency – not here – when I was thirteen. She always tried to find something happy to photograph or at least to find the good in a situation but thousands and thousands of people died there. She felt different to me after that, like she never really came home.'

Arlo remembers that quake. A cracking yawn that split the earth wide open. There were so many bodies that the authorities had to pick them up with diggers. Had he seen Mizuki's mum's pictures of it?

An echo of the terror of waking up in his hotel room as if he were being shaken and sucked into the ground rumbles through him. The sudden violence of it.

'That's why you wanted to get out of the city,' he says. 'The earthquake.'

Mizuki kneads great handfuls of sand at her sides, packing it against her thighs and knees, trying to keep herself together.

'And why I came with you. You seemed so lost too – I thought we could be like anchors for each other,' she says. 'So, anyway, she was weird after the earthquake and last year she went away again to take pictures of a chemical gas attack. There were children, I think. She only stayed for a week when she got back from that one.'

'Mustard gas, like at the factory?'

'Chlorine.'

Arlo feels like gas himself, as if he might float away.

Words burst out of him like bubbles. 'My friend Luke, he's dead.'

'God.'

People often mention God when they talk about death. Then, after a while, they don't say anything at all, as if the dead person were never even here.

'It was my fault.'

Mizuki waits for more.

'He tripped into a swimming pool.'

'That doesn't sound like it was your fault.'

'I think he's got blossom in his lungs.' Arlo's voice cracks right down the middle, splitting him open. 'The pool and putting trees in it were my idea. I left him up on the roof. Wherever he is he won't be able to breathe.'

'They give you new lungs in heaven if you need them,' she says.

'I don't know if I believe in heaven.'

'Wherever he is, he doesn't need his lungs. I promise.'

Mizuki seems certain of this.

His dad died with fluid on the lungs. What kind of fluid? Blood, pus, urine. Rain, puddle, seawater. What if he's floating on a raft somewhere, or drifting on a lilo next to Luke. What would they talk about? The only things they have in common: being dead and knowing Arlo. They could talk about how pit stop crews failed to restart both their hearts.

'You poor thing,' she says. 'You must be so sad all the time.'

The conversation plays out like a double helix, winding around itself. Sometimes they have to circle back down the ladder, climb up again together.

'Why are you doing all this?' he asks. 'The photos.'

He thinks he knows the answer: that it makes her feel close to her mum.

'I'm building a portfolio. I want to get a job at the agency she worked at, taking pictures like she did.'

'So you can feel near her.' He nods.

'I know if she's out there she'll still be reading all the photo credits, checking out the competition, and I want her to read my name one day. I want her to see my name in black and white, and I want it to hurt.'

Her voice is hard but she starts to cry again. 'A mum should want to know about her child.'

She'd as much as said it on their first train ride together: *I try to let everyone who might be missing me know exactly where I am.*

'It's like a test for her?' he asks.

'If she doesn't come back for me when she sees that then . . .'

Are you coming to get me now?

He can't tell which is her pain and which is his. This could be the first time he's hurt and doesn't leave. The first time he realises you can be sad and hopeful and scared and open at the same time.

'I don't really hate her, you know,' Mizuki says.

'I know.'

'Sometimes I wish I could but I guess I'm just one of those people.'

'One of those people who loves their parents?'

'More like if I ever love you, I will always love you.'

The light has changed again and the sand looks blue too now. The boat returns its passengers to the shore and collects another group.

'Tell me the truth about the acting thing,' she says.

'My dad wanted me to be famous. I don't really remember him but he named me.'

Arlo has definitely had this part of the conversation before, on another beach, with another girl, another him.

'My mum had to talk him down from Agamemnon.'

'Dear god,' she says.

'Exactly.' Arlo can feel a yawn coming. He walked away from everything to come here, and the thought of it is almost boring. 'I've spent a decade, since I was ten, working towards something and I don't think I want it any more.'

'Why don't you want it?'

'I used to get this kick from it but it hardly happens any more. And I've realised I can get the feeling without it. Maybe even a better one.'

'So don't do it. See the world, go to college, do something else.'

Relief runs golden inside him.

The flashing blue of the squid blurs to a neon puddle as Arlo's eyes fill. He scrubs the tears away.

Only his mum and Luke have ever been this kind to him.

He tells Mizuki about the darkest summer.

'Mum had to sit with me every night for weeks. She watched me while I slept – I think it helped her too. She was terrified I was going to hurt myself.'

'Did you think it would happen again when Luke passed – is that why you ran away?'

He nods. 'It's not as simple as that though; I could feel it coming before he died.'

The boat drops off its last human cargo, bobbing lower in the water this time. The squid do not dim.

It's gone 4 a.m. when they decide to go bed.

Arlo shakes sand from the sleeping bag, watching it flap like an empty chrysalis while Mizuki goes up to the loos. She takes her camera and he finds himself wondering whether or not she's coming back. She could have a genetic predisposition for running away; abandoning before being abandoned.

'I'm back.'

'Hey. Find anything to photograph in the bathroom?'

'Very funny.'

He zips them inside the tent. The spaces they're sharing are getting smaller and smaller. Mizuki curls against the canvas wall on one side while he tries to grind the uneven sand beneath the base of the tent on his side into flatness. He settles, breathing into the space between him and Mizuki, thinking about whether he's inhaling anything that has been inside her lungs.

'I can feel you staring at me again,' she says.

'Sorry.' He can barely see her, just the dark curve of her cocooned body and the shape of the back of her head, hair splayed in black waves on the towel she's using as a pillow.

'You want me to watch you while you sleep like your mum did?' she asks.

'I'm OK.'

'Right, because it's creepy.'

They laugh until their eyes water.

The sea pushes and pulls on the other side of the door to their little canvas house. He's aching to touch her, to feel the tide of her breath lift her off the ground. What's more frightening:

being reached for or grasping into an empty space hoping to find something?

'Happy birthday.'

'Thanks.'

Twenty. Next year, twenty-one, then twenty-two, then older than Luke. Then, eventually, older than his dad.

After a minute or an hour, Mizuki whispers, 'I've spent time where you are now – you'll be OK. Things are still fresh.'

Her words are like magnets, pulling thoughts to his surface. A month of blankness, of running and distraction, starts to bloom. Arlo tries not to feel it but he starts to shake.

'Where does it hurt?' she says.

'Everywhere,' he answers for them both.

She unzips her sleeping bag, throws the rustling fabric over them both and cuddles into his side.

She hesitates and he nods into the dark.

Her fingers are on his skin in light shapes moving his blood. Circles, then infinities.

Contact.

The heat goes right down into his bones.

Arlo's breath judders but he stays as still as he can while Mizuki washes her hands over him, the path of her fingers raising neon lines on his skin.

Fix me. Draw me whole. Colour me in.

He's not sure what's happening: is she trying to comfort him or does she want something else to happen?

There have been fumbles in the dark before.

The first time, a summer visitor at the caravan park called Sarah had tucked his hand into her shorts. Her pubic hair had thrown Arlo off at first — somehow he'd managed to get to fifteen without realising girls outside porn had hair just like he did — and she didn't make the sounds like the women in the videos he watched. Unsure of which bit of her body was which, he'd pressed his palm over the whole hot area and ground gently until she'd lifted his sweaty hand away. They didn't talk for the rest of her week there.

The next girl told him he touched too softly, then told her friends he was too rough. Her name was Miri. Arlo had liked her a lot.

He'd waited a year and committed hours to internet research before trying again.

When he started on *The Beat* there were women in bars, arching against him while pretending they weren't. Him pushing back. Neither wanting to be rejected, both trying to give permission.

Mizuki keeps her hands moving. Arlo doesn't hurt any more; he doesn't care that he only has a one-pack or if he never sees home again.

The twitch inside his boxers seems to surprise Mizuki. Her thoughts are loud: *Did I do that? Is that for me?* She pulls her hand away, then a moment later, passes it over the area again as if by accident.

He reaches for her and says it. 'Can I kiss you?'

It comes out a bit too loud in the quiet tent but she pulls him in, yes. She tastes of melon toothpaste at first.

He tries to make her feel good with his hands as they kiss. Her charm bracelet catches in his hair.

'I didn't bring anything,' she says, after a while.

Arlo has condoms in his washbag, thanks to Luke.

The box is still in the cellophane. He rips it off and takes one out.

Should he ask again if this is OK?

'Here,' she says, reaching for the condom. 'OK?' He pulls off his boxers. She unwraps it and rolls it on to him, and he pushes himself inside her. He can hear his heart and nothing else.

Slow down.

The brambled in and out of Mizuki's breath warms Arlo's neck as he inhales her salty skin and lemony hair. He has to pull out and start again a couple of times to pace himself. He lifts up, watches the black centre of her eyes swallowing the colour.

He keeps moving until he can't hold off any longer. Feels himself light up like Venus, like he knows all the secrets of the universe. He wants to take care of her for ever.

Afterwards, he rolls over, unsure whether Mizuki came too and not sure how to ask. *What do people say after sex?*

'I never know what to say afterwards,' she laughs.

He traces maps into her back, outlining all the places they've been and washing future journeys into her skin as the afterglow flashes all along the coast.

TWENTY-THREE

Mizuki is back on her side of the tent in the morning and Arlo reminds himself that people just move in their dreams, it doesn't mean she wanted to get away from him. The colour of sleep hazes the ceiling.

She sticks a bare leg out of the side of the sleeping bag but doesn't wake. Arlo pulls on his boxers, ready to spend their first honest day together.

The tent heats up like a greenhouse as the sun's arms reach for them. Arlo opens the zip and sticks his head out to watch the sea waving good morning. He pats together a tiny sandcastle just outside the door and breathes in salty, honeyed air. What if they stayed here? They could live on turtle fat and gull meat, maybe even the magic squid if they stick around.

Mizuki stirs and kicks away her sleeping bag. Still too hot.

She cranks open her eyes against the light and makes a drinking motion with her hand.

She nods her head, one, two, three, and they draw: Arlo is rock and she is paper. His turn to go and get the water.

'Wait,' she says in her morning voice. 'I'll go, it's your birthday.'

'It's OK, I'll go. I need a quick shower. You wake up.'

'Then we'll celebrate,' she murmurs. 'Happy birthday.'

'Thank you.'

The sand is already warm as Arlo strides up the beach towards the bathrooms and water fountain. He rinses under the outside shower next to a couple of surfers who've already caught their waves for the day. Arlo watches them load their boards on to the roof of their car before he heads back to Mizuki.

More people have arrived; some have pitched tents while fishermen with big bucket-like nets sweep the water. The word is out about the magical squid.

Mizuki has fallen back to sleep when Arlo crawls back into the tent with the water. Dare he lie down close to her? He settles for closer than usual but not so near that it could freak her out when she wakes up. Is that her heart he can hear through the pillow? He could listen to it all day. *Slow down*, he tells himself.

He drifts on his sleeping bag, lulled by the calls of surfers and seabirds. Fragments of the conversation he'll have with his mum later start to prepare themselves in his mind. A rehearsal. Maybe he'll tell her where he is. Though her first question will be when is he coming home and he doesn't know the answer to that yet. He can imagine her telling his aunt in disbelief – half-livid, half-proud of his adventure.

He wakes for the second time. Opens his eyes just in time to see Mizuki dropping his phone into the front pocket of his bag.

'What are you doing?'

'Just checking the time,' she says.

'What time is it?'

'Birthday time! I'd give you the bumps but . . .'

'I can't believe I'm twenty.' He passes her the refilled bottle. 'Here's the water.'

She guzzles it down. 'Where would I be without you?'

'Lost,' he says.

'More lost. Or, at the very least, thirsty.'

'Forced to play rock, paper, scissors solo.'

They laugh.

'I'm going to get washed up, then let's go for breakfast,' she says. 'You can get these deep-fried maple leaves here, even out of season. I guess they keep them in a freezer. It's probably best not to think about it. I always eat them on my birthday, if I can get them back home.'

She grabs her washbag. 'I'll be ten minutes. Happy birthday again.'

'Thank you again.'

Arlo waits until Mizuki is out of sight up the beach and takes the gift he bought yesterday from his bag. A tiny rock, paper, scissors charm. The man in the shop had wrapped it in some tissue but Arlo wishes he'd got some proper wrapping paper now. It doesn't matter, Mizuki is going to love it. He slips the package under her makeshift pillow.

He puts on the only smart clothes he has with him, the ones he was going to wear for the audition. He tucks the shirt into the front of his crumpled chinos and pulls it out again. No need to go overboard. His hair is already drying funny in the hot tent so he uses some water from the canister to pat it down, takes a couple of sips and leaves the rest for Mizuki.

A ding noise comes from his bag. Probably his mum messaging to wish him happy birthday eve again – it's still yesterday there. Maybe he'll just call now and tell her everything about his trip and the truth about Mizuki, get it out of the way.

He pulls the phone out and unlocks it.

Luke's eyes meet his, staring out from the screen, a shade less certain than Arlo remembers but still blue as a huskie's.

He rocks back on his heels, unsteady.

Mizuki must have been going through his pictures. *Why?* He tries to think over the roaring sound of seashells jammed against his ears.

Arlo scrolls through the camera roll: pictures of the sides of him that he works so hard to keep private. His home, his family. The photo of him and his dad and the sandcastle. A few pictures of the swimming pool at various stages. Luke mugging for the camera on the roof, a selfie of the two of them with their city glowing behind.

The tent moves around him; the sleeping bags ripple and squirm.

Mizuki's camera shines in the corner.

It all makes sense.

She's been using him to get to his photos, looking for something to sell. She said she'd do anything to get her name credit.

How could she do this to me?

He'd told her things he'd never told anyone.

192

Did she plan this from the start?

He grabs her camera, jabbing the buttons to look through her pictures.

All the places they've been together: the school, the clinic, the bowling alley, the strip club, the tower, more and more. Their view from the top of the castle. For a second, Arlo feels as he did up there with her. Whole, home. As if he was a human, not a concept.

He pulls the camera free from its case. Something drops to his side. A memory card. He swaps it into the camera and scrolls. Hundreds of his faces, none making eye contact. Him sleeping on trains, silhouettes of him in the sea, petting deer, the top of his head on her shoulder as he'd slept on the boat to Rabbit Island, even a few from the first day they'd met.

Nausea rises. Mizuki has been tricking him for a month. He's so stupid.

He has to leave before she gets back. Can't stand to look at her face while she lies to him.

He rams his stuff into his backpack. Rage and humiliation drive him through the fluttering tent door, up the beach to the road. He ducks behind a campervan so Mizuki can't see him from the showers, as if he were the one who should feel ashamed.

He has found his way back to the station before he realises he has no plan. Everything is hot and ruined. Looking around, everyone else looks unrocked by Mizuki's betrayal. The urge to shake them to shrink the gap between his pain and theirs is something violent and frightening.

The station clock says almost 11 a.m. Arlo grinds to a halt

under it. What now? He's caught between wanting to put as much distance as possible between him and Mizuki, and paralysis. Chemicals in his blood say go; something else is stuck and won't let him leave. He needs to get away from the station in case she comes to look for him here. It would be the most obvious place to find him.

He starts to feel dog tired, as if taken over by some sort of reverse adrenaline. Desperate, he looks around for a sign.

Across the street from the station a small hotel sits stained with sunlight. He could get a room, calm down, make a plan.

There are two small spotlights and a smoke alarm that emits an almost imperceptible flash every other second on the hotel room ceiling. Arlo's throat is arid, scratchy. There's no glass in the bathroom. He cups some water with his hands, rinses out his mouth and gulps down the rest.

The room is small, like all hotel rooms here. The receptionist said he couldn't get into the room until 3 p.m. so he'd bundled all his cash on the counter and said he'd pay for last night too. She'd finally handed over a plastic key card, baffled.

Two questions orbit in his head. How could Mizuki do this and how could he have let this happen again? He can't bear to go through his phone to see which images Mizuki might have chosen to sell, which might have best served to get her name in lights just so she could get the attention of a mother who doesn't want her.

Everything is in there, all his failures. A dead dad whom he never really knew, an alive mother whom he'd hurt, two homes he abandoned, a friend whose life he could have saved if he hadn't gone to bed, girls he'd failed to connect with, him as a lost child, even Neon the long-dead dog.

Arlo opens and closes the wardrobe, then the small fridge. It's empty save for a waft of cleaning product.

The fridge in the flat at home had started to smell a few days after he'd found Luke. The body. He'd taken Luke's food prep boxes from the fridge, tipped the contents into the bin one by one and stared down into the rubbish. Slimy peppers, cucumber. A slight fizz at their edges. Congealing meat. The next day, the bin men had come and taken everything away.

His stomach winces at the memory of it all.

There's a mini bar mounted on the wall next to the wardrobe. Rows of miniature bottles lined up like the tinctures and potions he and Mizuki saw at the abandoned clinic, like he's seen on beaches everywhere. None look like the magic potions they drank last night.

Arlo's not much of a spirit drinker, but he needs something to dull the world's sharp edges so chooses two at random. One clear liquid, one wasp yellow. The sound of the seal breaking is satisfying as he unscrews them.

Crack, twist, crack, twist.

The liquid tastes like battery acid but he lets it pour down his throat into his empty stomach.

The day tilts into evening and he finds somewhere else to drink. An American sports bar. Flags, beer, pool tables. Big muted TVs suspended in the corners. A jukebox near the bar. Is this country music? Lonesome, manly men singing sad, homesick songs.

Arlo has never been in a bar alone before, other than waiting for a few minutes to meet Luke.

He orders a beer but barely touches it, preferring a more efficient means of getting the alcohol into his blood stream. Shots the colour of morning-after urine.

They don't help.

Arlo looks around for something or someone to make him feel better. It's mostly groups of young men, a few older men by themselves. Mainly foreigners like him. His drunken eyes finally land on a woman. She could be any age between twenty and thirty. She watches him looking at her, rippling against the wall like a threat.

Eye contact.

She looks lonely. He looks sick, his shirt stained with spilt something.

They choose each other anyway.

'What's your name?'

'Arlo.'

She doesn't hear him over the music.

'Low?'

Low. Lost. Lonely. Love. Loved less than the others.

'Luke,' he says.

Her name is Melissa. She works for a family here but they've gone on holiday without her.

'What do you do?' she asks. Or maybe it was, 'How are you?'

'I'm famous as fuck back home.' He's slurring now but carries on. 'I'm a soap star.'

She laughs. 'Yeah, me too.'

'I've got two million followers on Instagram.' A lie.

'Isn't that kind of the same as being Monopoly rich?'

Arlo doesn't understand. 'More shots.'

They clash glasses.

'Happy birthday.'

'It's not my birthday,' she says.

Later, they slow-dance. Arlo can see Melissa's reflection in the window, one sad eye staring out over his shoulder. He clasps her hair, dry and bleached to the colour of old teeth.

Back at his hotel, his legs start to go as they swing down the corridor to his room. She takes the key card from him and enters the room first. He can't tell if she's impressed. Looking around, there is no reason why she should be.

He's nervous, needs to pee.

Melissa is under the sheets when Arlo gets back, moving, rolling like white waves, making him seasick. The sound of the sea in his ears again.

She's swapped the overhead light for a lamp in the corner. Low light. He strips down to his boxers and gets into the bed. They kiss, push against each other. Drunk and clumsy. She climbs on top of him.

Her dehydrated hair hangs in his face, scratching his skin. He swats it away like a string of flies. She pulls a band from her wrist and ties it up into a complicated knot. He blinks away the image of the knot on the shutter of his hotel capsule, the knot his mother tied to keep their home from sliding away, the knot on the notebook he hasn't drawn in for weeks.

He's never going to draw in it again, he knows. What's the point? He'll never get the chance to show Luke where he's been.

Melissa grips his thighs with hers, nuzzles his neck, whispers something in Arlo's ear.

His mouth fills with saliva. He's going to be sick. Pushes her off.

'Hey,' she cries.

'Sorry.'

No time to get to the bathroom.

He leans over the side of the bed and vomits on to his crumpled shirt on the floor. Wiping his mouth on the back of his hand, eyes stinging, he says again, 'I'm sorry.'

Melissa is already out of the bed and pulling on her clothes. 'You're wrecked.'

'I'm sorry. You stay, I'll go.'

She's at the door now.

He continues, 'Please. The room is already paid for. I'll go if you want me to.'

Her face softens.

'You can't go anywhere – look at the state of you.'

He can't bear to look down at himself or the mess on the floor.

'I'm going,' she says.

'At least let me help you find a taxi.'

'The doorman can get me one. You take care of yourself, Luke.'

'It's Arlo.'

'Kayleigh.'

She leaves.

Arlo feels sick again, ashamed.

He rolls up the shirt and drops it into the bath, covering it with water to soak. He should go after Melissa. Kayleigh. Make sure she's OK. A car pulls up outside. Pressing his face against the cool glass of the window, Arlo sees its driver open a door so she can get in the back. The engine purrs and she's gone.

He makes it to the toilet just in time to throw up again.

The flush is complicated; a million buttons and icons that don't make sense to him. Arlo puts down the lid and presses them all.

He tucks himself into the space between the side of the bath and the toilet, resting his arms across its metal lap. His mum would be so disgusted with him for behaving like this. *Kayleigh was using me too. Women do it as well.* His only defence.

He tries to look through the bathroom wall, the shell of the hotel, through the town to the coast, over land and sea, and back home.

He doesn't cry. At least not as much as he wants to.

TWENTY-FOUR

Morning cringes through the curtains. Heat sits heavy on Arlo's face and chest. The acrid taste of vomit coats his tongue.

What a difference a day makes.

A wave of gravity tries to smash him backwards when he gets up to pee. The urine is dark, the scene in the bath revolting. Arlo pulls the plug, squirts the entire contents of the complimentary shower gel on to the shirt and turns on the shower to rinse it some more.

Once it looks clean, he climbs into the bath, shifting the shirt to the other end, and blasts himself with the water. It's like being hammered by boiling hailstones.

He can't get Mizuki out of his head. Of all the people he'd thought would ever hurt him, he can't believe it was her. *This is what happens when you let people in.*

In the mirror, his tongue is swollen and white. Teeth marks

at the edges. Dehydration. He guzzles water straight from the tap, slurping until he can't take any more.

He wrings the shirt out over the bath until his hands turn red and tries to dry it with the shitty hairdryer. Futile. He shrugs himself into the still-damp sleeves, fumbles with the buttons. Hands shaking from the alcohol.

He has to call his mum again – it's still just about his birthday where she is.

His phone is full of birthday messages.

Maybe one of them is from Mizuki – an apology, an explanation. Of course it's not; she doesn't even have a phone. Or maybe that was a scam too.

The first email is from his mum.

Thank you – I feel a lot better knowing you're OK. Been a long time since I've seen that face. Who took the photos? Where are you? CALL ME, PLEASE. Lots of love, Mum xx

Thank you for what? Whose face, what photos?

Oh god, he must have sent her something while he was drunk.

The last email in his sent items is to his mum. No message but five attachments. Arlo opens the first one. His face downloads in front of him. Eyes closed, peaceful. *What the hell?* He opens the rest. All photos of him sleeping.

'*She watched me while I slept – I think it helped her too.*'

Mizuki must have taken and sent them. His ribs get smaller.

'*You want me to watch you while you sleep like your mum did?*'

Oh god, she'd done something so sweet and kind so his

mum wouldn't worry on his birthday and he'd left her all alone on the beach.

He has to get to her.

He has to make her understand how sorry he is.

The tent flaps are closed but not zipped.

Yesterday's sandcastle has subsided. It's still standing but definitely more of a lump than a palace now.

'Mizuki. I'm so sorry. I know what you were doing with the photos. I want to say sorry.'

She doesn't answer.

'Mizuki?'

She's going to jump out, he knows it.

Déjà vu.

Time slides again. Arlo steps out on to the roof. The lilos. The trees. The drizzle.

Panic rises, takes hold.

The soles of Luke's shoes at the bottom of the pool.

'Mizuki? Please come out.'

Luke's empty room. The police. The wake.

'Mizuki.'

A coffin disappears behind curtains. His own face, sleeping, sleeping, sleeping.

The tent door flaps open in the breeze.

It's empty. All the stuff is gone except for one sleeping bag, his water canister, and something under it.

A piece of paper folded into an envelope.

Arlo runs his hands over the edges, trying to feel what it says with his fingers. He steps back from the tent and faces the sea.

Unfolds the paper.

It's a note.

He's on the sand now.

I know you won't see this but the memory card full of you was just for me. I'm sorry.

No email address, no kiss, no nothing.

The universe and everything inside him turns 180 degrees.

She's gone.

TWENTY-FIVE

The answer comes to Arlo after three nights without sleep.

Three days of waiting for Mizuki to come back with no way of reaching her other than sending out messages to the universe. Three days of knowing he could actually have prevented losing this one.

She'll come back. She knows what it's like for someone to walk out and not return.

Arlo sits on the rough sand, guarding the entrance to their empty tent like the most loyal of dogs. He waits for her to reappear with brown paper bags of fruit or deep-fried maple leaves.

The more tired he gets, the easier it is for him to imagine her returning. Every detail of her comes alive as she crosses the sand to him in his mind. He can see the grease soaking through the paper bag on to her fingers, the leaves inside like tiny battered starfish. Her mouth at first cross then turning up into a smile as she drops down beside him and crawls into the tent, tired from her long walk, the shadow of her missing mother beside her. Camera zipped away and retired for the evening. The stench of warm fruit, the sensation of folding hard pips with his tongue and spitting them on to the sand. All conjured from hoping, from being awake too long.

Arlo only leaves his spot on the beach to go up to the bathroom, refill the water canister or grab food from the 7-Eleven just past the car park. After three days of subsisting on sugar he feels as if his teeth will never be clean.

For three days, sweat runs in rivulets from his temples, crawling down his body into the sand until it darkens around him. His hair curls with dampness behind his ears, longer now on the back of his neck. T-shirt and cap smeared with sunscreen but skin still growing darker under the violent sun.

At night, he shivers, not allowing himself the comfort of the sleeping bag. Seabirds gather along the shoreline to devour the dead and dying squid, their blue lights gone with Mizuki. Huge gulls size him up, pecking the sand around him as he slumps, waiting.

The more tired he gets, the hotter Arlo is during the day and the colder he is at night curled up in the sand.

In the dark, he allows himself to turn his phone on and use up some of the battery. Mizuki's photos of him sleeping glow on the small screen as he scrolls through them. Proof that he is capable of sleep. But not now, not with nobody to watch over him.

His skin crawls, swollen with bites from things that live in the sand. Flies, crabs, who knows?

The twitches started on night two. Minor misfirings in Arlo's muscles. Now, twenty-four hours later, they evolve into fireworks under his skin, great tectonic shifts making his limbs spasm as he tries but fails to ignite sleep. Hypnic jerks, the internet calls them. Other people get them too. *It's normal.*

Should he get some sleeping tablets? Something to reset himself, something to fold into yogurt and force down his throat to get better? Would he be able to get the right thing over the counter here? Nothing addictive, nothing too overwhelming.

He feels the tablets stick in his throat, invisible, impossible to swallow like hunks of stale toast. Finds himself halfway up the sand to the shop without remembering the decision to get up and thinks, no, no, he won't get any, before returning to his vigil.

The sea starts to sound like drowning after a while. Arlo heads to the waves and stands among the beached and dying creatures, wondering what to think about the ocean that hasn't already been thought.

There's just a faint silvery line where the blue neon scribble was now.

Animals flip flop at his feet. There are too many to throw back into the water and it wouldn't help them anyway. He watches a few be poisoned by the air, backwards drowning, and scoops sand over them. The tide carries away the burial mounds faster than he can make them, revealing the small dead bodies over and over again.

The sea keeps calling.

Arlo stands firm at the waterline. It wants him. He stands and stands and stands until the sea backs away from him, slowly, slowly, slowly. Finally he leaves it before it can leave him, launching himself back up the beach and collapsing outside the tent.

Time keeps sticking again. Slowing down, glitching, rolling over him to catch up with itself.

His steps to and from the bathroom and the shop grow less steady. But the less sleep that he banks, the more Arlo earns from the earth, the more it grows generous with its signs and secrets until, finally, it reveals to him where to find Mizuki.

For the first time in weeks, he opens his notebook. He folds Mizuki's Rabbit Island map into the pages.

He retraces their every step in his mind, seeing their path wind out like a piece of bright string tangling across the country in criss-crosses and loops, tiny knitted knots where they stopped to stay a night or talk with someone else for a while.

Early on the fourth morning, the packed sand beneath him becomes a gurney. He sinks down into it, crushing the remains of the sandcastle. And there he finds the answer.

Arlo plugs his phone into the socket at his feet and sits back in the train seat. He feels himself powering up; broken video games reanimate in his mind and he's sucked inside among bouncing cats and magic mushrooms.

It had taken him a while to find the address of where Mizuki will be. He'd closed his eyes, trying to visualise it written in her big, tidy letters on a slip of paper. He couldn't remember it properly and had to scour the internet for possible locations before he found a street name that looked familiar. Finally, he'd found the right place.

The train gallops on.

Giddy up, giddy up.

This anticipation is better than anything.

He solved the puzzle.

Is he God – is he controlling this train?

Somewhere, songs play just for him.

His mind spins in his seat, on the spot, on a pinhead.

Nobody is going fast enough to keep up.

He's too fast.

No sleep.

C'mon, keep up.

Try harder.

She'd taken the charm present; there's hope.

It's a test. He'll pass.

I'm coming to get you now.

The building is like nothing else Arlo's seen so far – bleak yet awe-inspiring. He imagines the pictures Mizuki will take. Not black and white like The Play's. She'll bring its shadows into the light somehow. He should make a start before she gets here; she'd like that.

But first he has to sleep.

Arisu was right: this dark place is full of places to rest.

The gurney creaks as he crawls on to it. There are no sheets. Arlo pulls his sleeping bag over himself, too tired to unlace his shoes as the dripping walls of the abandoned hospital close themselves around him.

TWENTY-SIX

Two days later, Arlo has cleaned three of the ground floor wards.

Whatever forced the hospital to close had dispatched the neighbours too. He can grunt as he hefts the beds around. No need to flinch as their metal legs scrape along the dusty floor.

The leftover cleaning materials that he found in a storage cupboard don't stretch far and he can only get water from a tap in the grounds, so it's been slow progress when you factor in that he has barely slept during that time. Too busy haunting the wards, being angry at the other ghosts.

Arlo flips through his notebook. Scratches and symbols mark the pages. Lines leading to other lines. Children's drawings done without looking at the page or taking the pencil off the paper. What is this language? One he doesn't speak any more.

He decides to change tack. Mizuki will be here soon, he can feel it, and he wants it to be special when she arrives. He runs the couple of miles to the nearest shopping centre to buy balloons, streamers and garlands.

Next, gifts. The apology requires a grand gesture but he doesn't know what so he decides on lots of small ones.

Mizuki is going to love her presents. Arlo swings the bag of gestures until the handle gives way. Everything scatters on to the pavement. Red plastic maple leaves, marshmallows, strawberry toothpaste, sachets of vitamin C powder, a disposable underwater camera, a string of international flags, a bag of cherries and persimmons, bottles of magic hangover potion, a novelty spoon and – the thing he's most proud of – a jar of actual holy grail peanut butter-not-cream. Arlo scoops up the treasure and carries it all in his arms like a baby.

His apology is pitch-perfect now. He's practised it out loud. *'Keep it simple – just say sorry. No secretly trying to make it the other person's fault,'* his mum used to say.

There's still some magic in him; all the crossing lights are in his favour on the way back, green lights for ever. He gets the last box of Krispy Kremes at the 7-Eleven.

Back at the hospital, Arlo chooses the cleanest corner in the ward closest to the main entrance and strings up the decorations. He arranges the gifts along the side of his bed. He's forgotten to get wrapping paper again but it doesn't matter; Mizuki probably doesn't approve of wasting paper like that anyway.

When he's done, Arlo takes a photo. It doesn't look how he hoped. The scene is less jubilant reunion and more someone having a tragic last birthday in a hospital.

He unpacks a few of his things to make it seem more homey, though he knows from unpacking in his dorm at school and back into his room in the caravan at the end of each term that this doesn't work.

Maybe home has to be inside yourself.

He throws the last of the water on to the windows closest to his bed – the gurney he selected when he checked himself in – and wipes them down with a pile of moth-ravaged towels. Cress-like plants grow along the windowsill, fragile as old people's hair. The sides of the window frames are thick with the sticky caress of fallen spider webs. He rubs all that away too. Light pushes past the trees outside to stream through the cracked panes, landing on the bed and floor in luminous zigzags and shadows.

Through the tangled vine of his thoughts, Arlo realises he should try again to get some sleep before Mizuki arrives. The greyness of his skin is starting to show even under his tan. There's a rash on his neck from too much sweat and sugar. Eyes like bruises. He needs to shave but can't find his razor.

He rinses himself and his T-shirt under the outside tap, shovels in some doughnuts and a can of lemonade, and lies back down on the bed. The ceiling is stained and dark. It can't be blood. Not all the way up there. Defunct smoke alarms. Peeling plaster and thick cobwebs like fishing nets clogged with dried-up creatures, possibly squid. He imagines them lit like blue stars above him.

His mind revs with sugar and chemicals and an energy he's never felt before as branches scratch at the window near his head. He shines his torch out on to the leaves. They're riddled with black pits and scars. Diseased. Dark, tar black.

The tree could die at any moment. Could come crashing through the cracked windows and that would be that. When

Arlo closes his eyes he hears toxic roots twisting and tangling under the building, the desperate stretching of its arms reaching for him. He can't be sure but it looks like a giant, dying relative of the tree that he and Mizuki had sat under when they met. Her tree. Bronze twisting through two-tone blossom.

When will she get here?

It's a special kind of loneliness that Arlo feels, close to superiority at night. Everyone else is wasting time sleeping. What idiots, what clowns, those losers. He lies listening to the static and beeps in his head, a machine silently sending messages in the dark.

Mizuki is coming, he can feel it.

She's coming to get me now.

Of course she's coming. She had all those photos of him. She'd done the kindest thing for him and his mum. *Maybe she loves me.* He doesn't know what all this means but it can't mean that she hates him. He knows that much.

The universe will deliver. It's withholding the only other thing he needs: to slip between clean sheets and sleep for days.

Glass shatters somewhere up a ladder or down a corridor. A scolding voice says something foreign and muffled. A showing off sort of laugh follows.

Mizuki.

No, male voices.

A metallic rattling noise like someone running a baseball bat along radiators. The squeak of rubber soles along cold floors.

Arlo can't translate what the men are saying but they seem uncertain. Voices inflecting at the ends of sentences as if deciding on a plan. Explorers, not security then. They sound agitated; he doesn't want to surprise them with his presence.

He could hide in the storage cupboard and pray they don't open it. Maybe it locks from the inside. But they'd still see the balloons and presents. No time to hide everything.

The footsteps and voices get louder. Two men, possibly three.

The leaves scratch and point from their vantage point at the window, directing Arlo towards a visitor's chair a few beds down. He unfreezes himself, grabs the chair and shoves it under the ward door handle just as Luke showed him how to wedge the fire door shut on the roof.

Holds his breath.

Seconds later, the door handle turns. A shoulder shoves the other side and the frame shudders. Should he just reveal himself? Whoever is here would be able to tell he's harmless. Maybe they'd be friendly like Arisu and James. They could help him find Mizuki.

What if it's Luke?

The handle turns again.

Mum?

A frustrated slam reverberates through to Arlo's side of the door before the footsteps and voices move away.

The banging in his chest subsides as they grow more distant. He turns to look at his pathetic party display at the other end of the derelict ward.

Painful clarity crackles over him. All this straining against his roots has taken him too far.

You've really snapped your tether this time, kid.

Mizuki could easily track him down if she wanted. One

Google search would lead straight to his agent, assuming Russell still is his agent.

She isn't coming.

He is unhinged, a vacant space where a door used to be, and he needs to get out of here before he gets caught or hurt.

TWENTY-SEVEN

The castle, the sea, and the hospital seem like distant concepts now Arlo is back in the neon capital. Existence Doubtful.

He's still looking for Mizuki but pretending that he isn't. During these last nights of neon, every low ponytail, every spine in the dark, are a reminder of her. Sometimes he thinks he sees Luke. Maybe his dad too.

He'd left a note in the empty peanut butter jar on one of the gurneys telling Mizuki he'd be in the same hotel as before.

In his different but identical room, he's found numbers to keep him company. Calculations. The sums are inside him, flashing, demanding to be solved despite his exhaustion.

If there are seven circles on the ceiling, how many are extra, how many are missing?

If I send one text home and receive two back, who is coming to get me?

If I go to sleep now and get up then, I'll have this much sleep. If I sleep ten minutes in every hour, I'll have that much.

He can time travel now too; with all the extra waking hours, two weeks to everyone else is three weeks to him.

If I never sleep again, I'll have a third more waking life than everyone else for the time I'm alive but won't live as long.

If I get a message from somewhere eight hours behind, someone will come and get me in eight hours' time.

Arlo spends some of the extra time that he's now in possession of mining the deep caves of the internet. He keeps digging until he finds what he wants: confirmation that this lack of sleep will end in more tragedy. Boy, does history deliver. Top of the lists: a nuclear crisis, an exploding spaceship, a devastating oil spill, a plane crash. All attributed, allegedly and in part, to sleep deprivation.

First: expect palpitations, a dead libido, forgetfulness.

Check, check, check.

His vision has never gone like this before but then he's never been this tired before. Lines appear like glimmering chasms cutting holes through the world. They start in one eye, crossing to the other, until there are blurred portals everywhere and the edges of everything leak like neon in snow. His head pounding, the only option is to push on through this virtual reality.

All his days run backwards; he wakes up exhausted, goes to bed wired.

But at least there are places he can go when he can't take another night of listening to his brain talking to itself in the hotel quiet. When he can't take staring at the ceiling any more, he heads out to the diner. When he gets back, he'll clean his teeth with melon toothpaste so that he tastes like Mizuki until it fades.

The fluorescent lights in the diner are more offensive than he remembers from his first night here. Maybe they were installed to keep those who could sleep – the waitress, the security guard, the guys on their way home from a late shift – awake. There's a persistent hum in the air.

These types of places have existed throughout time. Hadn't they studied a painting of a view through a window into a diner like this one at school – *Nighthawks*? This one is brighter, and seventy-five years later.

Arlo prefers this night-time crew. The earlier evening crowd are more animated; they travel in pairs and packs. The more people there are in here, the lonelier he feels. He waits for the man he gave his ramen to on his first night to turn up again, but he never comes.

A 4 a.m. ice cream sundae sits in front of Arlo on the counter, melted back into milk. He eats the too-sweet cherry, aware of his stomach and the tubes leading to and from it.

He stirs the dripping mess, mind fraying, following every thought to and way beyond its natural conclusion.

Ice cream reverts to milk but you can't get it back in the cow. Unless the cow drinks it. You can't un-toast toast or unboil an egg. What comes first, the waking up or the falling asleep?

It's fascinating to Arlo, this inability to switch off. Thoughts starting somewhere and ending up somewhere else entirely. Anything but think about Mizuki touching him, making him alive. Anything but think about Luke being dead.

He can feel his mind disintegrating. Thoughts loop and loop and loop through waves of mania and dullness. Rapid then treacle-slow cycling. Buzzing in his ears, the sound of neurons frying and connections fraying. Occasionally he falls down the rabbit hole of trying to figure out why he's like this. Where was the start of this particular episode, or is his life just one long programme of it? *The Arlo Show*. Airing 24/7, but only in his head.

If someone wrote his life down in a timeline, plotting events, they would make links that aren't really there. People love to attach causes and cures where they don't belong. This happened because that happened, x wouldn't exist without y. Why, why, why? It's in our nature to try to make sense of things.

Am I a missing person because I am missing people?

He was fading before that. Lost in space in his seven-year-old self's bedroom ceiling. Spinning globes in libraries, trying to hurl himself out of his location. The cracks appeared long before anyone started looking for them.

The waitress mops the melted ice cream from the counter in front of him but doesn't take the glass flute full of goo away. She recognises him. Not because he's famous. He's been here a few nights now and he still looks out of place. What does she think of him? *Oh, there's that foreigner who never sleeps.* There'd be nothing left of his identity if he became a sleeper now.

She folds the cloth over to find another clean part and dabs it along the counter – bored, Arlo assumes, but not showing it. Their communication has been the usual dance of pointing and a few phrases, but she doesn't need to explain that people prefer mess to be contained. The long spoon shakes in Arlo's hand as he lifts it so she can clean the surface underneath. She swaps the soggy bar mat for a clean one.

He shifts the sundae to the right in case she wants to clean the rest of the counter too. The world drags and zaps as he moves. Her outline blurs. There's a tremor underfoot. Three seconds, maybe more. Arlo glances round the diner. Nobody else has noticed.

A couple of minutes later, the floor rumbles again. Muscle memory awakens in his feet. He has felt this before. Earthquake. No, not that. An underground train pulling itself through the tunnel beneath him.

The ice cream isn't working. Whatever chemicals he was riding for a while have run out. Green lights never.

Arlo does more sums with the menu, puts some bills on the counter and heads through the automatic doors out into the streets.

He heads back to the hotel to scour news sites for photos that might be Mizuki's, finding no comfort in the knowledge that she's probably doing the same looking for her mum.

Maybe she'd given him a fake name. Hadn't he wished he'd done the same at first – and he'd told Melissa/Kayleigh that his name was Luke. Why can't he remember the names of any of her friends?

Probably she would have told him her real name eventually. He tests all sorts of alternative names but can only see her as a Mizuki Gray.

All Arlo wants is to find a way to get a message to her, even if it has to be via a news agency. He needs to tell her how sorry he is, that he understands she doesn't exist to reassure him and make him feel more whole. Just one message; he's not going to hound her. After all, she could easily find him if she wanted.

The certainty that she even existed is starting to go watery, though he has photos of her lifting a blonde rabbit's hind leg and their names written in dust to prove it.

He googles and googles and googles but finds no trace of her. He even logs in to the Twitter account that Lottie mans to see if Mizuki's tweeted him. She hasn't. His Twitter alter ego has been quieter than usual: just a few tweets by Lottie about his last episode coming up and how much he misses his castmates.

He can't find a Twitter account for Mizuki either but decides to send her a clue so she knows he's looking for her in case she tries to find him on here. None of the words that come to mind make any sense when he types them out so he tweets a picture of The Play's lost egg.

There are hundreds of mentions waiting for him. Mostly words of love, peppered with heart emoji, and a few people telling him he's shit. Those are the ones that stay with him. A few people have sent him gifs of himself. It's like looking at a bodysnatcher. People are already retweeting the lost egg. Arlo closes the app.

The ceiling seems lower than it was last night.

If he could just sleep.

The internet tells him to try hot milk, magnesium supplements, bananas for the potassium, but he subsists on a diet of hotel porn and nature documentaries, things that are on late at night. He's too tired to come but he's seen a hundred mouths like red pockets and watched two documentaries about penguins before sunrise.

TWENTY-EIGHT

The side alleys of this infinite metropolis are still a maze of lanterns and desire but the humming buildings and five-way zebra crossings of the main streets are familiar now.

There are signs all around sending Arlo messages about what to do next; he just needs the code to decipher and connect them. One more night without sleep should do it.

Pulled along through the swarm of masked strangers, he almost misses the screen on the side of the cavernous shop where he'd seen the teen metal band singing on his first night here. It's one of those stores that sells souvenirs and 'tat', as his mum would call it.

Footage of some kind of tournament beams from the huge digital panels on the wall above. Counter-flow, he steps through the pouring crowds into the gutter to get a better view. On the screen, two girls stand either side of a man dressed in an umpire shirt. The shot switches to the audience: thousands of girls and young women dressed in bright costumes – animals, flowers, monuments, characters Arlo doesn't recognise.

A passerby says something to him that he can't understand, pointing to the queue of traffic flashing him out of the road. *Why don't they just beep?* Arlo steps back on to the edge of the pavement.

The on-screen girls stare at each other; one is fighting back tears. Each holds an arm out in front of them. Fists touching, trembling with anticipation. The umpire calls something out.

The fists withdraw, then return to the centre: one paper, one rock.

The crowd erupts. Flowers jump up and down, the Eiffel Tower dances with a furry orange creature.

The owner of the paper hand looks at it in disbelief. She clutches it with her other non-triumphant hand and raises it over her head like a champion before falling to her knees, weeping.

She's won.

What, Arlo is not sure, but it's very important, that much is clear. The other girl helps the new queen to her feet, admiring the winning hand – the true hero of this event – and they embrace.

It's a sign.

Mizuki's here.

He feels a bit cheated that it turns out rock, paper, scissors seems to be something of a national pastime here rather than his and Mizuki's special thing but the relief that they'll soon be reunited is dizzying. Arlo slumps against the storefront next to three white racks laden with shiny tat. Yawning down great lungfuls of oxygen, he closes his eyes, allows himself to slide down the wall. His kneecaps feel pointy in his hands. People will think he's drunk but he doesn't care.

He takes some deep breaths. The chance to apologise starts to buoy him. He should go back to the hotel to wait for Mizuki. He pushes himself to his feet. Head rush. Arms reach out to find something steady. One of his hands grabs the closest rack. It rattles and, for a second, Arlo can see the whole thing toppling down on to him – key rings, charms, the lot. Two small arms and two bigger ones reach out next to him to steady it. A child and his father.

The kid is upset and pointing under the rack where he's dropped something – a dummy or a favourite toy. Arlo scrabbles for it. Pulls something out.

He doesn't even need to look to know what it is. The edges and curves draw themselves in his mind. Mizuki's rock, paper, scissors charm.

She must have dropped it. Her heart will be breaking to have lost it. The look on her face when he returns it to her will be worth missing the chance to give it to her the first time.

On his knees, Arlo holds the sign out triumphantly to show the man and his son.

The man takes the charm and returns it to its place on the rack with a million other identical pieces of tangled tat.

Maybe if Arlo were more famous, Mizuki would see him on TV. Maybe the casting people haven't found anyone for the film yet. Russell said they'd really liked him so even if that part has gone, maybe they'll want him for another one. A bigger one.

Back in his hot hotel room, Arlo makes his first phone call for weeks.

'Hi, it's me.'

'Who is this?' Russell's voice doesn't sound as warm as he remembers.

'It's me. Arlo.'

'Jesus, Arlo.' A pause. 'Are you OK? It's the middle of the night.'

'I'm sorry I blew the screen test.'

'That was six weeks ago and you're just calling now? And, by the way, you can't blow something you don't turn up for.'

'I know. I'm sorry.'

'Are you OK? You sound strange. Where have you been?'

'It doesn't matter. I thought you could get me another audition.'

'Someone saw you at the airport looking like a junkie.'

'Junkies don't look how you think they do,' Arlo tells him.

'With all due respect, that's not really the point here.'

Oh.

'So am I fired as a client then?'

'You'd be a hard sell right now. Studios don't want to hire actors who aren't reliable.'

'You're firing me.'

'I'm not firing you. You need to take some time. Some more time. Unless' – Russell laughs a flat sound into the phone – 'you want to try to pass this off as some kind of performance art thing.'

'What about . . . could you get me back on the show?'

Another pause.

'Sorry, mate, I don't think they'd have you back. You didn't answer my question. Where are you?'

'But they didn't want me to leave. They offered me more money to stay.'

'They've got new cast members.'

'All the more reason to have old ones back. Has my last episode even aired yet?'

'No.'

'We could talk to them. Maybe the writers could have us found after all.'

'I'm sorry, Arlo. Really I am. Valerie's back on the show. She's saying she felt intimidated by you.'

He'd forgotten about Valerie. They'd played boyfriend and girlfriend for two years. She'd blamed him for being written out, though that obviously hadn't lasted long.

Arlo's insides churn as if a great hand were reaching into him to stir up old things.

'Tell her I'm sorry,' he says and hangs up.

Valerie.

She was dumb as dirt like the rest of them on that show. *No, she wasn't.* He googles pictures of them together and wonders if he's in love with her. When he logs back in to Twitter, his picture of the lost egg is gone. Either he dreamed it or Lottie has deleted it. Damage control.

Arlo takes a cold bottle of Coca-Cola from the mini bar. Russell always gave him a coke when he went to his office. Bubbles fizz at the base.

He shakes it and they rocket to the top and disappear as he stares at the seven circles on the ceiling and wonders why they seem incomplete. *This planet is missing.* He's lying on Earth. People lie about Earth.

(A joke: I wish all those flat-Earth fanatics would fall off the edge to prove their theory.)

On his back on the cold tiles, he imagines a view beyond the seventeen ceilings above him where Mizuki climbs higher and higher to get her perfect shot, an image nobody has ever captured. She could zoom in on him if she wanted, but she's disappearing from his view.

Come back.

You're going the wrong way.

Was there a point when everything changed? He'd knocked on some wrong doors and they'd opened but which one was the critical one?

Maybe that crane swinging the moon overhead near the roof at home had spun everything off its axis.

Maybe he'd broken something when he'd hung planets on his ceiling and smacked a globe into orbit.

Maybe it had been when he'd closed his dorm door at school for the last time, when his dad had been wheeled away through double doors into surgery, when he'd shut the fire door behind him on the roof leaving Luke alone, when the aircraft door lock had been sealed for take-off, when he'd crawled into his subterranean capsule and tied the shutter with a knot, when he and Mizuki had stepped into the threshold of a chemical past on Rabbit Island, when they'd forced open the door at the abandoned school, when he'd pushed his tongue between Mizuki's teeth, when she'd slid him inside her, when he'd left the tent doors flapping behind him as he fled, when the dolphin-train doors had shut behind him. *Which time – when, when, when?*

The bathroom doesn't answer but Arlo gets it now.

He went forward at the moment when he should have gone backwards. When he found Luke in the pool and he felt time stop, shift, restart, he'd gone in the wrong direction.

He has to find his way back through all those doors and corridors, un-choose all those turns. He'd forgotten to leave breadcrumbs to follow back.

Arlo doesn't want to leave Mizuki but he can only fix things if he returns to the start.

TWENTY-NINE

Arlo doesn't really remember the flight. He must have slept.

He hands over his passport to be checked – 'Welcome home, sir' – and finds himself on a glassed-in bridge crossing between two buildings in the airport. A place of literal transition, stuck, then carried across by a moving walkway.

It's so strange to be back here. *What happened to the person who wasn't allowed to take their flight?* A twinge that it's so easy for him to move between places.

Half an hour later, he is through Customs and at the counter of a busy fast food place. The workers call to each other in stunted sentences.

'More, faster. More, faster.'

'Two medium, one large.'

'Need sauce.'

A minute more and salty fries hang out of his mouth like

spider legs as he flips through a magazine that's been left on the table. Thin, filmy paper and an interview with a boy band member, whom the journalist describes as looking like the love child of Mick Jagger and a teddy bear, talking about how much he loves romcoms.

Arlo watches a group of beefy lumberjacks nursing espressos and booming over their pubey beards. Nobody seems to recognise him.

Home.

Almost.

He feels more sure of himself as he makes his way to the train station.

He settles into a window seat where he knows he'll get the best view later and leans back as the decrepit train pulls away from the crowded platform. It's a long journey, though nothing compared with the twelve-hour flight.

Queasy from the greasy fries, Arlo dozes and wakes later to find they're in a tunnel. He recognises this stretch of the track. There are a series of coast-side tunnels on this leg of the journey.

The train emerges into light clotted by cloud. It'll be dark soon but he can still make out the sea to his left, a wet top-sheet keeping a lid on whatever teems beneath. There's a dark patch further out, over a shipwreck perhaps. Squares of pale blue and pink give the impression of houses on the other side of the inlet. The beach is as waterlogged as he remembers.

A dead whale washed up near here once. Luke told him it exploded but maybe that wasn't true.

Not far distance-wise now but there is only a single track along this part of the coast so it'll be another forty minutes or so.

It's an old train. Dark inside now they're losing the light. Arlo yanks down the window in the door and hangs his hand out until the guard warns him that's the fastest way to lose his fingers.

Rock, paper, scissors.

It's darker still when he steps on to the platform but he knows the sign says 'Home'. The station is smaller than he remembers and, of course, there are no taxis. It doesn't matter; he knows the way.

One of the straps on his backpack was somehow ripped in transit so he drags it bumping and scraping along behind him. He experiments with carrying it like a child to keep it quiet but it's too bulky and he needs a hand free to light the way with his phone. No street lamps.

The caravan site smells the same when he gets there. He knows his way around, even after two years, even in the dark.

Past the café where he'd washed dishes every summer, down the track to the main house and the fancy newer cabins at the top of the site. Past Mr Swanson's shed, which they were never allowed in, near the barbeque area and the rec room where the end-of-season parties happen, then down over the rougher patch of grass past the static caravans towards the sea. A few lights on but nobody out and about now.

Arlo finds the tree easily in the dark. Its shadow looks the same falling across the cream caravan. It smells the same too. Old pine and dry earth. In tree years, no time at all has passed. It's not quite as close to the beach as he remembered but he can smell salt and seaweed too, and hear the gentle wash of the waves.

He feels around the base of the tree's trunk. It's so familiar.

More recent smells too. Wood and flowers. Rot and growth. House and home. He can almost feel Mizuki by his side.

What happened to his head torch? Better to do it by the glow of the caravans anyway; a bobbing torch might attract attention. Arlo pushes harder against the soil, waiting to feel the bulge of a root.

There.

That's it.

His hands know what to do now. He loosens the root, long-dead but buried in the soil pretending not to be, and burrows with both hands until they hit glass. His stronger hand – the rock, paper, scissors one – forces its way underneath to lever it out. Arlo falls back on the ground as it comes free.

Pushing the loose soil back into the hole, he shoves the root back into the earth too and pats the area around it. He'll check again in the morning to make sure it looks undisturbed.

The oblong lengths of the glass jar are warm in his hands. The metal cap is stiff, won't budge. He'll open it inside.

Arlo wades through childhood memories up the three steps to the door, wraps a jumper round his fist and punches through one of its flimsy panels. The handle inside turns easily and the door opens. Arlo picks up the jar and his bag, feels for the light on the inside wall and goes in.

New curtains. His mum had made the old ones. Did she take them with her or were they thrown out like garbage?

A stale ghosting of gas clings to the walls and the carpet. It hasn't been aired out for a while. The hole in the door will fix that.

The door to his old bedroom is closed. He opens it. It's

even smaller than he remembers, smells like laundry put away wet. The same thick-tog duvet on the bed that he had hoped would press out some of his bad blood if he stayed under it long enough.

He leaves the door ajar to let some air circulate. It dawns on him that the Swansons don't rent this caravan out, the runt of the litter at the edge of the park. They're letting it rot rather than pay to scrap it.

He doesn't want to go inside the bedroom. He'll sleep on the sofa.

He and Mum had both slept in the lounge for weeks during the black summer. She had let him have the sofa while she nested in the chair in a full-body halo of cushions.

He had crawled into her lap where he hadn't been since he was in single digits; the idea of her changing his nappies and nursing him now so distant it seemed an impossible trace, something embarrassing. He'd cried into a cushion leaving it wet and smelling like the sea. She'd tried to squeeze him whole until his arms went dead and weren't his any more, just a fizz of pins and needles.

He must have gone back to his place on the sofa because he remembers the sound of her opening and closing the kitchen cupboards and crying into the sink.

Arlo opens the cupboards now. There's crockery and cutlery, a leaky bottle of squash next to several sticky orange ring marks, but no food. In the one under the sink: bleach, a plunger, metal scouring pads. By the kettle, the terracotta dish his mum used for teabags is still there.

She used to lose it when he put hot teabags in the bin. 'Makes the rubbish stink.' Brick-coloured tea. Lipstick marks on the rim. The way she used to beam at him when he made her a cup. He'd been embarrassed by all her love.

Arlo runs a hand over the counter, feels the tea towels. Stiff and dry where they used to hang soggy after she'd made him do the washing-up.

This old caravan. Where would it take him if the wheels hadn't been removed?

He imagines his mum closing her eyes and conjuring him. Could she see the curling wallpaper? Hear the long grass outside rustling against her old home and smell the scent of tears blowing in on the wind? He sends her a text.

Remember when you used to tie the caravan to the tree?

She replies.

Arlo! I've been trying to reach you for days! How are your meetings going? When are you going home? xxx

Then another one:

I never did that. You always wanted me to because you were scared we'd roll into the sea after Luke told you a silly story. xxx

Arlo doesn't reply. He lies down on the worn sofa with the jar on the floor next to him. He's finally motionless but still feels like he's moving.

Lines are forming and connecting in his mind again but he's

too tired to dig for the notebook to let them out. His eyes close.

He's come such a long way to get back to the start.

It's not a game and it doesn't have a name but, if it was and if it did, it might be called Run Until You're Lost Then Try to Find Your Way.

Arlo sends a last message to Luke.

Home. See you at the beach?

Fingers grip the back of Arlo's neck, yanking his hair. He tastes cushion.

Bright light.

'What the hell do you think you're doing in here? This is private property.'

The arm belonging to the fingers pulls him from the sofa. Arlo flails, scrapes his nails across something, the side of a hand smacks his eye. Somehow the intruder gets both Arlo's arms behind his back so he can't lash out.

He's marched from behind towards the door and catches the reflection of his captor in the window. A ghost. No, an older Luke.

'Mr Swanson, it's me.'

'Nice try.'

'It's me. Arlo.'

Mr Swanson frees Arlo's hands and spins him round so they're facing each other.

'Jesus, your face. What are you doing here?'

Arlo doesn't know.

'You don't half look a state.'

'I'm tired,' Arlo says. Mr Swanson looks tired too.

'I should say so.'

'Please let me stay.'

'I'm hardly going to kick you out in the middle of the night, am I?'

'How did you know I was in here?'

'The light was on. I came over to check it out and the door was forced, as you know,' Mr Swanson says.

'Sorry. That was me. I'll pay for it.'

'I don't think we'll tell Mary about it, OK.'

'OK.'

'Come on then.'

Arlo doesn't move.

'You coming?'

He doesn't want to go up to the house yet. Not with Luke's empty bedroom upstairs.

'Is it OK if I stay here?'

'In the van?'

Arlo nods.

'You need anything?'

'No. Thank you.'

'Right, then,' Mr Swanson says. 'Get some sleep, why don't you, and we'll see you in the morning.'

THIRTY

Mr Swanson is at the kitchen table doing something to a piece of parchment when Arlo knocks on the open door at almost midday. He'd been absolutely hammered by exhaustion and finally felt safe to sleep. It's a different table to the one he and Luke used to sit at but almost everything else about the kitchen is the same. It smells the same. His stomach knots.

'Does that need to be done where we eat?' says Mrs Swanson. Her husband turns his chair away from the table and carries on doing whatever he's doing to the thick paper in his lap.

'Come here and give me a hug,' she says to Arlo. Her hair is dyed as black as Mizuki's but grey bits have grown down the parting since the funeral.

She hugs him as tight as she had that day and Arlo wonders if he might fall apart when she lets go, but he doesn't.

'Sorry I didn't come earlier. I slept late.'

'We're glad to see you anytime. What happened to your face?'

Arlo doesn't miss a beat. He doesn't want Mr Swanson to feel bad for lamping him last night. 'I tripped a couple of days ago.'

'Looks like a fresh bruise to me.'

Arlo shrugs.

'Well, we want to hear about what you've been up to and what you're doing here but, first, does your mum know you're with us?'

'I was going to call her later.'

'You can use the phone in the hall.'

'I'll just use my phone.'

'When did you last speak to her?'

A greasy question. He wants to talk to her, especially now that he's back here, but the sound of her voice might break him. And what if she panics and thinks being there will make him sad again?

'You'll use the phone in the hall then,' Mrs Swanson says, leading Arlo out of the kitchen. 'You like the new wallpaper?' It looks the same to him. Same old smell, same mirror with the ugly frame by the stairs. 'Need me to dial for you?'

'I can do it.'

Mrs Swanson takes a few steps away but makes it clear that she won't be going any further until Arlo dials.

He taps a few buttons. He doesn't even know his mum's number. *Who knows anyone's number?*

'Hi, Mum, it's me. Yeah, I'm OK. How are you? How's Auntie?' he says over the dial tone. 'Yeah, the site looks great.'

Mrs Swanson smiles and leaves him to it.

Arlo witters to himself for a couple of minutes, being sure to leave pauses long enough to give the impression that his mum is talking. Hardly the performance of his life but he manages a few fake laughs, catching himself in the mirror as he does. His eyes are puffy, the one Mr Swanson caught with his hand more so than the other. The beach glow has faded, leaving him sickly looking, and his stubble is patchy.

'Hi, Jean,' calls Mrs Swanson from the kitchen.

He hasn't heard his mum's actual name for a while. Jean.

'Mr and Mrs Swanson say hi. OK, I'll tell them.'

'She sends her love,' he says back in the kitchen. Why would they suspect anything – he's an adult now, too old for silly games and tricks.

'We heard. And how many times do we have to tell you to call us Bobby and Mary. You're too old for this Mr and Mrs Swanson business.'

'Sorry.'

'Now, not to be rude, but what on earth are you doing here? It's been, what, two years since you've been back?'

Should he say he's researching for a role? What role would that be – himself? He's tired of lying. 'I just wanted to get away for a while.'

'It must be strange in the flat without Luke.' She turns to face the sink. 'We should send for his stuff really.'

No need to tell them he hasn't been there all this time. He hears her take a deep breath, pulling herself together.

'Well, a bit of sea air will do you good,' she continues. 'I never have understood how people can live landlocked like that.'

The way they speak sounds like an accent now. He hadn't noticed it at the funeral. Time away has hardened the way Arlo talks but none of them mention it.

'How long are you sticking around for?' asks Mr Swanson.

'I'm not sure. I was wondering if . . .'

'You can stay as long as you like. I'll make up Luke's room for you,' says Mrs Swanson.

Three pairs of eyes glance up to the ceiling as if expecting to hear Luke lumbering about up there. Mr Swanson gets up from the table.

'Would it be OK if I stayed in the van?' He couldn't remember ever sleeping in Luke's room. They'd usually just camp out or crash in the lounge.

'I don't go in his room much either. He took most of his stuff when he moved out but I still think of it as his. You could take the spare room? It's small but it gets the sun in the morning.'

'Really, the van is great as long as that's OK with you.'

'Home, sweet home,' she says.

'Here. Couldn't find any peas.' Mr Swanson holds out a bag of frozen sweetcorn. 'For your eye.'

Luke used to say frozen vegetables were better than most fresh ones – something to do with the distance they'd travelled and the way they're kept.

'It doesn't hurt,' says Arlo. It's true; being in Luke's old kitchen has pushed him back into numbness.

'Humour me.'

The ice burns his face.

'Right, I've got cabins to sort,' says Mrs Swanson. 'It's changeover day today. You remember how busy we get for the solstice – it always sends the summer people a bit mad and it's going to be a scorcher this year.'

The solstice.

Back to the start.

It's fifteen years to the day since Arlo and his mum moved here. Since Luke invited him to swim in that patched-together paddling pool. How strange that things have carried on the same without them both.

'I should get going too,' Arlo says. 'Thanks for letting me stay. I hope it's not weird.'

All their eyes are shining.

He wishes he had something to give them to help make them feel better, something to connect them to Luke. If only he hadn't lost the medal. It should be theirs to keep, not lost somewhere on a plane or in a park.

Mrs Swanson hugs Arlo again and excuses herself.

Mr Swanson takes the frozen sweetcorn from Arlo, shoves it back in the freezer then goes to the row of keys on hooks on the wall. He holds one out but doesn't release it until Arlo meets his eyes.

'Anything you want to talk about, Arlo?'

'No, no, everything's good. Well, not good but, you know.'

'Girl trouble?'

'Nope.'

'Boy trouble.'

'No. Nothing like that.'

'I see you're taciturn as ever,' Mr Swanson says. 'Do you fancy giving me a hand today?'

Arlo needs to find a tool shop to buy something to open the

dug-up jar with. No doubt Mr Swanson has tools but Arlo doesn't want to answer questions. And then he wants to go to the beach, but it could feel really good to do something to help the Swansons.

The site looks more or less as Arlo remembers it, though nobody lives here any more – it's all holidaymakers, and the big cabins have been renovated. Bright decks and designer gas canisters.

Part of him thought that the black weeds might wrap themselves around him again the second he got back, but he just feels empty. Maybe it's the jet lag, but all that frantic energy that had sent him on his hunt to the hospital and around the city has fizzled away. The Arlo who thought that tatty charm was a sign seems like someone else.

There's a voice in the back of his head telling him that episode wasn't like the black summer. It wasn't just grief either. It had been bubbling up before Luke died. It had too much colour, too much bad magic. The same voice knows he needs to get to the doctor before he flies back up or crashes again.

The heat is oppressive by 11 a.m. Mr Swanson turns a gurgling hose on himself, dousing the back of his neck and splashing his brow, then offers it to Arlo, nodding at the sky. 'Needs to storm.'

They've been planting seeds in the allotment. Mr Swanson explains that they don't plant them all at once but stagger it so that the crops can be harvested at different times to give a constant supply. Of course, otherwise they'd end up with all the food at once. It's so simple but Arlo would never have thought of it.

'Proper thunder and lightning job,' adds Mr Swanson.

'Yeah.'

There was a hurricane here when Arlo was ten. The next day he and Luke went down to the beach where the wind had thrown all the beach huts up in the air and scattered them like Monopoly houses. It lifted trees and carried them on to the beach, throwing them down like giant splinters impaling the sand. Maps surely changed overnight.

They'd been digging the caravans out of sand drifts for days afterwards. Arlo had his arm in a plaster cast – he can't remember why. He had picked up a sharp shell and dragged it through the filthy cuff until there was a ten-centimetre rip at the top. He levered it open, like ripping through old cardboard. The skin underneath was pale and hairy, and smelled like derelict clinics, rotting carpet. He had to do it. He'd needed his hand free to help clean up their home.

It was his rock, paper, scissors hand.

'Better get on and get things ready for the kids' party,' Mr Swanson says. Arlo follows him to his shed, clenching and unclenching his fingers.

It's really more of an outhouse but they've always called it the shed. At one end inside is a workbench littered with tools and paper with a washing line strung with what looks like oversized, misshapen bunting on it.

'This way.' Mr Swanson leads him to the other end. 'See if you can find the paddling pool in that lot, would you?'

This end of the shed is a graveyard for decorations from end-of-season parties gone by. Paper lanterns, dragons, inflatable palm trees, grass skirts, Village-People hats. Arlo shunts boxes aside, untangles some patio furniture then shifts parasols and loops of fairy lights until he locates a cardboard box depicting a large paddling pool. It's a new one, of course. Bigger, more robust. 'Got it.'

'Great.'

Arlo takes a last look at the bunting as they leave the shed. It looks as if it has sketches on it.

'We'll set it up near the barbeque.'

Arlo hefts the box on to his shoulder and winces. The skin is sore at the back of his neck. Must be sunburn.

Mr Swanson starts inflating the pool with a foot pump. It reminds Arlo of the lilos on the roof; he busies himself shaking out imaginary kinks in the hose.

'Get those out of the tree, would you?'

Arlo reaches into the branches to pull down a bunch of deflated balloons. There's another lot hanging further up, shrivelled like used condoms, leftover from one of the summer people's parties. He hooks them down with the barbeque tongs and shoves the whole lot into a bin bag.

Mr Swanson tells him to hang up some fairy lights in their place. They attach them to a portable generator but don't switch them on. It won't be dark for hours. The longest day of the year.

'Been a while since you've been here for the solstice.'

The last one was when he'd been twelve, around the time he and Luke had stopped being friends. His last birthday here had been the month before and Arlo had left for school soon after.

Mr Swanson hands Arlo a bottle of fluid. 'Put some of this in the pool in case the kids decide to water it themselves.'

Arlo squeezes a few drops of the liquid into the water. It comes out as blue as TV-ad blood then dissolves and disappears.

'Squirt a bit more in.'

Arlo dumps another few capfuls of the fluid in. It makes the water smell cleaner. Chlorine.

Luke.

The party area is starting to take shape. In truth it looks more fun than the boring parties that Arlo had to get suited up for to go to with Valerie Pitch and the rest of the cast.

He spies a football and gets a tingle of an idea, the urge to make something.

'Can I use some of those bottles?'

'Sure.'

Arlo lugs ten of the 1.5 litre ones over to the tree where he arranges them into a triangle, then takes two long pieces of bunting and lays them out parallel, running away from the bottles. For a second, all he can see are the cracked pins of the derelict bowling alley that he and Mizuki photographed. He grabs the football and rolls it between the lines marked by the bunting and knocks down seven of the bottles.

'Bowling alley,' he says.

Mr Swanson gives him the thumbs up. 'Can I have a go?'

Arlo sets the pins up and passes him the football.

'Maybe I'll just kick it.'

'Any means necessary.'

Mr Swanson kicks the ball down the makeshift alley. Eight bottles clatter over.

Arlo retrieves the ball and Mr Swanson boots over the remaining two.

'Strike,' Arlo calls.

'I think you mean spare, but I'll take it. Luke would love this.'

They fall silent for a while.

'Chuck some more of that stuff in the water, would you? One of these years I'll get round to building an actual pool. You boys were always on about wanting one.'

THIRTY-ONE

An earthquake in Arlo's limbs shakes him awake. He's drowning. Space water, a whirlpool, amniotic fluid, a tsunami, something lapping over him. The outside of his body won't move. Inside, it shivers and jerks.

His mind shouts Mizuki's name but the echo doesn't reach her. A conversation comes back instead.

'So is twenty a big deal back home?'

'Not as big as eighteen.'

'Twenty-one is the big one for us.'

'I've just always wanted to be twenty.'

'I always wanted to be seven. Seven is a big deal for girls here, you know.'

'Can you remember being seven?'

She could. She had remembered everything. She had gone to the park with her mum and dad, her last birthday there, just before they'd moved away. A celebration of her turning seven and Thanksgiving.

The edges of everything blur but the map to Mizuki sharpens.

He knows how to find her.

Not yet, but on her birthday.

'Twenty-one is the big one for us.'

She had given him so many clues.

'I'm here until autumn; hopefully I'm meeting someone then going home.'

'It was my last birthday here. We had a picnic under a tree.'

'Those are birthday shoes. I had the same ones.'

'We can't go to where I'm going for my birthday. I'm a fall baby.'

'I'm coming back in the fall when the leaves are red.'

She'll be at the park where they met, waiting for her mother under the tree with the twisted branches and the triple colours.

She's a fall baby. He springs forward into autumn.

There she is, waiting.

Soap opera voices.

'Are you running away from something or running to something?' she asks.

'Both,' he says.

She holds his cheeks with the pads of her fingers. Their hearts thump. No static.

Stars fall. When they get to the ground, they're red leaves.

Her rock, paper, scissors hand reaches for his.

'Let's can't sleep together.'

'Let's get lost together.'

He hates films. The stupid things they put in his head.

In another universe there's a Mizuki and an Arlo who are doing it better. Copies. A copy of him who sleeps. A copy of him in full technicolour.

But in this universe, cold, antiseptic water fills his nose and trickles down his throat. It burns. His eyes open. Stinging, watering.

Hot meat in the air. Leaves and balloons ripple through the veil overhead. Fairy lights. Further away still, clouds. He's outside.

On the roof?

No.

Underwater.

His lungs take action, expelling water and air. He bursts through a sheet of chemical water, arms thrashing. Gasping for air.

Is this a dream?

Mrs Swanson has his arms and is pulling him out of the water. He's flat on his back now. Hands pulling at grass. Cartoons inked on to plastic walls at his head.

Mrs Swanson is solid.

Eyes streaming, Arlo looks around.

A giant clap followed by a flash above.

'You must have passed out. What on earth were you doing in the paddling pool?'

Arlo tries to sit.

Clap, flash. Less time between them this time.

'Don't sit up yet.'

Clap. Flash.

Thunder. Lightning.

An electrical storm, just as Mr Swanson predicted.

Arlo forces himself up anyway.

'What happened?' His eyes and throat are burning.

'We thought you'd gone back to your van.'

He's shivering.

'What a state to get in,' Mrs Swanson says, not in a mean way.

'I did go back to the van. I was asleep. I didn't feel well.'

'Sun stroke, by the looks of you.'

'I'm freezing.' None of this makes sense. 'How did I end up in the paddling pool?'

'You tell me. I came out to make sure the barbeque was out and there you were. Gave me the fright of my life.'

'I'm sorry.'

The sky splits and little rocks of rain start to jab them.

'Can you get up?'

'Yes.' The shock is wearing off and embarrassment starts to set in. 'Don't worry, I can get back to the van by myself.'

'Your mother would never forgive me if I left you alone in this state. Come with me.'

Arlo is too dizzy and nauseated to argue as Mrs Swanson leads him past the shed into the big house, upstairs and into a bedroom.

'I'm soaking.'

'There are pyjamas in the third drawer down. Leave your wet gear on the landing.'

He does as he's told.

I smell like Luke.

Mrs Swanson comes to check on him, does a double take.

'Are these Luke's?'

'Yes. You don't feel like you need to throw up, do you?'

No, he shakes.

She puts a damp sponge on his forehead.

'I feel like Florence Nightingale.'

Arlo's throat aches and he wants to cry. He is nothing but sadness and tiredness. Mrs Swanson pats him on the hand and makes a few comforting noises.

'I miss him,' he says.

'I miss him too.'

There's a hand on Arlo's shoulder.

The same fingers that made him taste pillow. A kinder touch this time, but causing searing pain on his burned shoulders.

'Don't wake him. You're not supposed to wake sleepwalkers.'

'Should we lock the door?'

'I'll keep watch. He could have electrocuted himself being out in the pool in this weather.'

The hand steers Arlo and puts him back to bed where serrated sheets tear his skin as he counts his way back down the ladder.

Thunder claps through his body like the shock of a defibrillator.

Down the ladder he goes, over the congealing beach, under the sea until he's caught in the nets with the rest of the trash.

'Well, I think we've solved the mystery of how you ended up taking a nap in the paddling pool.'

Mr Swanson making light of it the next day takes the edge off the situation.

'I don't remember you being a sleepwalker,' he adds.

'I'm not.'

'I'm going to have to disagree with you on that one. Maybe we should put another lock on the door. Don't want you wandering into the sea in the middle of the night.'

Arlo's head is pounding. He needs to get the jar undone and get to the beach. His skin is still raw.

He downs some water and holds his hands under the tap to

cool them. Chlorine lifts from his skin, renewed again by fresh water. The kitchen surface holds him up as he leans into it, his mouth filling with saliva. Sunstroke is worse than a hangover.

'Sorry if I scared you.'

'I think you scared yourself more. Though you might let Mary know you're OK and assure her you won't be going for any more midnight swims.'

THIRTY-TWO

Being shipwrecked on the sofa where Mrs Swanson sets him up in their lounge is torture. It's the stillness, the not being able to keep moving and shake all his thoughts off. A kind of reverse motion sickness from finally stopping.

The fever from his sunstroke shuts Arlo down and he curls into the cushions and disappears inside himself for a day or two to sleep it off.

When he emerges, he's too weak to do much more than try to quench his insatiable thirst. His piss comes out darker than usual despite all the water. Mrs Swanson tells him a hundred times not to peel his sun-blistered skin because it'll scar.

Mr Swanson has brought Arlo's backpack up from the caravan. Maybe he's old enough to look after himself when he's ill but Arlo gives into it and unpacks a few things – some bathroom bits, his notebook. He waits until he can hear Mrs Swanson in the kitchen before pretending to call his mum.

'Yeah, sunstroke. I feel awful,' he tells his phone. 'Don't worry. The Swansons are taking great care of me and I'll come and see you as soon as I'm better.'

Mrs Swanson hovers in the doorway pretending not to listen while her shadow falls across the living room.

Too dizzy to get up, Arlo watches documentaries on the nature channel to distract him from the sweating and his racing pulse. The best one is about hoopoes. Mysterious-looking birds. Orange headdresses, zebra backs and wings. Might as well be pterodactyls for all the hope he has of seeing one but maybe he'll make one some day.

He finds himself thinking about school a lot, maybe because it was the only other time in his life that he was without Luke and the time he was most invisible. Why hadn't he been able to make other friends there?

Once he'd walked in on four of the other students – or Artists as they had to call themselves there – smoking drugs in one of the studios at night. Two of them had ignored him completely and one had simply held out a smoking piece of foil and a thin tube. Arlo had turned and walked back out.

One of the girls had followed him. Popular. A troublemaker. Maybe he had been in love with her. 'You won't tell, will you? My parents would kill me.'

'Crack will kill you,' he'd said.

'It's heroin.'

He didn't tell. Looking back, perhaps he should have. Maybe she'd needed help, maybe she hadn't been one of those Artists who went round shrugging on and off others' pain like old costumes.

He'd seen her at a fancy Halloween party a few months after he'd left but she hadn't seemed the same. He'd left early and spent most of the evening in a chip shop called Frying Nemo or something like that. Invisible again.

Now Arlo finds himself thinking maybe it wasn't a choice for her either. She might have just been a kid hoping for something brighter too.

At the end of these long days on the Swansons' sofa, they have proper dinners together in the evenings before Mr Swanson disappears to his shed.

Arlo is still a bit out of it, probably still feverish from the sunstroke. There's a Luke-shaped hole at the table. A hole in the conversation, in everything.

Arlo sits outside the Swansons' circuit, watching them contain their heartbreak, passing it back and forth between them, taking turns to bear the weight of it. The three of them sit round the table, clinging to each other and the life raft table without actually touching.

Arlo's mum is missing from the table too. He sends her a short, cheery message. She asks about his meetings and he tells her he'll be coming home soon. It's harder not to speak to her now he's somewhere they used to be together.

She needs me to be well.

He offers to wash up after every meal and when they finally accept, Arlo takes it to mean that they think he's better.

The next day Arlo is steady enough to walk down to the beach alone. He takes the jar with him in the hope of finding a tool shop on the way.

Not much has changed at this end of the esplanade. Even lit by the blazing June sun, it's an area so dead that neglect doesn't hurt any more.

The seafront holds the same old buildings. Vacant properties and a string of greasy spoons named after women – Patsy's, Liza's and what used to be Dolly's but is now Doll because part of the sign has fallen off.

Arlo keeps walking, Luke's ghost by his side, asking him what's behind all the doors, telling him to try a new route, that they've walked this way a hundred times.

Next are the familiar amusement arcades, all christened with the suggestion that they'd much prefer to be elsewhere – Las Vegas, Monte Carlo, New York, then, further away still, Planet Electro, Electric Boulevard, Starworld.

The hotel on the front has been renamed The Hope.

Arlo walks on until he hits one of the two cash points in town. Better grab some money while he's here; he'll need to sort out food for the caravan later if he doesn't want to eat every meal in the site café. The screen is cracked and the buttons defaced but it's just about usable. He inserts his card and punches in his PIN.

Beep, beep, beep.

Insufficient funds.

The machine spits the card back out. Arlo tries again. Same answer. *Shit.* He hasn't checked his balance for weeks. He puts the card back in and checks his transactions. Seven pounds off the overdraft limit that he didn't even know he had.

There's a few hundred pounds' worth of foreign currency still in his wallet that he can change back, plus the eighty or so quid he already has on him. There should be another two hundred emergency dollars divided and stuffed into various socks and in the washbag in his backpack.

It's plenty to live on for now but where has all his money gone? He knows the answer. Last-minute long-haul flights, train fares, taxis, hostels, hotels, doughnuts and 4 a.m. ice cream sundaes. The donation he'd made in the middle of the night to a nuclear refugee charity to appease his guilt for suggesting he and Mizuki go and see the boars. Generous tips to waiting staff who made him feel less lonely.

Maybe the landlady of the flat will give him a refund on some of the advance rent he'd paid.

Fuck, though.

He'll have to find some work pretty quickly.

He needs to call Russell again. Maybe Mr Swanson will give him a job on the site for the rest of the summer.

The back of Arlo's neck is starting to feel hot, as if it might be burning again. He needs to get out of the sun so finds himself under the pier at the tourist beach looking up at its thick metal and wood underside. He and Luke used to pretend the pier was a road on stilts and that they had to be careful of its legs in case it decided to run away somewhere.

Rubbish lies in heaps around the pier's legs. Arlo gathers up an armful of cans – soda, lager, WD40 – and carries them up to the bin. Bits of dark plastic glint like a smashed disco ball among the sand. A tangle of green fishing net strangles one of the pier's legs.

Arlo picks the mess undone and smooths the metres of net

out. The end won't detach from the pier leg and he has nothing to cut through it with. Instead he stretches the net out and ties the other end to the next leg over. Perhaps he can catch some more litter this way when the tide comes in.

The treasure he might find if he comes back to check the nets – glowing blue squid, Luke's broken camera, The Play's egg finally found, his and Luke's lost atlas, Mizuki, both their mums.

The underside of the pier darkens as the sun dims above. Could be a summer shower coming or another storm. Better get moving to the other end of the beach before the bad weather hits. Arlo grabs as many more empty cans and bits of plastic as he can carry and heads back up to the bin.

He's so busy fighting through seagulls to shove the litter into the overflowing recycling can, and trying to remember whether or not there is actually a tool shop in town, that he doesn't notice the spectre on the other side of the pier until he's started walking again.

He sees the turrets first. Blue and green rather than faded pink but otherwise exactly the same. His breath sticks.

A castle.

How desperately he needs it to be real.

Arlo takes off down the esplanade and reaches metal gates. A big circular sign announces: 'Sea Island Adventure Land'.

He pushes his way to the front of the ticket queue. 'How long has the castle been here?'

'We reopened last month. It was a massive build – everything's upgraded or new,' says the guy behind the counter. 'Free entry then three pounds a ride. Some of them aren't ready yet though.'

Arlo is through the gates before the guy can finish. The rides are running with no one on them. Something with giant yellow claws swings and spins over his head.

The teacups where his mum had tipped the boy twenty pence and the intimidating High Striker game are gone. In their place, a passengerless Ferris wheel wobbles round its circuit. A two-lane water slide has been constructed to hang over the side of the park above the sea.

Everything reminds Arlo of something. The lemon patterns on the side of the dodgems are like the yellow lichen growing over gravestones in the churchyard where they buried his dad and grandpa. The huge arrows around the park like the polystyrene raft The Play sailed away on. And neon everywhere he looks.

Small tangles of coloured metal hang like highways, as if the earth had yawned and spat out this unrecognisable network. A mini rollercoaster. Also new.

The area around the castle is taped off. It's so new it might not even be on maps yet. Existence Doubtful.

How tempted he is to climb it.

The door to the sea-side turret isn't in place yet. The staircase twists around inside like a snail shell. Arlo can almost hear his footsteps echoing against the fibreglass walls.

One of the workmen clocks him skirting around the edge of the castle. 'You can't go in there. It's not open yet.'

'I'm leaving anyway.'

As he says it, he realises it's true. He can't climb it without Luke, without Mizuki, and he needs to get to the other end of the beach before the sun sets.

Arlo runs out of the theme park and heads away from the pier.

The beach he remembers had Fanta-orange clouds and a big yolk sun, gulls that glowed flamingo pink in the light. A giant vitamin sea and sandy puddles that fizzed like sherbet. It had him and Luke and games and a scribbled-on atlas that was scratchy with sand and buckled with water.

Today their beach has tangles of seaweed with blisters like necrotic skin, matted with feathers and sea glass as if some ocean monster had crawled up on to the beach in the night to arrange it.

The tide is out. Great swamps and wet trenches scar the sand, boiling under the scathing sun. A couple of boats sit stranded and slanted in the warm mud waiting for the tide to lift them up on its journey back in again. In the distance, inconsolable, wet muscle. It'll be a few hours before it comes back in, by Arlo's calculations.

This was his and Luke's favourite beach, less popular with the tourists because the top part is stony. They liked it because it's the biggest, it was as simple as that. They'd run along it, sliding over and picking themselves up, covered in muddy sand. Hands squelching through muck and treasure as they pushed themselves back to their feet.

Arlo always looked back to see if his mum was following. *Prove that you love me. Come and get me. Show me love is safe.*

He sits down on some shingle against the wall at the top of the beach away from the sand and hot puddles, setting the jar in the bag down next to him. A low whistle sounds nearby but there's nobody around to respond. Big, black birds that Arlo used to know the name of line up along the beach, jumping and foraging. Gulls mewl, bringing messages in a language he doesn't know any more.

Dog walkers fling things for the animals to retrieve. Arlo has always wondered how dogs are able to find things underwater. The seabed must be carpeted with tennis balls and sticks, along with all the other lost things. You've got to go to the sea if you want to get really lost. He used to think that all time. Maybe he'll catch some of it in the nets.

A couple of beachcombers step up and down the beach, swinging strange machines that crackle like police radios and Geiger counters, sending Arlo's mind back to the roof with Luke and talk of radioactive boars with Mizuki.

Still he sits.

Arlo has the stretch of beach to himself now. He sits and sits to give the place a chance to feel like home again, wondering if it was really him who could have disappeared into the sea at Squid Beach.

Looking back over his trip, it's cast in a different light. Even though he'd been hurting for a lot of it, he'd been so lucky to spend time in that beautiful country. Maybe he'll go back one day. Probably not, but there's a bit of it inside him still. Wild and bright.

Arlo looks down at the stones. Maybe he could use one to open the jar. He chips away at the seal for several minutes until it finally loosens. The canvas bag that he'd carried it in works as a makeshift mini blanket so he won't lose anything in the stones.

Arlo twists off the lid and tips out the contents, half expecting the gush of formaldehyde and the plop of a dismembered ear tumbling on to the bag. Instead, pieces of paper screwed up into small balls spread like marbles. Some blue, some green.

He lays the spheres out in front of him, arranges them by colour. The blue ones, his. The green ones, Luke's. Sorts them again into descending size order.

He's sweating, wipes his face with his T-shirt. Weeks of rotating a shirt and three T-shirts to climb over fences and through broken windows has left his clothes with holes in.

Arlo picks up one of the blue globes, rolling this miniature world between his thumb and forefinger before unravelling it and revealing its secret. A picture of two boys, an alien and a dog. His words:

One day we'll have our own planet.

His handwriting has changed. It's messier now, as if his grip on letters has unravelled in the ten years since he and Luke filled the jar with their hopes and confessions, and buried them under the tree.

Too late for that wish to come true.

He picks up one of Luke's and tries to imagine what it might say. Opens it. Green paper, greener letters. Reads its revelation.

I'm sorry I threw our atlas in the sea.

A shiver passes over Arlo's shoulders and down his arms as he absorbs the decade-old words from his friend. His eyes prick and fill as he rubs his thumb over the paper.

It could have said anything, the impact would be the same. A new message from someone he thought he'd never hear from again.

The beach goes blurry. Arlo slumps back against the warm wall, trying not to feel anything.

Everything hurts anyway.

He pulls his knees up to his chest and wraps his arms around himself, holding everything in. If he starts to let it out, he won't be able to stop.

I'll drown.

He sucks air through his teeth, trying to push it all back down, but there's no more room. He wants to run but something won't let him. Black tides fill his insides, glistering sharp in his blood.

The unfairness of it all. All his missteps and mistakes. Everything that's broken and missing.

Luke and the roof and Mizuki and the castle. The hospital. Luke's parents, trying their best. His dad. Mum. *The Beat* and the audition. The smashed tree pots and the lost medal.

Luke again, and again and again. His prone body in the pool.

I'll never seen him again.

No more racing through the city calling out doors or buying trees for a garden they don't have. No more building their own private world on the roof or arguing about who didn't take out the rubbish.

He's not coming back.

Arlo feels himself splinter, shattering like glass the way he always knew he would. He breaks loudly, a howl pushing up through his body and out on to the beach. The black birds flap and stare. Arlo doesn't care. He can't stop now, doesn't want to any more.

Hot tears in his eyes. He lets his hands drop into the stones beside him as they spill down his face, making the neck of his T-shirt damp.

He sobs for all the hurt in the world but mostly for Luke and for himself. Fists clenched, heart torn. All this stuff pouring out of him into the stones.

He lets his head roll back against the wall and closes his eyes. Feels the sun on his wet face and tries to breathe.

In, out. In, out.

Still.

For the first time Arlo gives the pain his full attention. Grief washes out of him and he lets it keep coming, wave after wave after wave.

Briny eyelashes, hollow chest.

He breathes, letting the beach hold him until he's ready to see the world without his friend again.

All sense of where he is has gone when he finally opens his eyes. He wipes his face. Tears and snot streak the back of his fists but he hasn't drowned.

That's enough for now. He'll hurt more later, tomorrow. It's the only way out of this.

Luke's messages glow on the bag in front of him. Green lights for ever.

A little colour in the sea now where the sun has started to set.

THIRTY-THREE

The next morning, Arlo hears Luke's voice coming from the Swansons' kitchen. Booming, unmistakeable. His accent less changed than Arlo's though he'd been away from home for longer.

'Fail to prepare. Prepare to fail,' Luke says.

Arlo is frozen on the sofa. The pillow damp with sweat and last night's quiet tears.

Another fragment of Luke. 'Let me know what you think. I love you guys. Thank you for everything.'

Arlo is half asleep still. *It must be Mr Swanson.*

But it isn't; he'd know Luke's voice anywhere.

He came home.

'I've been doing this secret project with my best friend,' says Luke. 'He has the most amazing ideas sometimes. I love it.'

Arlo swings himself off the sofa and into the kitchen.

Mrs Swanson is at the table with an old laptop. Tears in her eyes and a tissue in her hand but no Luke.

'Are you OK, Arlo?'

He was so sure. So sure Luke was here. 'I thought I heard . . . it doesn't matter.'

'Luke?'

'Yes.'

'Oh, I'm so sorry, love. I was just watching some of his videos.'

Arlo holds on to the back of a chair to steady himself against the disappointment.

'The police finally sent us the memory card from his camera,' she says. 'I thought it would be nice for his supporters if I uploaded some of the footage. There's nothing' – she swallows – 'nothing from his fall on here. The police watched it all to make sure. Do you think you could give me a hand?'

Arlo pulls up a chair next to her and together they watch Luke giving a tour of their roof. He hangs the camera over the ledge, pretending to drop it down on to the street below then turning it back on his grinning face.

'There's so much I didn't know about him,' Mrs Swanson says. 'I wish I'd asked him more questions. I wish I'd been there.'

She means she wishes she'd been there when he died, Arlo thinks. He wishes he'd been there too.

'Sunburn's almost gone,' she says.

'Yeah.' He twists to show her the back of his neck and the top of his shoulders where all the dead skin has peeled away or come off in the shower. 'I'm sorry.'

'No harm done. You just gave us a fright.'

That's not what he means. 'I'm sorry I let Luke die.'

Mrs Swanson clicks pause on the video and stares at Luke's frozen face for what feels like for ever. 'Now listen to me, Arlo, you didn't let him die any more than I did.'

She's going to hate him when he explains the truth. 'I left him on the roof.'

'Did he ask you to stay?'

'He told me to go to bed.'

'Arlo.' She's looking right at him and using his name like his mum does when she really needs him to hear her. It takes everything he has not to look away. 'Even if Luke had asked you to stay, it still wouldn't be your fault. It was an accident. An awful accident.'

It's even worse that she's having to comfort him now. He should be making her feel better. A deep breath later, Arlo says, 'I know.' He can barely hear himself but it's enough to make it a touch more real.

'Your mum will be thinking the same about you, you know. That she wishes she could hold on to you. I know what you boys are like, but go and see her when you can.' She squeezes his shoulder. 'Shall we watch some more?'

Arlo moves the cursor and clicks on Luke's face.

Luke reanimates, showing off their work on the pool, zooming in on the tiles Arlo scrubbed the day he cut his hand open. He pans out to show the trees clustered together in the middle.

'This is the best bit. We've started a forest in the pool. It's going to be awesome.'

Arlo and Mrs Swanson smile at the screen through wet eyes.

It hurts him to see his friend's beaming face again, but not quite as much as never seeing it does.

Arlo makes spaghetti for the Swansons that evening. It's chewy and the sauce is a bit watery but they eat it all and tell him it's delicious.

Mrs Swanson washes the dishes then heads upstairs while Mr Swanson puts on the TV. 'Isn't this that show you were on?'

Arlo turns to look at the screen. It is. And it's utterly bizarre to think he used to be inside people's TV screens like that, walking around saying stuff other people told him to, wearing other people's clothes.

Mr Swanson hands him a mug of something.

Arlo sniffs it.

'Hot toddy.' Mr Swanson nods. 'It's medicinal. Drop of whisky.'

Arlo thanks him and downs half of it, looks back to the TV. This must be a few episodes after his character went missing. His on-screen parents look distraught, the feud between his on-screen dad and Valerie's character's dad now resolved as they work together to try to find them.

A new shot. Valerie Pitch in the back of an ambulance with another young woman. It looks as though Valerie's character has been found while Arlo's remains missing.

Wait.

It can't be.

The woman with her, hugging the silver foil blanket around Valerie's shoulders. That smile. *Jessica.*

Her skin is several shades more natural but it's definitely her.

267

'Reality TV stalwart and aspiring actress' Jessica Start. Her arm around Valerie as they comfort each other in the back of an ambulance. She must be one of the new characters that Russell told him about on the phone.

Arlo can't help but laugh. Mr Swanson jumps. 'Sorry,' Arlo says, turning the laugh into a cough. 'Drink went down the wrong way.'

They keep watching. Jessica is good. Really good, in fact. It might not be visible to the untrained eye but Arlo can see what she's searching for: connection.

Do she and Valerie ever talk about him? Maybe there was a cursory conversation when they met. Probably about what a douche he is. They have better things to talk about, he knows.

'Reckon you'll go back?'

'I don't know. Depends on Russell.'

'Russell!' Mr Swanson almost shouts, jumping up. 'Something came for you from him while you were out of action. I forgot. Hold on.'

He fetches Arlo a padded envelope with Russell's office address stamped on it. Arlo opens it. There's a compliments slip from Russell – 'This came for you. Call me when you can' – and another envelope inside. The second envelope is made of newspaper folded around on itself, a sprig of plastic maple tucked into it.

Arlo's hands shake as he loosens it.

Inside is a bundle of sketches. Maps and routes to secret places. Their scale is slightly off. Each has a date in the corner.

Mizuki's maps.

He pores through them, memories flooding him. All those

nights spent creeping through strange doors into stranger places.

On the final page is a neon blue scribble, the suggestion of a line between the beach and the sea. There's a castle like the one drawn in steam on the hostel bathroom mirror. A tent and two stick figures.

'What is it?'

'Something from a friend,' Arlo says, blood rushing hard in his veins.

'Just a friend?'

'There's no such thing as just a friend.'

Friends are everything.

Arlo looks at the picture of Squid Beach again. Notices the date in the corner. It's smudged but he's sure it says next year.

She wants to see me again.

The carpet swims.

'I need some air.'

Mr Swanson looks doubtful. 'You look like you've seen a ghost. Maybe you should stay here.'

'I'll stand just outside,' says Arlo.

Mrs Swanson is tramping about upstairs. They both glance up to the ceiling. 'OK, but I'm coming out with you. If Mary comes back down and I've let you wander off into the paddling pool again, I'll get it in the neck.'

'That was just the sunstroke. It was an accident.' It's very important to Arlo that Mr Swanson gets that. It's very important that he himself understands it.

'No arguments.'

Arlo slides Mizuki's maps into his notebook and brings it with him.

They stand outside the front door. Another hot day has given way to a warm evening. The thimble of whisky is working its magic, fuzzing Arlo's edges.

'That's Venus,' Mr Swanson says, pointing up.

'Really?'

'I don't know. It could be.'

He's right, it could be.

Its light is bright, bright, bright. Glowing sharp like a squid but green. Having seen the stars from somewhere else puts a special shine on them tonight.

The caravan site is full of laughter, from the fancy cabins up at the top right down towards Arlo's van closer to the sea. The air is smoky; someone is having another barbeque. Outside the front of one of the cabins, a row of kids in sleeping bags are getting their first taste of a night camped out under the starry sky.

Arlo feels safer than yesterday. Here on his patch on this mad planet, a place he walked out on but which welcomed him back anyway.

What a strange thing to have once felt indifferent about living in this magical hive. To have paid no attention to any of it. To his mum, who had made everything as easy as she could for him and to whom he had given no credit. Embarrassed by her lack of achievement when everything he'd done had belonged to her.

They step away from the house and lean against Mr Swanson's shed.

Arlo looks through the window. The odd bunting is still hanging over the desk. Long, oval strips.

'Come on then. Can't have you breaking in and pretending you were sleepwalking, can we?' Mr Swanson opens the door and Arlo follows him in.

'You're the first person I've let down this end. This is my workshop.'

Arlo leans over the desk to peer at the bunting. Its pieces are the shape of the parchment Mr Swanson was working on at the kitchen table on Arlo's first day back here. That seems like centuries ago. The frozen sweetcorn, seeing the castle at Sea Island for the first time.

He gets closer to one of the hanging strips. Faint black lines mark outlines and craters.

'What are they – flags?'

'Go around the desk.'

Under the table on the other side is a pile of spheres, some the size of beach balls, some closer to footballs. Arlo recognises bits of them from their end-of-season parties, his half-birthdays – a snowman's head from when they'd had Winter Wonderland, a pair of huge eyes from the Land of the Giants party, shimmering bubbles from the underwater theme, a disco ball from the 1970s one.

Mr Swanson dislodges one of the spheres. 'Here's my prototype for this season's party.' Strips of the strange bunting have been stretched out and stuck on to it. The effect is rough.

Globes.

'Planets,' says Mr Swanson. 'Space theme this year. I'm making a solar system – and I'm keeping Pluto because I like it, even though they demoted it.'

'The kids will love it,' Arlo says.

'I know you boys like your big audiences but this is what matters to me.'

He motions for Arlo to sit down and hands him the sphere.

Arlo sits behind the desk, cradling the world in his lap. He remembers holding another human on a beach the same way.

'What are they made of?'

'The proper handmade ones are resin or fibreglass. Or some are plaster of Paris. These new blank ones are just off the internet, while I'm practising.'

Arlo can see how perfect it needs to be. He rolls the planet over again. Some of the strips are peeling at their ends and there's bubbling along the seams like global warming.

'Every error is multiplied by pi if you're working on a sphere.'

Arlo isn't sure exactly what that means.

Mr Swanson continues, 'Wish I'd thought of this when Luke was a boy. Not that he could ever look after anything properly.'

He looked after me properly. Like a brother.

'He threw our atlas in the sea.'

Mr Swanson laughs. 'So I recall. I can't remember what you'd fallen out about but my god he felt awful when you made up. Made me swear never to breathe a word.'

'Doesn't matter now.'

'No.'

Arlo's notebook bulges against the back of the chair, the start of an idea poking him in the spine. To make something that matters, you sometimes have to start with something that looks nothing like the thing you want to create. To feel something, you sometimes have to start by feeling the opposite.

Arlo rolls the sphere a final time and wedges it back into its safe place under the desk.

They head back to the house. Mrs Swanson is quiet upstairs.

'You sure you're OK on the sofa?' asks Mr Swanson.

'Fine, thanks.'

'OK. Night then.'

'Night.'

The stairs creak as Mr Swanson climbs them.

Arlo shakes out the pillow and duvet and settles in. He leafs through Mizuki's sketches again. They're all of the last few steps to get to the ruins they chased, not the actual places themselves. Except for the final one of the beach.

Has she found her mum?

Does she miss me as much as I miss her?

An idea is starting to take shape in Arlo's mind. A way to make something that matters, something that no one has ever seen.

The thought is fragile. He has some of the materials he'd need: a notebook thick with his sketches, Mizuki's hand-drawn routes, his and Luke's messages from the buried jar. But he'd need other things too: time, money, for Mizuki to understand how sorry he is.

Her email address is written on the inside of the newspaper envelope. *Not yet.* He'll wait until he has the exact right thing to say to her.

Arlo sets the embryo of the idea aside.

He has a different call to make.

There's a question that's been playing on his lips since childhood: 'Are you coming to get me now?'

THIRTY-FOUR

The food in the café is as good as Arlo remembers. Sausage, hash browns, beans. A mudslide of brown sauce. Double side of toast. His head is full and breakfast is a good distraction.

The chef – a different one to when Arlo worked in the kitchen washing up – cuts round the rim of a pie, throwing the scraps out of the kitchen window to the gulls. Arlo can't decide if it's a waste or not; he might have been made from leftovers like that.

You know you're too sensitive when you're empathising with a pie that might have been.

Still, he takes it as a sign that the numbness is wearing off and tries to welcome it.

There's just him and a woman with two children inside today. It's the second day of their holiday; the kids are chattering about wanting to go to the arcades again after breakfast. Their favourite is Starworld.

The woman watches the kids eat – muffins, or breakfast cake as Luke called them – scraping her hair up and tying it off her face. She and the waitress – also new – talk about the cliffhanger on a soap they both watched last night. One of the shows that always outdoes *The Beat* at award ceremonies.

They introduce themselves. 'I'm Cara, by the way,' the waitress says. The other woman is called Sal. They talk about the characters on the show as if they were mutual friends.

'Can't believe she did that,' and, 'Her mum won't stand for that though.' It's nice, watching two strangers connect over something they have in common and he wonders if conversations happen like this about *The Beat*. He supposes they must do.

Cara slips outside for her cigarette break, straightening a sign on the wall as she leaves: 'Sea, sweat, tears. Salt water cures all.' The clock on the wall next to it says 10.15 a.m.

Arlo clocks Sal looking at him as he shovels in the hot food before it gets cold, her eyes following the fork to and from the plate to his mouth. She's really staring. He catches her eye and she looks away. It makes sense that she would watch *The Beat* too. Been a while since he's been recognised.

'Where's your breakfast, Mummy?'

'Mummy isn't hungry,' Sal says, counting brown coins into short stacks on the table. She reminds Arlo of the man he'd given his noodles to.

She's skipping breakfast to save money.

He picks up his plate of toast.

'Don't suppose you'd like this?' he offers. 'I thought someone was joining me so I ordered too much.'

She looks Arlo up and down. He's made an effort today, even dug out his sponsored razor for a shave after spending most of the night cleaning the caravan and fixing the door pane that he busted when he broke in. But when he looks down at his stained shirt – the cleanest one he has – he realises her look isn't 'Why is this minor celebrity giving me his toast?', it's 'Why is this wreck sharing his food when he clearly can't afford to?'. She takes the toast anyway and thanks him.

When they go, Sal lifts a couple of longish cigarette butts from the ashtray on a table outside.

Arlo's heart twinges at this. It's still sore from his breakdown on the beach the day before yesterday. Maybe he can find a way to give her some money before one of them leaves; he could put it somewhere for the kids to find.

He pushes the rest of the food around on his plate, watching the door.

'Anything else I can get you?' Cara asks. It feels weird to know her name when she doesn't know his. Maybe he should introduce himself, but he doesn't want her to think he's hitting on her.

'Not at the moment. I'm waiting for someone.'

'No problem. Let me know if you need anything.'

It's almost half ten now. They were meant to meet at ten.

She's not coming.

Of course she's coming, she said she would.

Arlo is at the counter paying his bill twenty minutes later when he hears the bell tinkle and the café door open behind him.

'Arlo!'

He turns around. Her face looks rounder than he remembers and she's caught the sun.

'Mum.'

The way she hugs him is the same.

'Don't put the teabags in the bin.'

'I know,' Arlo says. 'Makes the rubbish stink.'

They sit in the caravan lounge to drink their tea. Him fidgeting on the sofa, her dead still in the armchair that she once sat in to watch him sleep.

It's stuffy.

'I'll open the window,' he says.

'I'll do it.'

His mum pushes it as wide as it will go then comes and sits at the other end of the sofa. It's no cooler with the window open but the scent of the sea and pine drifts in.

'Shall I open the door a bit?' he asks.

'Neither of us is leaving this sofa again until you've told me where you've been and what's going on.'

So Arlo tries to undo the stories that he's been carrying around with him for the last two months. He lays it out for her the best he can but has to leave parts out. The bits about sleeping with Mizuki in the tent, Kayleigh, the hotel porn. Mums don't need to hear those kind of details. He leaves out half the reasons why he left in the first place, especially the bit about being scared of doing something that would hurt her.

Though from the look on her face, it seems he has done that anyway. With half of it missing, his explanation just sounds like he jacked in his career and went on an adventure.

'I don't understand why you didn't just tell me.'

Something about the way she keeps looking at him and being back in their old home together makes him feel like a child. He's caught between wanting to tell her it's nothing to do with her, that he's twenty now, and desperately wanting her help.

So he tries a bit more. 'I ran away.'

'Why – what were you scared of?'

'I thought I was getting sick again.'

He thinks he sees her flinch but maybe he's imagining it. 'Because of Luke?'

'Luke dying is the worst thing I can ever remember happening, but I could feel something happening before that. I was already trying to escape myself.'

'I don't think it works like that.'

'Evidently not.' His laugh is feeble.

'Arly.' He'd forgotten she ever used to call him that name; it was left behind years ago. She doesn't say anything else for a few seconds.

'I need to ask you something and it's very important that you tell me the truth.' Arlo looks at the threadbare carpet, waiting for it to fly him away from this conversation, back to the roof, to a beach somewhere. 'Arlo. Do you understand?'

He nods.

'Have you ever thought about hurting yourself? It's OK if you have.'

Only the doctor has asked him this before. It feels different coming from her, more real.

'I've never done it. I've never made plans.'

'That's not what I asked,' she says.

How can he tell her the truth when he knows how much it will hurt her?

The words choke him. 'I know you need me to be OK.'

'I need you to be alive, Arlo. You don't need to protect me. I'm the parent.'

He wonders if she's read about how to have this conversation on the internet, practised her most neutral facial expression.

'I have thought sometimes that I wouldn't mind if I didn't wake up.'

When they get to the end of her questions, there's a mound of cold teabags piled up on the counter.

Later, Arlo hears a familiar sound.

'Mum?'

She's standing by the sink, opening and closing the kitchen cupboards, looking for nothing.

Arlo gets up from the sofa and puts his arm around her shoulder. She's shorter than he remembers too. His mum sweeps the stale teabags into the bin, sending the swing lid rattling.

'Trashlandia,' she says, tapping the lid to still it.

How does she know about Doors? 'That's mine and Luke's game.'

She laughs. 'You kids think you invented everything.'

It's awkward, standing there sobbing into the sink with her, but it's better than anything else he's tried recently.

'Let me take you home, Arly.'

THIRTY-FIVE

Arlo takes the sofa while his mum sleeps in his bedroom. It's as bare as he'd left it; the wardrobe is mostly empty and his half-unpacked boxes still sit by the radiator.

Neither of them suggests sleeping in Luke's room and Arlo dodges his mum's questions about what he's going to do about the flat. The rent is paid for a few more months so he doesn't need to think about it just yet. Somewhere in the back of Arlo's mind though, he knows he'll probably move when the contract ends. Once he's done everything he wants to do.

It's strange, being together in a space bigger than their old one but getting in each other's way more. His mum is always in the bathroom when Arlo wants to use it; he's always standing staring into the fridge when she wants to make breakfast. They're so unused to each other.

Something that keeps coming to Arlo in the middle of the

night while she's sleeping is the idea that he's pathetic. Not so much for being sad but for needing his mum to scoop him up and bring him home.

What about the other twenty year olds who don't have that option – or those who are even younger than him? What about the person at the airport who was just trying to go somewhere to be safe and happy but wasn't allowed – did they have someone to come and get them?

The questions thread their way through Arlo's mind, tying it in knots until he realises that the thing he should do is be grateful. That's what he'd want someone else to do if they had something he needed but didn't have. Like if someone had a best friend who didn't die in an accident on a roof and they didn't find their friend's body, broken on the inside but looking the same as it always had, then he would want them to appreciate that. To be grateful and to do everything they could to hold on to it.

So Arlo is grateful. It's been nice having his mum here. And it's been suffocating.

Michael, the counsellor she'd arranged for him, had impressed on Arlo repeatedly that it's possible for something to feel like more than one thing at a time.

He'd thought the counsellor would be a woman for some reason, probably with a ponytail and glasses like in films, or maybe an older man with a tweed jacket and a beard like Santa. Michael has a shaved head and tattoos of big cats that poke out of the ends of his shirt sleeves. His laugh is a bit weird but Arlo doesn't mind him.

'Want to make dinner together before I go? Arlo's mum asks. 'We've got time. My cab's not coming for another hour.'

'Actually, I was wondering if you could help me with something?'

If he'd known it would only take such a simple request for help to make her eyes light up like that, he might have asked sooner. Probably not though.

Arlo owes the Swansons a box of things that he hasn't quite built up the strength to get together for them yet.

His mum follows him to the closed door opposite his bedroom and watches as he eases it open.

There's a trace of chlorine in Luke's room, or maybe Arlo just wants there to be. That familiar smell.

The curtains are open. The bed is made but the striped covers are rumpled, as if Luke has just got off it and is in the kitchen fixing himself a snack. The wardrobes are open where the police rummaged through them. Arlo straightens up the clothes inside and closes the doors.

Together, he and his mum collect the things that Mr and Mrs Swanson asked Arlo to send: a few family photos, Luke's signed school shirt, the swimming trophies. Arlo hasn't told them about the lost medal yet but he knows he'll have to.

They have to look through Luke's drawers to find the documents the Swansons mentioned. It feels like intruding but Arlo would rather he did it than them having to smell their son's room without him in it.

'Have you got something to send it all in?' his mum asks.

The lilos had come in a box but he must have thrown it out.

Arlo looks across the hall into his own room and clocks the boxes at the end of his bed by the radiator.

'Yes,' he says. He empties one of the containers on to his bed and brings it back into Luke's room.

'What are Mary and Bobby doing with the rest of his things?'

'They said I could keep what I want and they'll arrange for the British Heart Foundation to collect the rest.'

Arlo sorts everything into a neat pile on the bed and falters. His mum gently packs it and labels the box, and they put it in the hallway ready to ship.

He wonders if Mr and Mrs Swanson will unpack it right away and what they'll do with its contents. Will they put it in Luke's old bedroom, maybe still in the box, under the bed? Arlo writes 'Sender' and his name and address on it so they'll know what it is and aren't taken by surprise when they open it.

'That was thoughtful,' his mum says.

He doesn't want her to leave and he doesn't want to be alone. He wants her to leave and he wants to be alone so he can get on with his plans. The two feelings exist in his head at the same time and he tries to just notice them and let them be like Michael told him. It's not easy.

'I'll come with you to the airport,' he tells her. 'Help you carry your stuff.'

'You don't need to do that.'

'I want to,' he says. 'Someone needs to see you off the premises.'

It's a feeble joke but they both crack a smile.

'Honestly, just walk me down to the cab. I hate airport goodbyes and we'll see each other in three weeks when you visit. Plus, I know what happens when you get near an airport now.'

They share a weak laugh at this and take her stuff down to

the waiting car. It's hard to tell who is hugging hardest before she gets into the back seat.

There are a couple of new letters addressed to Luke in the hallway when Arlo checks the post after waving her off. Time sticks for a second. He breathes until he's ready to keep pushing forward again.

This is what it'll be like sometimes. Daily reminders.

He shakes it off and tries to focus on what he needs to do next. First step: drop the post off back inside the flat.

The lift is taking too long so he takes the stairs. When he comes out into the corridor there's a tower of cardboard boxes on legs wobbling towards him. For a second he thinks someone is stealing Luke's stuff but it's locked in the flat. Someone must be moving in. Or out. He and Luke had never met any of the neighbours.

'Do you need a hand?'

A woman's voice responds, 'Please.' She shuffles sideways so they can see each other's faces.

Dark hair.

Not Mizuki.

'Maybe you could take the top one so I can open the door?'

Arlo does as he's asked and follows the woman's invitation into the flat three doors down from his. It looks like a one-bed but otherwise it's pretty much the same as his and Luke's place. It'll always be his and Luke's place, never just his.

'Where d'you want this?'

'Maybe on the kitchen table,' she says. 'Oh, actually, I think the sheets are in that one so stick it in the bedroom. Whenever I move, I always make my bed first so it feels like home.'

'I'm Arlo, by the way,' he says, when he comes back into the kitchen.

'Nimah.'

She holds out her hand and they shake.

'Nice to meet you. I live just at the end of the hall.'

'Nice to meet you Arlo-from-the-end-of-the-hall.'

'Is there any more stuff to come up?' he asks. He'd be happy to help her really, but part of Arlo is itching to get on with what he needs to do to make things right now that his mum's gone.

'This is everything. Thanks for your help.'

'Anytime. I'll let you settle in then.'

Luke's bedroom door is still ajar when Arlo gets back inside the flat.

Of course it is.

He goes in and puts Luke's post on the bed for the time being, smoothing the rumpled sheets. It's a bit much having them look like Luke's just hopped off.

It'll be dark soon so Arlo draws the curtains. There's a clinking as the radiator comes on and he wonders if he should turn it off since nobody will be in here but doesn't. He leaves Luke's door open behind him as he goes and heads straight back out of the front door.

The morning air nibbles Arlo's fingers, twitching the rest of him awake.

The bed groans beneath him. Wait. It's not *his* bed. Too narrow. No pillow. The room is too bright.

He squints in the white glare.

Where am I?

There are seven cranes to the west and a chimney behind him.

The roof.

Arlo sits up on the decrepit sun lounger. Small summer leaves flutter from his face and torso into his lap. He rolls his stiff neck; it cracks – once, twice, again. The lounger's metal frame creaks under him as he looks over to the swimming pool and lets himself remember.

He had come up to the roof after his mum left.

He'd thought the landlady might have sealed the door to the roof after the accident, but it's a fire door so of course it still opens. The steps that used to lead up to the terrace have been filled in to form a concrete wall next to the fire escape. Arlo threw his water canister up on top of the wall and took a running leap. After weeks of scrambling over barbed wire fences, the wall was no challenge.

Someone had folded the pool cover neatly away but everything else was the same. The head torches were still in his and Luke's stash of equipment behind the defunct chimney. The battery on one was dead but there was still life in the other.

With both pairs of gloves on to protect his hands, Arlo had climbed into the pool. Their forest had grown sideways in a clump along the pool basin where he'd flung the trees in a heap in his rage.

In my grief, he corrects himself.

Saying 'my' grief still sounds weird to him, probably because he doesn't want it. Michael has told him it's OK to be angry but that he should apportion blame for that anger where it belonged. He could be angry at his loss, not at himself.

He'd whispered a thank you to the trees for not dying and spent the night picking the pieces of the shattered pots from the pool basin and out of the soil, before lying down on the sun lounger to rest under the stars and blipping planes. He must have fallen asleep counting things on the city ceiling.

Arlo dismounts the collapsing lounger and downs some water from his canister, then drops back into the pool with the trees.

There are seven plants, longer and stronger now, and one big clump of roots. He puts one of the pairs of gloves back on and begins the work of separating them.

Luke's voice is in his head.

'This is the best bit. We've started a forest in the pool. It's going to be awesome.'

Arlo isn't sure what he'll do when he's finished, he just knows that he wants to undo the damage he's done and give the trees each space to breathe and grow.

Maybe he'll order some compost and plant them properly in the pool. It was never going to be used for swimming anyway, he and Luke had both known that. It was just a game.

The sun shines down on him as he manages to divide the root network into seven distinct but still connected clods. Next, he needs to get them fully apart without wrecking the roots. The gloves make him too thick-fingered for the more delicate work. He's always been good at special knots but needs bare fingers to get in there properly.

The dirt dries his hands as he sifts through the strands, coaxing them apart. Some are like rope, others thin shoelaces, the rest as fine as baby hair.

He works with method and patience, stopping only to drink

some more water and share some with the trees. They don't need it. The summer rain had stopped them getting thirsty and they like the fresh air, but he feels so grateful that he didn't come back to their seven dead bodies that he can't help but give them water anyway.

It takes the rest of the morning to unpick months' worth of creeping and tangling. When he's shaken the last clump loose, Arlo lays the trees down side by side. *Like sleeping lions.* It'll take a long time to unpick the mess in his head but this act helps.

In his old spot on the side of the pool, legs dangling over the edge, Arlo is calmer than he can remember being for a while. The labour has made him the right kind of tired. It's a world apart from the time he'd sat in the smashed terracotta and roots, turning Luke's medal over and over in his hand, waiting for him to come back and tell him it was all a game.

The police tape has blown away somewhere, to some other emergency maybe.

Arlo leans forward with his head in his hands to rest a minute. He rubs his temples and his brain seems to slide forward in his head. He messed up his sleep routine last night, though he's not supposed to beat himself up about that either. He'll just try again this evening.

Making a start on fixing the trees and the pool has helped clear a small space in his brain.

The idea that he'd had in Mr Swanson's shed when he saw the decorations is starting to tickle the back of his mind. It swirls around in there with the jar, maps and notebooks. The glow of the squid and the park deer and their castle combine to create a vision of something new. Something he could make that would matter.

It's getting hotter. The thought of another bout of sunstroke is not appealing, so Arlo gets to his feet.

He surveys the trees and the length of the pool. A golden something catches his eye. A glint among the debris he tidied to the far end last night.

Luke's medal.

THIRTY-SIX

Russell motions to the chair in front of his desk. Arlo keeps his hand in his pocket so Luke's medal doesn't fall out as he sits.

'You look good,' Russell tells him.

Arlo knows he's looking better. He feels better. Not everything-is-fixed better, but better.

It's hard to tell if he's just going through a more stable patch. He's not sure whether or not he should trust it – what was grief and shock, and what was something else. Somewhere inside him is the sense that the black weeds or the too-high high of the hospital might come back.

His doctor has been good. She's not patronising and hasn't seemed particularly shocked by anything he's told her. Once he'd got out the words, 'I think I sometimes feel worse that I'm meant to, like, much worse,' it was easier to say more. He might tell her the rest at his next appointment.

They might try medication to stabilise his mood but the routine he's been trying to stick to and the counselling seem to be helping for now.

He's been meeting Guy at the gym. Arlo usually puts his earphones in and ignores the talk of protein and 'birds' while they work out, but most of the time he likes being there and he almost always feels better afterwards. He and Guy are looking for things to like about each other, reaching for similarities. Luke liked them both. That's a start.

Arlo's even been following Luke's meal plan on the fridge, taking some of his powders and supplements while he tries to build himself back up. He's fairly convinced that the latter are pointless and he's a long way from joining the protein cult that Guy seems to belong to but maybe this is the zombie apocalypse that Luke had been preparing for.

Arlo tries to go outside every day. Not on the roof though. He's been up a few more times to fill the pool with compost and put the trees to bed in it. Nobody else will climb the wall; they'll be safe up there. Arlo knows he won't go up there again either, but maybe this time next year he'll be able to see the tops of his and Luke's forest from the street.

He hasn't told the doctor or Michael about the other elements of his routine yet, the things he does when he's not occupied with the actions they agreed on. The endless 'what if' thinking and the fantasising about how he could fix things.

He thinks about Mizuki and all the things they did together, the incredible places they went. He thinks about leaving Luke on the roof.

Aren't people always saying that everything boils down to

sex and death – or is it sex and power? Either way, he also spends time thinking about sex with Mizuki, especially when he's masturbating. His body remembers the way she touched him and how it felt to be that close to her. Her lemony, salty smell and melon mouth. The way she'd laughed afterwards.

All he can do is hope she wouldn't mind that he likes remembering. Maybe she does the same. Sometimes his mind runs away with the thought that she looks at her photos of him while she's touching herself, but after he comes the idea seems less likely.

He also hasn't told Michael or the doctor that sometimes he just lies on the floor with his earphones in and turns the music up so loud that he thinks his ears might bleed and that he stays there until he can't feel anything except the beat reverberating through his body.

'You want a coke?' Russell says, as he always does.

'Sure, thanks.'

Russell hands him a can from the mini fridge. Arlo never feels as young as he does when he's in this office with Russell's arty furniture and desk strewn with contracts.

'Thanks for seeing me,' Arlo says. 'Sorry I didn't call you when I got back. I've had things to sort out.'

'I'm sorry about your friend,' Russell says. 'Twenty-three is no age. He was a talented kid.'

Funny how twenty-three is a kid to someone like Russell.

'Thank you.'

'How long have you been back in town?' his agent asks.

'Just over a month,' says Arlo. 'Well, I was just away visiting my mum for a few days, but I'm back again now. Obviously. Anyway, I wanted to say sorry in person about the screen test.'

'It's forgotten,' Russell says. Arlo knows it's probably not but he appreciates Russell saying it. 'You know the studio has moved on though? Filming starts next month.'

Arlo had assumed that would be the case but it's a gut-punch to hear it out loud.

'There'll be another part.'

'Maybe,' says Arlo.

'Let's get you some new headshots done, update your reel. Take it from there. Sound like a plan?'

Arlo practised his next lines with Michael and again last night with his mum on the phone. In the moment before he delivers them, he wobbles, but once the first line is out in the air between him and Russell he knows it's right: 'I just want to try being me for a while.'

'And what exactly will that entail?'

That's the thing that Arlo hasn't figured out yet. Maybe it means applying to university or saving for a gap year. Maybe it means having a rest and hitting the audition circuit again. All he knows is where it starts. 'I'm about to start working on something and it's going to take me some time. I'll understand if you don't want to represent me any more.'

'What sort of something?'

'I'm making something. Well, trying to.'

The truth is he's already been working on it for a month but he doesn't want to tell Russell about it yet. Maybe if it goes well, he might see some pictures.

'Let me show you something, Arlo.'

Russell types something on his laptop and turns the screen round so Arlo can see. Post after post of #ArlosArmy. Arlo wonders if 'he' has tweeted recently courtesy of Lottie, *The Beat*'s publicist, and what he might have said. He hopes he said thanks to all these people for thinking of him and for missing him.

'Wow.'

'You've got so much support.'

Arlo is grateful but it mostly feels like it's happening to someone else and he's had enough of numb.

'Look at how much they love you,' Russell says. 'That's not nothing, you know. You always said you wanted to make something that matters. Well, this is something.'

They circle round each other for a while longer.

Russell tries a different tack. 'Pilot season auditions are starting even earlier this year.'

Arlo knows Russell believes in him and he feels bad about throwing them off the course they'd mapped out together but he's said what he came to say. It feels like putting a lid back on a jar for a while; it'll keep.

They shake hands as Arlo leaves.

'We're having drinks next door tonight. Come by.'

'I've got to pick up some packages from the other side of town before work,' says Arlo. 'Another time, though.'

'Where are you working?'

'In a bar.'

'Like most actors,' Russell laughs. 'Tell me it's a theatre bar at least.'

'It's a pub near where I live.'

'Take some classes then. Keep fresh.'

* * *

Arlo turns on Luke's TV and sits on the bedroom floor next to the packages that he's just carried up five flights of stairs.

He needs a minute before he opens them and gets on with the next stage of his project. Seeing Russell was draining and it was a long shift at the bar, though he made good tips.

The punters who recognise him think he's researching for a role or something and he lets them imagine whatever they want. He'd promised Michael he would spend time with other humans anyway. It makes a difference, having people to talk with even if it's only about whether or not the head on their beer is too foamy. Sometimes it's even fun.

He's started watching films again. Tonight it's *Titanic*. Later, when it finishes, he'll tell himself that they could both have fitted on the floating door, that he could have not left Luke on the roof.

Once Rose and Jack have had sex in the car and the boat has hit the iceberg, Arlo is ready to get started. He used to watch it and expect a different ending. Not any more. Mizuki was right though, Rose's near suicide attempt could have been handled better. He pauses the doomed ship and goes to the bathroom where he retrieves a wet globe shape from the full bath.

A prototype. He'd left it overnight to see how it holds up in water. It's still firm; no obvious signs of water damage yet. He needs the material to degrade after time but not immediately. It looks as if this stuff works. Arlo dries it off with a bath towel and pulls the plug.

He puts the sphere down the side of Luke's bed with the others then tears open the packages and lays everything out in front of him. It took a while to save the money but he has almost everything he needs now.

His fingers ache with the possibilities. The chance to make something for himself and maybe even help Mizuki find her mum.

Fix me. Draw me whole. Colour me in.

THIRTY-SEVEN

There are days when getting out of bed is too much. Sometimes it feels as if the only thing holding Arlo up is a web of memories. Today is one of those days.

He sacks off meeting Guy at the gym and texts his manager at the bar to say he's sick and needs to take the evening off. He's heard all about how it's good to be honest if you can and telling his manager he has a headache feels like a cop-out but he just doesn't have the energy today. And it's not untrue; being sad hurts physically too.

The sun has set before Arlo manages to shower and put on clean boxers and joggers. He channels surfs for a bit. *The Beat* is on. There's Valerie and Jessica. He still owes Jessica an apology. He picks up his phone and follows her on Twitter. He'd prefer to say sorry in person but it might have to be this way. He's planning to tweet a thank-you message to Arlo's

Army as soon as he feels strong enough to answer some of the replies.

Arlo changes the password so Lottie can't tweet out any more bullshit on his behalf or intervene if Jessica follows him back. He turns off the TV and puts his phone under the sofa cushion.

He sits trying to figure out if anything in particular has made this feel like a bad day. Checking in, Michael calls it.

Maybe there isn't an explanation, maybe this is just how he feels today. It could be because he finished the final stage of his project last night and doubt is creeping in about whether or not it's turned out as special as he wanted it to be. He reminds himself that, whatever happens, he made it for himself above anything. Only tomorrow will tell whether or not it matters to anyone else. Tomorrow night to be more specific.

Arlo looks out of the window to Luke's car, grubby but still silver, tucked against the curb under the street lamp. A shot of adrenaline pulses through him. Enough for him to decide to load up the car tonight.

The boxes are already empty and waiting where he'd finally unpacked in his room. It felt silly for the sake of a couple of months left in the flat, but it does seem more like a real place where a real person lives with his things anchored within it.

There are a few more pieces of clothing in the wardrobe now too. Comfortable things that Arlo likes and knows he deserves. A warm coat and some new shirts hang above his old trainers. He hasn't got round to replacing those yet.

It takes over an hour to wrap everything in tissue, pack the boxes and make the several trips it takes to get it all down to the car. Arlo is sweating by the time he grabs the final two packages and is holding them against the wall to free his hand to press the lift button when Nimah appears from the stairwell.

'Oof, five flights,' she says. 'I think it's supposed to be good for you but I'm dying. Need a hand?'

'I'm OK,' he says. 'Thanks though.'

'OK. Nice to see you again.'

She carries on down the corridor.

Why am I making this so hard for myself?

'Actually,' Arlo calls after her, 'if you don't mind, some help would be good.'

'Of course.'

'If you could just press ground for me when the lift comes.'

Nimah walks over to him and lifts the top box from his arms. 'Easier if we just take one each. Not moving out are you?'

'Not today. Just taking some stuff home.'

After they've wedged everything into the car, Nimah taps the boot like people do in films to send taxis on their way. 'I don't know why I did that,' she says. 'It's like muscle memory or something.'

'Thanks for the help,' he says when they get back upstairs.

'No worries. Do you want to come in for a drink?'

Actually Arlo is gagging for a drink and it would be nice to talk to someone for a few minutes.

Nimah's place looks totally different to how it had on the day that Arlo had helped her move in. There's stuff everywhere. The fridge is covered in magnets and photos, and there are cushions and throws draped over the sofa and armchair in the lounge. Big abstract art hangs on the walls.

Arlo smiles at the potted tree in the corner and wonders if he might get one too.

'Beer OK?'

'Great.'

They cheers and sit down at the kitchen table. After a few minutes of polite conversation, they hear a key in the lock.

'My girlfriend,' Nimah says.

'I didn't realise you lived with someone.'

'Nobody knows anything about anyone in this building,' she laughs.

'Honey, I'm home,' comes a sing-song voice from the hallway.

A young woman comes into the kitchen. Big smile, smart clothes.

'Ooh, I see we have company,' she says, flinging her suit jacket on the back of a chair and yanking off her shoes. 'I'm Lucy. You know what, the patriarchy is making me think I have to wear these stupid clothes but I'm over it. Next week I'm wearing a bin liner and that's it.'

'This is our neighbour Arlo,' says Nimah, furnishing her with a beer and kissing her.

'Are you here for games night, Arlo?' Lucy asks.

'Games night?'

'Friday night is always games night in this household.'

'Will you stay?' asks Nimah. 'It's just us and our friend Olly. Nothing hectic and we could really use a fourth player to even things out. I'm bored of beating them at everything.'

'Thanks so much but I have work.' He pushes his chair back to leave.

'Call in sick,' says Lucy. 'Nobody should be working on a Friday night.'

Arlo looks at her and then to Nimah. The way they're smiling makes it seem as if they really want him to stay so he decides to just be honest with them.

'I've had kind of a rough day . . . I don't know if I'll be good company.'

'Well, Olly just got dumped so he'll be in a total state I imagine. I've been wearing this ludicrous lady costume and photocopying eight hours a day at my internship all week. And Nimah cheats,' says Lucy, 'so I'm planning to get so drunk that I can barely string a sentence together.'

'Basically, it's come as you are here, no judgement,' says Nimah.

'Plus, we have snacks and Cards Against Humanity,' Lucy adds, twirling a black and white box in the air.

'OK,' Arlo says, 'thank you. Maybe one game.'

THIRTY-EIGHT

It's cool and compact underfoot as Arlo pads towards the frothing seam between the earth and the muddy lilac sea.

He pulls off his trainers and abandons them to the lonely beach.

Nobody sleeps with their shoes on.

It had been a late night with Nimah, Lucy and Olly in the end and it had taken him hours to set everything up how he wanted it after the long drive. He'd spent the journey stuck on the image of his and Mizuki's clothes whirling round in a hostel washing machine together. She'd suggested they just use the one since they didn't have enough laundry for a full load each. He'd give almost anything to sit on a laundrette floor talking about everything and nothing with her again.

But he's done everything he can and now he has time to stand still for a while.

He steps over the torn edge of the world into the ocean, curling the sand and stones with his toes, planting himself among them.

Still, steady, in the shadow of the pier.

He stares out over the great body of water; nothing behind him but time.

The moon reaches for him over the deep sky as his mind searches all the seas and pools he's ever known, all the ways he's almost drowned.

The shallows lap his feet until they're numb, a natural anaesthetic.

It's been a happy day. It's been a sad day. A day like all the rest.

Arlo makes himself stay there in the ache while black tides of sadness batter him. He knows how to do this now. The weeds tighten and they will loosen.

Hot tears drop into the cold surf.

Bright minutes pass.

He's learned that it helps to try to think things about the sea and the sky that anyone who has ever seen them must have thought. How vast they are, how beautiful.

That others have felt like this makes him feel less alone.

When the weeds release him, Arlo wipes his wet face and heads back up the beach.

Everything looks exactly as he planned. A fragile flicker of an idea made real.

Tangled antlers of driftwood dot the beach, as if shed by deer in some other place and washed up here. Arlo repositions a couple of them, dragging them closer to the pier.

He's hidden a portable generator in a hole close, but not too close, to the tideline, patted sand over the top and trailed string after string of neon blue fairy lights from it. The wood sculptures will look extra magical lit up by the lights.

He's strung up rows of nets under the pier and tucked more twinkling lights into the transparent webbing so they'll look as if they're levitating, suspended between the pier's thick legs.

At least, Arlo hopes that's how it'll look. He can't draw attention to himself by testing the lights and he doesn't know if the nets will hold. They're just a backdrop anyway, a nice setting for the main event: his galaxy of shining globes glowing at the water's edge.

He checks they're OK again, nestling in the sand, waiting for the water.

Their colours in the starlight are like nothing he's ever seen. Delicate blue, the creamiest pales, mint. A perfect one among them, humble, blushing.

It took weeks to build and colour this universe the way he wanted it. Long nights after his shifts at the bar, easing pages from his notebook, spreading out Mizuki's maps, and laying out Luke's green words alongside his own blue ones.

He'd gone over their lines and scribbles to make them bolder, adding icons and secret clues. Winks to Luke and Mizuki. It felt right to use his friend's room as his workshop, as if it kept the space alive somehow.

Arlo's forefinger and thumb are calloused from pressing down a blade to cut pieces of parchment into the right shapes. He'd drawn positioning lines on them, stretching the shapes out and recutting them to the smallest degree of accuracy, sticking them down millimetre by millimetre on to the spheres, starting again if they bubbled or tore.

He'd painted and varnished, loosening a bit of every colour from a palette with a tiny brush. Delicate dabbing, furious stokes. He'd made land from green words, sea from blue. Recreated, imagined, and changed journeys. Built worlds and moons and other places.

It's all biodegradable, of course. Mizuki would not be impressed by him sending more plastic out to sea. Everything will dissolve after forty hours; he tested it again and again in the bath filled with salt and water. The floating candles will burn for about as long.

When Arlo invited her, he suggested to Mizuki that she brings her camera. When he lights the candles and turns on the neon lights, he hopes it'll be like nothing they've ever seen before, like nothing that's ever been photographed. Light after light, world after world.

A floating atlas.

A handmade universe.

An upgrade on the washing-up-liquid bottle and newspaper pterodactyl on his childhood ceiling.

He checks everything one last time. He's ready.

The borrowed boat is prepped too, slanted in the muddy sand. It's tied to the pier with a special knot and hooked to the beach by a dead-weight anchor. The tide will lift the boat but it won't go anywhere unless he asks it to. There might be a better view from out at sea.

Arlo tosses two sleeping bags into the hull. He checks the anchor is firmly wedged and climbs aboard.

He's early but they're coming, he knows they are. Mizuki and the tide.

The moon is wider than the sky now, so low in the sea that

it can taste its own reflection. Glimmering syrup. When the light moves round, the blue and green castle on the pier above will throw its image on to the water, shining back at them. They might climb it tomorrow; maybe they'll say a poem or give a howl for Luke at the top.

Arlo lies back, eyelids sealing themselves against the lunar light as he sinks further into the boat. The part of him that didn't trust the rest of him lets go and a cool silver sweetness covers him.

He rests. One warm dot waiting for another.

Soft stars and blossom fall like confetti.

Clouds smother the moon as he feels the creep of warm fingers into his.

ACKNOWLEDGEMENTS

The without whoms . . .

Clare Conville, rock 'n' roll philosopher, literary leader, and absolute dearheart. Every day I thank my lucky stars that you're my agent. Thanks to all at C+W, the best agency in town, and especially to Allison DeFrees.

Thank you to the team at Hachette. Polly Lyall Grant, my wonderful editor and a deeply cool human. Anne McNeil, always right and always gentle. Emily Thomas, I hope to be like you when I grow up. Special thanks to Naomi Berwin, Katy Cattell, Katherine Fox, Rachel Graves, Hilary Murray Hill, Amy Hoang, Kelly Llewellyn, Rebecca Logan, Alison Padley, Chloe Parkinson, Laure Pernette, Lucy Upton, and Natasha Whearity.

Thanks also to my eagle-eyed copyeditor and proofreader. Maura Wilding, you are a gift and a glory to behold.

Richard Skinner, that I am a published author remains pretty much your fault – thank you. Chloe Esposito, Felicia Yap, and all my Faber Academy friends – I'm rooting for you.

Dan Dalton, mender of broken stories – having your words on my wall made such a difference.

Dayna Brackley, my first reader and dearest bear.

Thanks to the places that inspired this story and to Mark F for showing me one special country in particular.

My heartfelt thanks to every reader, bookseller, author, journalist, blogger, reviewer, and friend who has supported my writing – I appreciate every one of you.

To my family, all my love, always.

READING GROUP QUESTIONS

1. Is Arlo a typical 'hero'? What do you think the author was trying to say about young men, mental health, and toxic masculinity? Do you agree?

2. What's unique or important about the places in the book - how would changing the settings affect the story? If you could visit one of the locations in the book, which would you choose?

3. What role do acting, drawing, photography and making things have in Arlo, Luke and Mizuki's lives and the overall story? Do you think it's important for people to have a creative outlet?

4. Is fiction a good place to discuss environmental issues such as climate change and pollution? Did any of the book's images related to this stick in your mind?

5. Mizuki has her own quest and motivations. What do you think they are?

6. What did you think of the author's writing style? Is there a strong sense of voice? How does the language used contribute to or mirror the story?

7. Did you find the ending satisfying? What did you like and not like about it, and what do you think happens after the final chapter?

8. Why do you think the author chose the title? If you had to re-name the book, what would you call it?

Lydia Ruffles is the acclaimed author
of *The Taste of Blue Light* and *Colour
Me In*. She also writes and talks about
creativity and mental health for media
ranging from Buzfeed to Woman's
Hour. Lydia is a graduate of the Faber
Academy and is based in London.

Find her on Twitter and Instagram
@lydiaruffles and on Tumblr at
lydiaruffles.tumblr.com